BAD KARMA

(A JACK MCCOUL CAPER BOOK 2)

DWIGHT HOLING

BAD KARMA
(A Jack McCoul Caper)
Print Edition
Copyright 2015 by Dwight Holing
Published by Jackdaw Press
All Rights Reserved

ISBN: 978-0-9911301-4-6

For More Information, please visit dwightholing.com.

See how you can **Get a Free Book** at the end of this novel.

For Family & Friends

1

Only a few months into the nine-to-five life and Jack McCoul was sweating more bullets than he ever did running a con. Working hard was hard work. Commuting to an office. Making payroll. Fighting off creditors. And that was only the half of it. The mobile app space was the wild west of high tech. Thieves showed more honor than start-up founders did. When he was on the grift at least he knew who was trying to stab him in the back. By the time Friday night rolled around, all he wanted to do was dive into a shaken, not stirred martini and hang onto the toothpick to keep from drowning.

Jack hoped Katie was mixing the cocktails as he rode the elevator to their San Francisco loft, but when he opened the front door, he got a bigger surprise than biting into an olive with the pit still in it. Bobby Ballena was sitting on the couch with Katie's feet on his lap.

"What's with the suit, bro? Someone die?" Bobby's grin shined as bright as a halogen light. His tan was deep and his curls sun-bleached at the tips.

"What happened to you?" Jack fired back. "Mistake saddle soap for sunscreen?"

Bobby laughed and kept rubbing Katie's arches.

Her smile was the same as when she was eating crème brûlée. Jack noticed right off she was wearing the periwinkle pashmina scarf he'd given her in Kathmandu. But it couldn't be. He'd left it gagging a monk the night he and Bobby stole a 400-year-old solid gold Buddha from a mountaintop temple.

"Hey, babe. Bobby bring you a gift?"

The usual sparkle in Katie's green eyes were softened by a dreamy look as she stroked the kitten-soft neck warmer. "Bobby remembered how much I loved the one I lost in Nepal. Isn't he sweet?"

"As Himalayan honey," Jack said.

Katie spread her toes and settled deeper into the leather cushions as Bobby started working her heels. The reflexology chart said they were connected to the stomach. Jack knew that because she had a life-size body map pinned to their bedroom wall. It resembled the Africa page in an atlas with all sorts of colored patches on the shoulders, back, and feet. Katie was big on massage therapy. Acupuncture, too. It was all part of her holistic approach to medicine and matrimony.

"Bobby's here on business and I told him he didn't need to stay at a hotel," she said. "He was telling me about the school he started in Baja. He teaches kiteboarding and lives in a house on the most beautiful beach in the whole wide world."

"Second most," Bobby said. "First is the one you're always looking for."

Katie oohed.

Vintage Bobby. He was always smooth with the lines. Jack wondered what he'd say about the pashmina. It was no coincidence he showed up with it. The scarf was going to cost him. The question was, how much?

"I'll go make drinks," Jack said.

He stopped off at the bedroom to change into a pair of jeans and a camp shirt. Solid black, no palm trees, and no hula dancers—not ever. A suit wasn't his natural skin but he'd been in court all day trying to block a crew of patent trolls from muscling in on his app. Bobby wouldn't have understood. The closest he ever came to a straight job was back in high school when he sold popcorn at a theater on the weekends. He lasted a month before the manager fired him for skimming all the little salt packets and selling them to shut-ins at a nursing home.

Jack checked his phone for messages on the way to the kitchen. He was hoping for good news from his patent lawyer but it was still radio silence. It was the latest in a string of setbacks that came with bringing a killer app to market. There was no escaping them—angel investors throwing their weight around and software glitches that popped up with more regularity than drinking one of Katie's prune juice and flax seed smoothies. Even with online banking there was always another report to print out and tax form to submit. Death wouldn't come either from being on the wrong end of a swindle or shanked in prison while stacking time; it would be by a thousand paper cuts.

He decided against shaking martinis into stemmed glasses. Bobby was sure to make some wisecrack about his new domesticity. *Oh, is it martini Friday, dear?* he'd say with a tone. It wasn't too far from the truth. Once Jack was without a care in the world, traveling wherever the next opportunity lay and earning a rep as one of the best artists in the game. But he'd given it up when he got married. Well, most of the time.

Now he settled for special occasions with special names to make them stand out. Like *date night*. Jack couldn't remember when Katie started calling it that. It was probably her best friend Laura who came up with it. She was always reading blogs on how to make marriage work. It was a full-time job for her since she'd hooked up with a Silicon Valley venture capitalist. Katie rushed to Laura's defense when Jack commented that she was another one of Dexter Cotswold's trophies to go along with his mansion and annual membership to the Forbes wealthiest list. "You have no idea how hard she works to keep him happy," she said.

Jack whipped up a pitcher of margaritas. He dumped some pink sea salt Katie professed was cardio friendly onto a paper towel as the blender whirred, wetted the rims of three thick tumblers, and twisted them into low-sodium drifts the color of pale roses. The shine on the sterling silver serving tray didn't get past Bobby.

"Man, have you come up in the world," he said. "No more swilling *chhaang* out of a wooden bowl?"

Katie sat up. "What I wouldn't give for a taste of Himalayan home brew. Those were the days. I can still remember when Laura and I walked into that adorable teahouse in Kathmandu and found you two sitting there. Certainly a lot more hunky than any of the mountain climbers. What a trip. What an adventure. Waking up to first light hitting the peaks. The smell of incense in the temples. The prayer flags fluttering. It was all so magical."

She sipped her margarita. It left a yellow caterpillar inching across her lips. "Let's go back right now. Jump on a plane and go. No more excuses."

Jack reminded her about the lumpy beds and squat toilets to head off Bobby from saying something cute about how that could land them in a Nepalese jail for the next twenty years.

Katie's arched brows mimicked a pair of minks getting ready to pounce. "Don't be so negative." She patted Bobby's knee. "Jack's been under a lot of stress since he started his new business. He's all serious all the time now. I'm trying to get him to do

TM." She paused. "I've always wanted to go back but time got in the way. You know what I mean?"

Bobby nodded. "Time doesn't stand still. People do."

That sent Katie oohing again. Jack took a gulp and wished he'd doubled up on the tequila. He noticed Bobby was playing with the periwinkle fringe on the scarf. The wool came from hardy goats that lived on Mount Everest. It was only a matter of time before Bobby got around to telling him why he'd risked coming back to San Francisco.

"What about some dinner?" he said. "I can fire up the grill."

Katie's brows arched again but this time into question marks. "Didn't you get my text? We're going to Laura and Dexter's tonight."

Jack nearly spit out his drink. He shot Bobby a look but the thief was preoccupied with wrapping the pashmina's fringe around his fingers. "Whose idea was that?"

"Mine, of course. I called Laura to tell her Bobby's back in town. She's dying to see him."

"I'll bet."

Katie went to get dressed. As soon as she closed the bedroom door, Jack started right in on Bobby. "How long have you had it in the works?"

"Had what in what works?"

"Whatever it is you're planning."

"Who says I'm planning anything?"

"You think you can drop in and I'll suit up like old times? Wave that scarf around and threaten to tell Katie about us sneaking out of the hotel and hitting the temple, me taking her scarf in case I needed a mask, not thinking I'd have to gag a monk with it."

Bobby waggled a finger. "Which technically you didn't need to do it since all the monks there cut out their tongues." He gave an exaggerated shudder. "And I thought some of the stuff they made us do at Saint Joe's was twisted."

"You're forgetting. I'm legit now. I got a mobile app business."

Bobby shook his head. "Katie's right. *Señor Negativo*. You need to chill out, bro. Do some transcendental meditation like she says."

"Well I'm *positivo* you've got something planned. This isn't about seeing your old girlfriend and reliving Nepal. It's about Laura's husband, who Dexter is, and, more importantly, what he's got."

Bobby gave it a few beats and then his eyes turned sly. "And from what I hear it's plenty."

2

Woodside was once home to hippies and rock musicians; now it was a Silicon Valley sultanate. The founders of Oracle, Intel, and Intuit lived there. So did Dexter Cotswold, and he was doing his part to make it the wealthiest and most exclusive ZIP code in the country.

Jack drove up a long, redwood-lined driveway and parked his Prius in front of a newly built mansion a little smaller than Downton Abbey. By the time he climbed out of the car, Katie was already clanging an antique door knocker that hung from the jaws of a brass lion's head.

Bobby took a deep breath and blew it out with a wry smile. "I love the smell of money. Especially new money."

The thick oak door swung open to reveal the lord of the manor. Dexter was a stubby guy, a good foot shorter than Jack. Laura had confided that her husband had a complex about it. It was why he was always letting everyone know he'd attended Cambridge or Oxford or one of those stuffy colleges where stuck-up British kids went and how he made his first billion picking winners before they were even start-ups.

Bobby offered his hand to Dexter after being introduced. "Thank you for honoring me with an invitation to your beautiful home. Now I know why I never stood a chance with Laura." Then he bowed and adopted a Confucian accent. "He who wins and honors he who lost is the most honorable of all."

Dexter beamed, Katie oohed, and Jack stifled a gag. Laura came galloping across the limestone-tiled entryway like a long shot stretching for the wire at Golden Gate Fields. "Bobby, baby," she cried and threw her arms around him and planted a big wet one right on his lips.

The kiss involved an exchange of tongues but Dexter didn't seem to mind. Jack figured it was probably because the crown Bobby set on his cue ball head blinded him. Katie took Dexter's arm and guided him back into the mansion. She told him how pleased she was he'd taken her up on her landscaping recommendations. Drought tolerant plants and edible native herbs covered the front yard. Bobby and Laura followed right behind. They walked shoulder to shoulder, and Bobby cupped Laura's toned and shapely gluteus maximus, a testament to her dedication to yoga and Zumba.

The mansion's living room was as long as a cricket pitch and the art and furnishings looked as if they were shipped over from Buckingham Palace. The stone fireplace was big enough to roast a Highland bull. The guests sat on overstuffed couches as Dexter went into a big show-and-tell by opening a magnum of wine. He called it *claret*. Babies were delivered with less drama with the way he went on and on, coaxing the cork out and then cradling the dusty green bottle.

Bobby winked, and that's when Jack knew he was thinking the same thing: It took Dexter longer to extract a two-inch piece of bark than it did a doctor to pull a 9mm slug out of someone's ass. Specifically Bobby's. He'd been on the receiving end years ago when they got caught lifting an eighteenth century icon they needed for a con from an Old Believers' museum. The night watchman had unloaded his Marakov at them. Luckily for Bobby the old duff was half blind from nipping vodka to keep himself warm in what passed for springtime in the Baltics and missed hitting any vital parts. Even luckier was finding a veterinarian who didn't take much persuasion to do the lead extraction. Though Bobby was still hurting as they made their escape, Jack kept it light and said he should be thankful the doc didn't neuter him.

Dexter finally got the wine poured, and Katie and Laura started chatting like they hadn't seen each other in years even though it had only been a day. Bobby walked around the room, cataloging the paintings on the walls, the bronze sculptures, and the glittery chandeliers that displayed more sparkles than a pair of vintage Elton John sunglasses.

Jack could all but hear Bobby's mental calculator clicking as he figured out exchange rates on the black market. To cover he said, "So tell me, Dex, what's new on the far horizon?"

Dexter never let anyone forget he had landed on the cover of *The Futurist* more than once. He waved his wine glass and dove right into a lecture about houses that could track the occupant's health, artificial intelligence aids imbedded in earrings, and personalized virtual reality televisions sets. Jack only caught about half of what he said as he kept an eye on Bobby to make sure he wasn't pocketing a Picasso.

"What about you?" Dexter asked. "What is it you're working on again? A children's game?"

Jack kept his smile pasted on. He'd told Dexter about his start-up the last time they had dinner. He even presented him with a business plan in hopes the rich twit would get in on the second stage of funding. But Dexter turned him down flat. Said all his investments were already budgeted for the year. The very next week he went out and bought a Gulfstream G350 on a whim.

"Actually it's a specialized travel app. Allows international business travelers to locate special services no matter where they are in the world."

"Really?" Dexter pronounced it *Ruh-ley*. "That's right. You did mention it before. But I also seem to recall there was a bit of a sticky wicket regarding your patents."

That triggered Jack's radar. The trolls had surfaced since the last time he'd spoken to Dexter. "The Valley has more rumors than Vegas has hookers. You know how it is. Every tech company, whether start-up or legacy, has to watch out for lowlifes trying to scam a quick payoff by alleging patent infringement. The rights to my intellectual property are bullet-proof. Just today I was dotting the i's and crossing the t's on the IPO prospectus." He sipped some wine. "I hope you've already put in a trade order."

Dexter recoiled in mock horror. "I buy companies, old chap, not shares."

Jack's radar pinged louder. He started to excuse himself so he could call his attorney, but a dwarf dressed in saffron robes with a third eye drawn between his eyebrows waddled into the room. He was wearing traditional Nepalese slippers with the toes turned up.

"Dinner, *memsahib*, is served."

Katie and Laura started clapping and Dexter beamed. They proceeded to a room decorated like a tented Himalayan teahouse, right down to the pounded brass tables and hand-loomed floor pillows. Beeswax candles cast a golden glow and smoke curled from incense sticks. Fresh lotus flowers floated in glass bowls. A trio of musicians played traditional instruments in the corner. One guy drummed a *dholak* and another clanged a pair of brass *jhyali*.

Katie gasped and clutched Jack's arm. "Oh my God, we've died and gone to Shangri-La."

Jack pulled away. "Not before I hit the can first."

The guest bathroom smelled of Chanel No. 5. Jack leaned against the pink marble counter and speed-dialed Tingly Meyers, the bus-stop lawyer he'd hired to secure his patents. The call went straight to voice mail. "Call me ASAP," Jack said. "I got a feeling we're going to have to double down on our defense against the trolls. They could have a deep pocket behind them."

Back in the dining room he squeezed in beside Katie. Bobby was laying on the compliments thicker than yak butter.

"You are correct. I am an Asiaphile," Dexter said from his perch on a fat pillow that gave him a height advantage. "I do appreciate the many cultures of the Orient, having traveled there so often. My firm took sizeable positions in call centers in India, manufacturers in China, and logistics in Seoul."

"But you're more cognoscenti than connoisseur," Bobby said.

Dexter sniffed. "One does get so much more out of life when one is informed."

"One does." Bobby sounded as if he'd stepped off a flight from Heathrow. "Knowledge is what separates a collector from a hobbyist. I'm referring to cultural artifacts of course. Discovery and preservation are foremost. Appreciation of the actual form, well, it really is quite secondary. Wouldn't you agree?"

Dexter raised his chin. "Quite right."

Bobby pressed on. "Is there a particular religion or tribe you focus on?"

"There may be one or two."

Bobby winked at Jack. He was planning something, all right. Jack was sure of it. It was only a matter of what and when.

Dexter picked up a carved stick with a fuzzy animal hide attached to one end and banged a gong near his place mat. Immediately the tent-like fabric draping the walls parted.

Servants dressed in gold silk pajamas paraded in, holding aloft serving platters and bowls.

Bobby inhaled deeply. "Ah. Curried baby goat. My favorite."

AFTER A DESSERT of gunpowder-green tea ice cream that left Katie moaning like someone was working her soles with an eggbeater, Dexter invited Jack and Bobby to the library for cognac and cigars. He led them down a wide hallway to a pair of doors that looked sturdy enough to stop a Mongolian horde. Bobby pretended not to pay attention as Dexter placed his palm on a wall-mounted scanner. A silvery light flashed and the doors swished open.

Jack was expecting dark paneling and leather bound books in floor-to-ceiling shelves. He was right about the shelves but wrong about the books. Row upon row of antiquities covered the walls. There were Ming vases, jade figurines, terracotta sculptures, lacquer boxes, and ivory animals. Handwoven tribal rugs that reflected more colors and countries than Katie's reflexology chart covered the teak floor.

"Exquisite," Bobby whispered in the same way he did when he and Jack used to creep a target.

Dexter opened a humidor and extracted three cigars the size of Gurkha truncheons. He handed them around and they took turns using a solid gold lighter engraved with the logo of their host's firm, Capital Dexterity. As the smoke billowed, Dexter flicked a switch. The gray cloud formed into a whirling column and disappeared through a ceiling vent.

"I designed this centrifuge system myself," he boasted. "It removes tobacco smoke and alcohol fumes from anywhere in the room, thus eliminating the risk of nicotine staining the artifacts or odor permeating the fabrics."

Bobby puffed his stogie, the ember at the tip matching the gleam in his eyes. "Sucks it right up the air shaft and spits it out into the night sky, does it?" He eyeballed the grate that was about the width of his shoulders. "Brilliant, old boy. Brilliant."

It had been years since Jack worked a job with Bobby, but he could still read him as easily as a blueprint to an underground vault. He shook his head at him.

Dexter launched into a series of anecdotes about how he acquired this piece and that. All his stories shared a common theme: He'd outsmarted the seller, beat out the competition, and never paid full price.

Jack was no stranger to arts and antiquities. He cut his teeth working plays with his mentor, Henri LeConte, who was considered to be one of the greatest forgers in the tradecraft. Every piece in Dexter's library was a prized collector's item except for the gold lighter on his desk and a heavy bronze statue that served as a paperweight. The eight-armed figurine depicted Benzai-ten, the Japanese goddess of love, language, wisdom, and the arts. It was an obvious reproduction and surely a gift, but that stood to reason. Dexter wasn't about to use a centuries-old artifact to keep papers from being blown around every time he turned on the ceiling fan. The entire collection had to be worth $30 million easy. And that's what a fence would pay before putting it on the black market. Buyers who didn't worry about a piece's provenance would be willing to pony up ten times that.

Jack finished touring the private gallery and rejoined Bobby and Dexter. They sat in green velvet wingchairs, clutching crystal snifters. "Here's to you, Dex. The San Francisco Asian Art Museum can't hold a Tibetan prayer candle to you."

Dexter accepted the compliment with a shrug that was supposed to show humility. "One does what one can. As Robert here so eloquently stated, preservation of a culture is paramount. I would also add it is one's duty."

Bobby swirled his cognac until the amber liquid mimicked a hypnotist's spiral. He tilted the snifter so that it caught a beam from one of the overhead spotlights and discreetly aimed it at Dexter's eyes. The crystal acted like a prism and made the fractured lights dance.

"Dexter, old boy," Bobby said in a soothing tone. "I'd hazard a guess there is a special *objet d'art* that holds fascination above all others."

Dexter fixated on the spinning sparkles and didn't seem to hear. Bobby asked him again using the same hypnotic voice. Dexter finally nodded. He put down his glass without saying a word and walked across the room as if in a trance. A narrow Japanese scroll depicting a samurai and geisha locked in a Kama Sutra clench hung on the wall. Dexter tugged it as if signaling a butler for tea. A motor whirred and a hidden panel next to the scroll slid open.

A solid gold Buddha smiled from atop an ornate pedestal. The foot-high antique was as shiny as the day Jack and Bobby stole it.

3

K atie's snores purred louder than the hybrid's engine as Jack drove home. He angled the rearview mirror so he could eyeball Bobby. "How did you know Dexter had Little Buddha?"

Bobby shrugged. "Kim let me know the statue changed hands last year."

Kim was a taciturn fence that dressed like a North Korean dictator and controlled a significant portion of the antiques and artifacts black market in the Far East.

"Old Kents and Sunglasses. He still smoking three packs a day?"

"Like a Shanghai steel factory."

Jack hit the mental playback on the religious icon's history. He and Bobby had been running a simple bait and switch involving an antique Cantonese porcelain vase to pay for expenses during an extended tour of Asia. Unbeknownst to them the mark was a notorious one-eyed opium trafficker who wanted the vase as an urn for his recently departed mother. When he discovered his purchase was the fake, he dragged Jack and Bobby to his lair and threatened to throw them into a pit filled with Komodo dragons. Bobby offered to snatch the legendary golden Buddha guarded by a secretive order of monks and trade it for their lives. They were in Kathmandu plotting the heist when they met Katie and Laura. Bobby and Jack held up their end of the deal and the one-eyed trafficker lifted his fatwa on them. He got caught in the middle of a turf war six months later and wound up bartering the gold relic for his own life.

"Last I heard some Saudi prince had Little Buddha. What happened?" Jack spoke softly so as not to wake Katie.

"Kim said the prince ran into cash flow problems after he tried launching the first Islamic online dating site." Bobby's eyes were as bright as the headlights reflected in the rearview mirror. "I've always said today's must-have high-tech gadget is tomorrow's must-take to the recycling bin. Stick with antiquities, the older the better. They never go out of style."

"Maybe the statue's curse is true. You remember the story. Little Buddha brings bad luck to anyone but monks who tries to hold onto him."

Bobby laughed. "There's no such thing as bad luck. There's only cause and effect."

"Since when did you start reading Emerson?"

"Who?"

Jack exhaled. "I take it Old Kents and Sunglasses served as intermediary again with Dexter as the buyer?"

"You got to like Kim's business model. He gets a commission coming and going. I hear he's buying up beachfront in Phuket. He's the silent partner in a new luxury golf course in Chung Mai even though he's never swung a club in his life."

Jack concentrated on the road ahead. Interstate 280 was a beltway that linked Silicon Valley and San Francisco. This time of night the CHP made their quota red lighting speeders who treated the eight lane as if it were a virtual racing game. That got him thinking about Dexter and the remarks he'd made about

Jack's app. During cocktails and dinner, the half-pint tycoon acted like he was in on a big secret, all but bragging that he was responsible for flushing Jack's start-up down the crapper to become the next skid mark on the information superhighway.

It was as if Bobby was reading his mind. "Dexter may have lots of money, but Laura deserves better. I've always regretted I didn't marry her after we left Nepal."

"No, you don't," Jack said. "You're too in love with yourself."

"Ouch. Why so harsh, bro?"

"Just saying it like it is."

Bobby was silent for a moment. "Fine, I'll say it like it is. Dexter Cotswold deserves to get taken. Period. Our little gold friend? He's still ours. We stole him fair and square. Every place he's landed since has been couch surfing."

"There is no *we*. There is no *ours*."

"*Señor Negativo.*"

"How many times I got to tell you? I'm legit now. I got a wife, a business, employees. Don't think for a minute I'll help you. You'll never get away with it. Dexter's got his house wired to the teeth."

"I've never met an alarm system I couldn't disarm, and I'll bet you a grand he doesn't even have that fancy exhaust vent wired. It's a simple pop the top and drop, then bag and tag. Whoosh, right back up the chimney like Santa Claus. We'll make our getaway in your Prius. Dexter will never hear us coming or going."

"I'm warning you, don't try it. Dexter will blame me."

"That's the beauty of it. There's nothing he can do. He can't report the statue's been stolen because he doesn't have any paper. It's not like Kim gave him a sales receipt. And no way Little Lord Fauntleroy filled out a customs declaration." Bobby laughed. "It doesn't get any easier than this, bro. There's absolutely no chance for blowback."

Jack started to contradict him. There was always blowback. And certainly when it came to something as valuable as Little Buddha, curse or no curse. He drove the rest of the way home in silence. Convincing Bobby to take a pass was pointless. All he could do was try to stay out of the way.

4

The next morning Jack walked to his office. It was located on a gritty stretch of Market Street. Not long ago the faded low-rise was a flophouse for people one paycheck away from homelessness and the occasional tourist who'd misread TripAdvisor. But then Twitter moved in up the street and speculators hoping to cash in on the latest high-tech gold rush quickly followed. The property was sold, the scruffy lodgers booted out, and the tiny bedrooms offered as office space to technopreneurs and mobile app developers. All leases were month to month, not because the tenants were still transients, but because it allowed the landlord to ride the skyrocketing rental market.

A woman wearing a straw fedora with a black band frowned as Jack entered what served as the lobby to his fourth floor office suite. "I hope you brought a bag of beans 'cause we're fresh out. How you expect us to work if you don't fuel us?"

Jack smiled. "Top of the morning to you, too. It's another bright and sunny day in Silicon Frisco, don't you know?"

Moana Akauola crossed her arms. Polynesian tribal tattoos blued her shoulders. "As soon as you start laying on that brogue pidgin, I go looking for a bulldozer. You haven't landed any investors have you?"

Jack maintained his grin. "I got a hot one coming in any day now. They told me their funds are tied up for the moment. A Belarusian currency scheme recently buffaloed their offshore bank so they're scrutinizing their wire transfer policies. It's a paper jam is all."

"Please." She dragged the word out. "You're starting to sound like those last *pulalifulu* I worked for. They actually believed there was a mine that produced metal for Bitcoins."

Jack hadn't hired Moana so much as inherited her. The previous tenant went bust and left behind a couple of scratched workstations, an overgrown philodendron that snaked up an exposed drainpipe, and a mouthy receptionist-slash-book-keeper-slash-office manager.

She'd been watering the potted plant the day Jack moved in and greeted him with a question. "So what business we in?"

Momentarily dumb struck, he told her he wasn't looking to add to the payroll. "We're still in the embryonic stage."

"Embryonic?" Moana's laugh rumbled like the volcanoes on her native Tonga. "Trust me, *palagi*. You need me. We can talk about salary later."

She'd turned out to be right. Jack soon found her indispens-able. Whatever he needed—managing his schedule, setting up vendor accounts, leasing equipment, fending off creditors—she got it done. She even found his start-up's secret weapon, a young programmer right off the bus. Moana snapped him up at the coffee shop downstairs before a bounty hunter could sell him to one of the boomtown companies willing to pay top dollar for coders.

"My name's DuPree Davis, sir," he told Jack when Moana had introduced them. "But everyone calls me Do Pray."

"Show Jack the game you designed, the one with the alligators and water moccasins and all those other creepy crawlers the player has to dodge," Moana said.

Do Pray was as thin as she was wide. His scalp was buzzed and he possessed the long arms and legs of a professional basketball player with none of the tattoos. He shyly handed over his phone. "It's nothing, really. Something I made up on the Greyhound coming 'crost from Naw'lins."

The game involved a couple of characters dressed in old-timey prison stripes. As the soundtrack from *Oh Brother, Where Art Thou?* blared, Jack guided the prisoners through a swamp teeming with poisonous snakes and vampires while being chased by baying hounds the size of dragons and guards toting everything from RPGs to samurai swords.

"You architected this on a four-day bus ride?" Jack didn't bother to hide his skepticism.

"Well, two of the days, sir. On the other I wrote an application for sharing sketchpads. That one really wasn't my idea. See, these kids sitting 'crost from me were playing games and one says to the other wouldn't it be cool if they could share drawings back and forth. They were pretty noisy so I figured I could get them to hush up if they had something to keep them busy. Their grandma was riding with them and she sure appreciated it."

"So you designed an app right there. On the bus. And it worked?"

"Well, it was pretty simple coding. Basic core data with limited Cocoa bindings. The color palette was device dependent but, well... yes, it worked."

"What did you do on the fourth day, create the stars and planets or did you rest?"

"Stared out the window mostly. That and edited the film I made of my trip. I never been out of Lous'ana before. You want to watch it, it's on ZippCast. Already got six thousand views."

Moana beamed. "He's what we've been looking for. He can get our app up and running, *wikiwiki*."

"What sort of application y'all need help with?" Do Pray asked.

Jack gave a quick explanation.

The young coder nodded. "That sounds simple enough. Mainly a search and sort with user profile and input functions. Y'all got the algorithms yet?" When Jack shook his head, Do Pray said, "I can write them."

Jack felt the weight on his shoulders grow a little lighter. He hooked his thumb toward his private office. "Give us a moment, would you Mr. Davis while my... er... associate and I confer on a couple of matters."

As soon as they were behind closed doors, Jack said, "Smart kid. He's a born natural. But how are we going to pay him?"

"He's a *pêpê* in the woods. Give him a hundred thousand founder shares and keep the pizzas and Monsters coming. He'll be happy to sleep on the couch. He won't even know he's not getting a paycheck until after we hit it big." When Jack hesitated, Moana applied the coup de grace. "The landlord came around again. I had to promise to go out to dinner in exchange for him not barring the door. See what you're reducing me to?"

"Okay, okay." Jack threw his hands up in capitulation. "Sign him up. And make it two hundred thousand shares. Anybody who can design apps on a bus without blowing chunks is worth every dime. Keep me posted about every one of his designs. I need to lock them up tight with patents."

JACK'S private office had peeling paint and water stains on the ceiling. The narrow window was always streaked no matter how many times he wiped it with Windex. His desk was a closet door laid atop two file cabinets. It still had the knob and hinges. He didn't bother with guest chairs, preferring to hold meetings in restaurants and bars.

Jack swiped open his tablet and began checking e-mail. He'd barely gotten through the first few messages when his phone buzzed. Caller ID said, "Restricted."

"Speak," he answered.

There were a couple of clicks and then a hum as the signal ricochet from satellite to satellite, from one cell tower to the next.

"Hullo, Jack," the caller finally said.

It was Anders, his inside man at the Cayman Island bank where he kept a numbered account, a holdover from his days on the grift. In an earlier life Anders had been an unassuming Danish bureaucrat with a knack for hiding millions of kroners for whichever political party was in power. A hacker exposed the system on WikiLeaks and the politicos made Anders the fall guy. He exchanged Copenhagen for the Caymans where the island nation's unregulated banking community welcomed people with his discretion and skills.

"How's the sunny life?" Jack asked.

"Boring." Anders replied in his typical morose fashion. "It's all sea, sand, and topless sunbathers. I miss home. I miss the cold and snow. I miss seeing women wrapped in bulky turtleneck sweaters and puffy down jackets. They're like Christmas presents. It adds an element of surprise."

"So turn up the air conditioning when you're entertaining." Jack paused. He could count on one hand the number of times he'd spoken to Anders by phone. They usually conducted business via encrypted e-mail. Any fund transfers were always done by wire that bounced from one offshore bank to another before landing in Jack's account. His suspicions grew. "What's up?"

"Bad news, I'm afraid. Your balance has dropped below the

bank's minimum depository requirement. Your account is in danger of being canceled."

Jack looked out the streaky window. A panhandler was sitting on a filthy piece of cardboard on Market Street. For all Jack knew he could've been a designer whose app went from being the top download one week to an orphan the next. Such was the high-tech marketplace where customers too young to drive, much less vote, dictated success and failure. Jack had been withdrawing from his secret stash to keep his fledgling start-up afloat.

"I'm outraged. I'm a long-standing client who's never flinched at paying the bank's exorbitant monthly fees. I expect some goodwill."

"May I remind you that discretion comes with a price."

"So does extortion."

"May I respectfully offer some advice?"

"Shoot."

Anders cleared his throat. "It's quite simple. Return to your former career. At least that produced a generous cash flow on a predictable basis."

"Good idea. And if I get busted I'll tell the cops I was operating under my banker's advice."

The phone went silent. Anders finally spoke. "I believe they call that gallows humor."

"I wouldn't know. I've never worked that side of the street."

Jack hung up and stared out the window. Maybe Anders was right. Maybe a play was the answer. He'd given his word to Katie he'd never do it again but as the old saying went, desperate times called for desperate measures. He nearly tipped over when his phone blared with a special ringtone signaling who it was.

"I was just thinking about you, babe."

"Guess what?" Katie sounded excited. "Bobby remembered

Two for the Road is Laura's favorite movie so he rented a convertible and they drove up to the wine country. The Audrey Hepburn look is really back in vogue. Laura's redone her entire wardrobe."

Katie knew what she was talking about when it came to fashion. It was all part of her approach to women's health—equal measures of organic food, exercise, sex, and stylish clothes.

"And what's old Dexter think about that?"

"He's British. He likes that cropped hair and classic silhouettes look."

Jack blew out air. "I meant about Laura and Bobby. Dexter's not worried they're going to be grabbing each other instead of lunch at Auberge du Solei?"

"Don't you love the rooms there?" Katie's voice turned wistful. "Remember? We watched the sun set over the vineyards from that big comfy bed. I loved the sheets. Egyptian cotton with 800-thread count."

"You called to tell me Bobby and Laura are playing getaway?"

"I wanted to know what you'd like for dinner. I was thinking of making that veggie quiche because it's only going to be the two of us. The one with egg whites and gluten free flour."

"Meaning Bobby won't be joining us, he being stuck in Napa with Laura. Drinking wine and looking at sunsets. Catching up on old times. Maybe counting sheet threads."

Katie laughed. "I mean because of rush-hour traffic. Bobby has to take her all the way down to Woodside and then drive all the way back to our place. He'll be lucky to get home by midnight."

"Poor Dex. Left all by his lonesome."

"Oh, Dexter won't even notice. He's always working on one deal or another. Laura says he hardly ever leaves his office. He's probably there right now missing out on all the fun. Bobby arranged for a private tour and a tasting at Cliff Lede. I love their Cab. It's big but not too big."

A shaft of sunlight hit the window and shined in Jack's eyes. Along with it came a bright idea. "Sounds like the old boy could use some company," he said. "Go with the quiche. I'll be home in time for dinner."

5

The short stretch of Sand Hill Road between 280 and Stanford University featured clusters of unassuming buildings that blended in with their residential neighbors. Most could be mistaken for suburban medical offices but no pediatrician or orthodontist could afford to hang a shingle there. The occupants were venture capitalists who wielded more wealth and power than kings and presidents. Their seedlings sprouted into tech companies that reshaped the world.

Jack pushed open the door to Capital Dexterity's headquarters. A woman sat behind a desk in the reception area. She had her hair pulled back in a tight bun. A gold and jade Siamese cat brooch gleamed from the breast of her suit jacket and a Chinese amber bracelet etched with fans and butterflies encircled her wrist.

"I'm afraid Mr. Cotswold and his partners don't accommodate drop-ins," she said with a frozen smile. "If you would like to submit your name and proposal by e-mail, someone will get back to you, time permitting."

Jack turned on the charm. He pointed to her jewelry. "I see

you're a fan of Asian baubles like my old friend Dexter. Give him a call. Tell him it's Jack McCoul."

"Mr. Cotswold has many friends and they all make appointments." Her eyes dropped to a computer screen and she resumed keyboarding.

Jack tapped his foot. He fired off a text to Bobby Ballena. Seconds later his phone pinged with an incoming text. It was a picture of Laura toasting the camera with a glass of bubbly. He found Dexter's cell number on his contacts and forwarded him the photo. The phone made a whoosh. Then he rounded the desk, leaned in close to the woman, and said, "Cheese." She looked up and he snapped a selfie.

The wheels on her chair all but smoked as she pushed away. "What do you think you're doing?"

"Letting Dex know his pal's out here cooling his heels. Trust me, he'll get a kick out of it." Jack attached the photo to a text and hit send.

A blue light on her headset blinked instantly. "Yes, Mr. Cotswold. Yes, he's standing right here, but I had nothing to do with—" She listened and then nodded. "Yes, sir. Very good. Right away."

She ushered Jack down a hallway and stopped in front of a black door trimmed in white Victorian casing. Two brass numbers shined in the middle.

Jack cocked his head. "Ten, as in Downing Street?"

The woman stiffened. "Mr. Cotswold is waiting." She twisted the handle and stepped aside.

Dexter looked imperious, sitting behind an enormous mahogany desk. Framed magazine covers featuring his portrait hung on either side of a painting of Queen Elizabeth. A Union Jack was draped from a staff. He cleared his throat. "Good to see you, old chap, but I do have a business to run. What is the meaning behind sending me these photographs?" He held up his phone.

Jack shrugged. "Just a way to get your attention. Electric fences show more warmth than your receptionist."

Dexter's throat clearing was on par with a morning gargle. "Miss Nash is not a receptionist. She is my executive assistant. I am sure you understand a man in my position requires an able administrator."

"Like Queen B on the wall over there has her palace guards in bearskin hats. I get it but I was hoping the snaps would brighten your day. Remind you that your real friends are flesh and blood, not spreadsheets and business plans."

Dexter sighed. "This is about your start-up, isn't it? I am sorry, old boy, but I thought I made myself perfectly clear. Mixing friends and business is rarely good form. Mixing friends and a bad business?"

"That's where you're wrong. My app is a good business. It's the financing that's lousy. You could change that. You know better than anyone what it takes to launch a new product."

Dexter's swivel chair was the type used in England's High Court. It squeaked when he leaned back. "You are right about that. I have launched hundreds of companies. But even the good ones do not always make it. There are so many variables that can make the difference between success and failure—financing, competitors, human resources, the marketplace, public tastes." He grimaced when saying *public*.

"I can make this one work. All I need is some seed money to keep it going."

Dexter and his chair both groaned. "I can see you have become attached to this... er... travel app, correct? But personal attachment is folly. It will blind you. You must have the discipline to sever all emotions when making financial decisions. Who was it who said, *You must kill all your darlings*?"

"William Faulkner but he died thirty years before the Internet. I'm talking about the here and now."

Dexter waved his hand in dismissal, his fingers wiggling like fat sausages. "Listen, Katie is a wonderful girl—she is my wife's best friend, after all—and I would hate to see her suffer because you clung to a dream that will never fly. Jack, old boy, think of her. Your business is not going to make it. Take my word for it. If it were worthy of financing, someone would have already stepped up. Leaders make decisions about funding start-ups before the idea is even put to paper." He shook his head again. "You must let it go."

"The app will work. I know it. It's going to be a hit. I have the coding equivalent of Frank Lloyd Wright architecting it"

Light from an overhead spot reflected off Dexter's pate. "You don't say? I probably know him. It's my business to know all the young talent. What did you say his name is?"

"I didn't. *She's* a total walk-on. Straight out of a community college in Seattle. Goes by one name. Bird. If only she'd wash her hair." He made a face.

"A female programmer? Well, if she's as good as you say she is, good luck keeping her. And I doubt she will make a difference in your app's marketability. But I will say one thing for you, you are a born salesman. Shame to let that go to waste. Tell you what. I have hundreds, no thousands, of business contacts. Say the word and I will pick up the phone right now. You will have dozens of invitations for job interviews. Only too happy to help." He paused. "And I might be persuaded to put in a word for any of your staff as well. If this Bird person is as good as you say she is I am sure I can find her a spot somewhere."

"You can help by writing a check. I'll give you whatever points you want. All I need is a few hundred grand. Just enough to finish writing the code and finalize a marketing plan. I'm close. Real close. Once the beta is finished, the app will sell itself."

Dexter stood. The floor behind his desk was raised. It put him eye level with Jack. "Do not let this come between our friendship. My decision is final. If you decide you want my help obtaining interviews for a sales job, let Miss Nash know. Now, excuse me, but I really must return to business." He reached for a folder and started shuffling papers.

Jack breathed in, breathed out. It was a yoga technique Katie was always trying to get him to do. Centering, she called it. Sometimes it worked. Most times it didn't.

"You don't want to know about the picture of Laura?"

Dexter looked up. "What of it?"

"Do you recognize the location?"

"Should I?"

"Take a look and you tell me."

Dexter picked up his phone and studied the screen. "It appears to be Napa Valley. I can see vineyards in the background. I do not recall the precise locale or the occasion. Some celebration with you and Katie, I should imagine."

"It was taken a few minutes ago. She's having lunch with Bobby Ballena. He sent it to me."

Jack had made his living spotting tells. Everyone had one. Dexter included. The corner of his left eye drooped slightly.

"Of course. She told me this morning when I left for the office. Luncheon and a little wine tasting. Good for her. She needs a break now and then. Redecorating our home has been a tremendous amount of work. I am sure she is having a lovely time."

"I'm sure." Jack put a couple of beats between the set up and what he really wanted to find out. "So Dex, speaking of bad business deals, you might want to think twice about bankrolling those trolls chasing after my app. You're going to burn up a lot of money on lawyers. My patents are sealed up tighter than a nun's underwear."

Dexter's left eye sagged. "Whatever are you talking about, old boy?"

Jack left Dexter's inner sanctum and closed the door behind him. Miss Nash was waiting. A tall man with a sharp nose and the unblinking eyes of a hawk stood alongside her.

"Here he is," she said with an icy tone. "I tried to keep him from bothering Mr. Cotswold, but he played a trick on me."

Jack sized up the man quickly. He was wearing a light gray turtleneck underneath an expensive dark suit jacket. Jack offered his hand. "Jack McCoul. Dexter and I are old friends. Our wives are besties. And you are?"

"Arjun Chopra. I am afraid you gave Miss Nash quite a fright. Our firm has a strict policy regarding unscheduled visits." He smiled thinly. "We ask everyone to conform to it, including husbands of best friends. I am sure you understand."

"Actually I don't. It doesn't sound very neighborly."

"We must take every precaution against armed robbery given the times we live in. There is a societal element that mistakes venture *capital* for venture *currency* and believes we keep such on the premises."

Jack showed him a grin. "You don't exactly strike me as a security guard."

"I am the firm's managing partner."

"Let me guess. Dex hired you because you both went to school in England. The old boy's a royalist through and through. I have a thing for reading people. I'd say you're Silicon Valley by way of London School of Economics and, wait, wait, central—no, make that western—India. State of Maharashtra if I'm not mistaken. Mumbai, right?"

"Very clever, Mr. McCoul. Good day."

Jack faked a modest bow. "Wasn't that movie *Slumdog*

Millionaire filmed there? It's one of my favorites. A little guy takes down the big guys. Lies. Corruption. Love. Redemption. A big over-the-top Bollywood ending."

Chopra blinked very slowly. It was as if he had a bird of prey's third eyelid. "Everyone is from somewhere, Mr. McCoul. The question is, where are they now and what did they do to get there?"

6

A buelita's was a holdout against the gentrification of the Mission District. The traditional Mexican restaurant still served refried beans cooked in lard and menudo made with fresh cow tripe. Hark was splashing hot sauce into a bowlful when Jack found him seated at one of the café's back booths.

"Your grandma catches you messing with her recipe, you know what she'll do," Jack said.

Hark grinned. "Like she always does, *vato*. Smack me in the shoulder with that big metal ladle. Lets me know she still cares." The former gangbanger spooned up some of the spicy hangover medicine. "What the doctor ordered. You want a bowl?"

Jack could still taste the pride curdling in his mouth after his meeting with Dexter. "I could use something spicier. Maybe she's got some carnitas verde ready."

"You know she does. Woman's going on eighty and still puts in fourteen hours a day behind the stove. I talked to her about retiring. You know what she told me?"

"I got a good idea and you don't have to translate." Jack

nodded toward the kitchen. "I'll go say hello. You want me to bring you back a beer?"

"You got to ask? You know menudo's only half the cure."

Abuelita's was Jack's home away from home when he was growing up. He lived a few blocks away but dwelling under the same roof with an Irish father whose temper was as hot as the fires he fought didn't always make for a sitcom family upbringing. Jack's visit to the kitchen resulted in hugs and blessings from Hark's grandmother and assurances that she would bring him a plate. He reached behind the bar and snagged a couple of Pacificos along with a handful of lime wedges on his way back to the table.

"How's business?" He set down the beers.

Hark wasn't one to watch his weight no matter how much he wanted to. He loved food as much as he loved his '64 Impala lowrider. "Good, *'mano*. Even great. I got two sprayers and four metal pounders working for me now." His custom paint and body shop was right around the corner. "I put up a website. You should check it out. The photos of the rides we customize will make you ache. I got an online store now where low lows can order T-shirts and fuzzy dice and chrome chain steering wheels. I'm telling you, it keeps going the way it's going, I may trade bricks for clicks. You know what I'm saying?"

Jack shoved a lime down the neck of a bottle. "Didn't know they figured out a way to paint a car online yet."

"Give them time. It's the way it is. Way it's going be. They got these 3D plastic printers now you can crank out all sorts of things on. Lot of the old 'bangers I used to run with are printing out plastic guns now."

"Zip guns made out of recycled zip ties."

"Tech's everywhere. The only downside in my business is when some *cabron* Yelps my ass. It's not like the old days when you got disrespected and settled things with a baseball bat. Now it's anonymous. And you can't get it deleted from the web no matter how hard you try. You lose a star on your rating, it costs. Big time."

Hark's grandma brought over a platter heaped with carnitas swimming in green sauce. She watched Jack take a first bite.

"*Delicioso, abuela,*" he said.

She crossed herself and flashed a gold-toothed smile.

When she was gone Jack said, "Guess who showed up at my front door? On my living room couch, to be exact."

Hark grunted as he spooned his bowl clean. "Not Katie's punk brother. Don't tell me he's in trouble again."

"Bobby Ballena."

Hark grimaced. It stretched the big gothic letters tattooed on his neck. An inker had misspelled his given name, Geraldo, with an *H,* left off the *o,* and then added angel wings. That's how Hark got his street handle.

"Dude's trouble from the get go. Always has been. The way he was when we went to Saint Joe's? He made us look like altar boys. And his thing with the ladies? I never did get what they saw in him." Hark gestured at the kitchen with his spoon. "He looks like one of those dudes on the *telenovelas* my *abuela* watches. What's he doing here anyway? Isn't he riding a warrant?"

Jack nodded. "He's casing a score. A big one."

"Then you better keep your distance now that you're on the straight and narrow. You don't want to get sucked into his shit again."

"Hard to do, seeing he's bunking on my couch. Katie invited him."

Hark drained his beer in one gulp and belched loudly. "Katie's the best. I mean that. One smart, beautiful woman, all due respect. But having Bobby Ballena as a houseguest? That's asking for trouble."

"Tell me about it." Jack continued eating. The pork was juicy and tender, and the sauce triggered a sweat.

Hark rolled his empty bottle around. "What kind of score? I'm only asking. You know, theoretically speaking."

"Theoretically?"

"Yeah, theoretically. I bought this new app. Cousin of mine designed it. Vocabulary builder. It's pretty good, too."

Jack exhaled. Apps. Who wasn't making them now? Maybe Dexter was right. Maybe he should hang it up.

"Did you ever meet Katie's best friend, Laura?"

"She was in Nepal with her when you two fell head over heels, right?"

"That's the one. Bobby and Laura were an item there, too."

Hark huffed. "Bobby dated every girl in the Mission. Kept more than a few from becoming novitiates. What's this Laura got to do with the score?"

"Her husband is one of the richest VCs in the Valley."

"Bobby planning to scam the ex-girlfriend's hubby?"

Jack drained his beer. "More like a B and E."

"For what?"

"A statue. A solid gold statue." Jack told the story about how Bobby and he filched Little Buddha to save their hides.

"How big is it?" Hark asked.

Jack held his palm a foot above the table. "Weighs around ten pounds."

"Not bad. Price of gold bounces around some but even at the low end of around twelve hundred an ounce that makes the statue worth a couple hundred large, easy."

"It's worth a lot more than that to the right buyer. It's at least four hundred years old. Whoever cast it left a little smudge on the bottom. It was probably an impurity in the gold. You know, iron, copper or silver. But in the right light it looks like a fingerprint. That adds to the statue's legend. The story goes

Siddhartha—that was Buddha's original name—touched it during one of his many rebirths. Some say the blessing bestowed the statue with a curse because anyone who tries to own it has nothing but bad luck."

Hark quit sliding the bottle around. "You believe that?"

Jack shrugged. "You went to Saint Joe's. You know my feeling about religion. But Little Buddha definitely has a track record of bouncing from owner to owner like a hot potato. Only monks who've reach a certain level of enlightenment can be entrusted with its care. That's because they don't lust after it. They've forsaken all worldly goods and earthly pleasures."

"You and Bobby didn't get burned when you had the statue?"

"Not yet but who knows? Buddhists believe the world wasn't created once upon a time but over and over again, millions of times every second. I guess there's still plenty of time for payback."

Hark laughed. "Knowing Bobby, he's not going let that stand in the way."

"Nope."

Hark started skating the beer bottle around again. "He's already asked you to help him, hasn't he?"

Jack nodded. "And the way my start-up is draining my bank account, I closely considered it."

"How close?"

"Close enough."

7

S ome people measured the passage of time by the changing of the seasons—trees leafing, birds migrating, fog pouring through the Golden Gate in summertime— but the start of a new year for Jack was Giants opening day. He was a shortstop while at St. Joseph's and won a full ride to play college ball at San Francisco State. The crack of a bat and the slap of leather told him all was right in the world even when a con went awry or the cops got close. When he got home from Hark's, Katie had the windows open and the cheers coming in from nearby AT&T Park mixed with the play-by-play blaring from the kitchen radio. She was peering into the oven of the six-burner range. Jack sneaked up behind and grabbed her hips.

"Dinner ready?" he whispered into her ear.

Katie yelped and spun around. "If you made my quiche fall...
"

He grabbed her and they kissed. Afterward, she laughed, and Jack felt his money troubles melt like the butter in the pan.

"Make a salad while I set the table," she said.

Jack bowed. "Right away, Chef."

He opened the refrigerator and pulled out a bottle of Etudé Pinot Gris along with a head of butter lettuce, pomegranate seeds, a blood orange, and a jicama root. He filled two glasses and went to work slicing and dicing.

"Any word from Bobby and Laura?" he asked.

"Laura texted she was a bad girl. She had the cow's milk *burrata* for a starter and the red miso sweet potato purée for her main. She's coming over bright and early in the morning and we'll go to step together." Katie led fitness and yoga classes in the building's private gym. "She's going to need a colonic after the carbohydrate overload she put herself through today."

Jack winced. "Ask her to do that at home, okay?"

Katie shook the spatula at him. "Be nice."

"Did Laura say if she spoke with Dexter?"

"She didn't mention it but I'm sure she did. She texts him about hundred times a day. Why?"

Jack peeled the blood orange and quartered it. Then he halved the quarters. He julienned the jicama and a couple of carrots. "I saw him today. Drove down to his office."

"You did? You're such a good friend. You weren't kidding when you said he needed some company."

"More like I need his *company*."

Katie glissaded across the kitchen and threw her arms around him. She started nibbling his ear. "Everybody knows you're a good egg but I'm the only one who knows you're a three-minuter."

"I'm pretty sure I last longer than that."

She punched his shoulder. "You know what I mean—what's inside that hard shell of yours." Katie went back to work on his earlobe.

"You keep that up and we're never going to get to dinner."

Katie pressed against him. "You know why quiche is like revenge?"

"How's that?"

"Both are best served cold."

THE GIANTS BEAT the Rockies six to four. The stadium lights were still shining but all the fans had filed out, some to keep celebrating at the nearby watering holes, others to board street-cars for the raucous ride home. Flocks of seagulls descended on the ballpark and fought over half-eaten hotdogs and spilled peanuts.

The loft's windows were still open. Jack and Katie lay entwined on the bed. He was humming "Strawberry Fields Forever" as he played dot to dot on the passion blossoms that bloomed on her skin.

"What did you and Dexter talk about today?" she asked, her voice turning sleepy.

"Work."

"Is he going to help you launch your app?"

Jack thought about telling her how he was sure Dexter was out to screw him over. "He says he's already committed."

"If he didn't give you any funding, did he at least give you some good advice?"

"Not really."

"I think he did."

"What makes you say that?"

She took his hand and held it against her breast. "Because when you came home, you certainly knew that all work and no play make Jack a dull boy."

Jack laughed and Katie rolled on top of him and pinned his arms to the bed. "Ready for that quiche now?" she asked.

"Something tells me we better leave it for breakfast."

A WOMAN BELTING out the blues pulled Jack from a deep sleep.
He and Katie were snuggled under the duvet, a yin and a yang.
She was using his arm as a pillow so he slipped it gently from
beneath her head and reached for his phone. It wasn't until he
had it in his hand that he was awake enough to realize the singer
wasn't his ringtone. Katie's phone launched into another stanza
of "Set Fire to the Rain" by the time he grabbed it and swiped it
open.

"Call back when it's daylight," he growled.

A woman's voice even louder than the ringtone shrieked,
"Oh my, God! He's not moving. Oh God, I think he's dead."

Jack sat up fast. He glanced at the phone's screen for caller
ID. "Laura, it's me, Jack. Katie's asleep. What are you talking
about?"

"Oh, my God. There's blood everywhere."

"Whose? Whose blood?"

"Dexter! His head's all bloody. Oh God, Katie. I don't know
what to do. Can you come here right now? I need you. Please?"

Jack stood. "Laura. Listen to me. It's Jack. Have you called
911? You need to hang up right now and call 911."

"Jack, is that you?"

"Yeah. Have you called 911?"

"Dexter's head. It's all bloody."

"What happened? Did he fall down the stairs?"

"I... I don't know. I was asleep. I heard a noise. He wasn't in
bed. I... I went to look for him. He's lying on the library floor.
He's not moving."

"Listen to me. I'm going to hang up and call 911 for you. The
paramedics will be there in minutes. You need to let them in.
Laura and I are on our way. We'll be there as quick as we can."
Jack carried the phone into the living room. The couch was bare.

Bobby's go-bag was gone. Jack took a deep breath. "What about Bobby?"

Laura's teeth chattered. "What about him?"

"Is he still at your place?"

"No, he left hours ago. Why?"

"No reason. Forget I asked. Hang tight. We're on our way."

8

Woodside was too small to warrant its own police department. The San Mateo County Sheriff's Department officially handled law enforcement but most of the town's billionaire burghers fielded their own private security teams. Flashing emergency lights were bouncing off the redwoods when Jack turned into the Cotswold driveway. A CHP officer wearing a Smokey the Bear hat waved a Maglite.

"Back up your vehicle right now, sir," he barked. "Go on home. Nothing to see here."

A half dozen emergency vehicles were parked at the end of the drive. Jack lowered the window. "We're not looky-loos. We're family. Radio the officer in charge and let him know Mrs. Cotswold's sister is here."

The cop hesitated before toggling his collar mike. "Roger that. I'll send them right up."

Jack pulled in behind a black Crown Vic blocking the mansion's porte cochère. He recognized the plates. A sheriff's deputy stood guard duty at the front door. He had a baby face and a uniform that looked a size too big. "You the family?"

Jack nodded. "Where's my sister-in-law?"

"In the living room. I'll take you to her."

"That's okay. We know the way."

Jack didn't wait for an answer. He put his arm around Katie and hustled her down the hallway. She broke free as soon as she spotted Laura hunched on the couch.

"I'm here," Katie called. "Everything's going to be all right."

"He's dead. Dexter's dead. I can't believe it." Laura lurched forward and Katie caught her.

"There, there girlfriend. Let it out. Let it all out. Don't hold back a drop."

San Francisco Homicide Inspector Terrence Dolan was seated in a chair next to the couch. He was dressed in his trademark blue suit, white shirt, and rep tie. He was another alumnus from St. Joseph's but unlike Jack, Hark and Bobby, he really had been an altar boy. Still was. He'd also been Katie's fiancé before she met Jack.

"What are you doing here?" Jack worked hard to hold his astonishment in check.

The former all-American's jaw jutted. "Since when does Katie have a sister?"

"Since the chipper out front tried to turn us around. You know Katie. She sees a cat up a tree, she starts climbing. Don't get me started about baby birds falling out of nests. You didn't answer me. What are you doing here?"

The homicide cop squared his already squared shoulders. "I'm the one asking the questions, got that?"

"Sure. Why all the fuss and bother for a slip and fall?"

"Who says it's a fuss and who says it's a slip and fall?"

Jack got what he wanted. He steeled himself. "What happened?"

Terry jutted his jaw again. He beckoned Jack to join him on

the far side of the room. "I got a dead man down the hall with his head bashed in. What do you know about it?"

Jack held up his hands. "Nothing more than Laura called and said she found Dexter on the floor. I dialed 911 and we jumped in the car."

"Were you and the victim as close as those two?" He gestured to Katie and Laura. The waterworks were still going full blast.

"Are you asking officially?"

"And I already told you I'm the one asking the questions."

"Since when does SFPD get involved in Woodside? You guys open a branch in the 'burbs?"

Terry's teeth clenched. "Same old Jack McCoul. Ask you if it's raining and you have to think what's in it for you before answering."

Jack shrugged. "It's clear as a bell outside. Satisfied?"

"A one eighty-seven goes out from a town that doesn't have its own force, and it's all hands on deck. I was in the neighborhood. Sheriffs and CHP aren't equipped to lead a murder investigation. I am. Now answer the question."

Jack knew all the cop codes. It was his business to know. "What makes you so sure it's a murder?"

"Answer the question. Were you and the vic close?"

"Katie's the closest to family Laura's got. Dexter and I were the plus ones. Sure, the four of us got together for dinner occasionally but that's about as friendly as it got."

"Did he know about you being in the life?"

"I believe the word you're forgetting there, Inspector, is *allegedly*. I'm a businessman. I have a tech company."

"Since when?"

"Since I got religion. What's it matter? It doesn't have anything to do with this."

"I'll be the judge of that." Terry looked over at the couch

where Katie had steered Laura. "What about the wife? She's a lot younger."

"And he's a rich nerd. They're the same as ninety percent of the other couples in the Valley. Both sides are outkicking their coverage."

"But none of them are lying on the floor with their heads bashed in."

Jack sucked his teeth. Dexter was a pompous little prick but nobody deserved that. "Was it a robbery?"

"Nine times out of ten these wind up being domestics," Terry said, his voice drifting.

"No way. Uh-uh. Laura and Dexter were gaga over each other. She'd never swat a fly. She's like Katie. She feels guilty eating an oyster."

Terry rocked back and forth in his spit-shine oxfords. "You've been here before, right? Cotswold ever show you his library?"

Jack nodded. "It's like a private museum."

"Let's go take a look. Maybe you can tell if anything's missing."

DEXTER WAS SPRAWLED on an antique Tibetan tribal rug with a sage and gold leaf pattern on the border. The back of his head resembled a split melon. A stain the color and consistency of motor oil spread across the rug. Jack had seen dead bodies before and remembered the coppery, cooked liver odor of spilled blood, but he couldn't smell a thing here. He glanced at the ceiling. The specially designed centrifuge was humming.

Two people in matching white Tyvex coveralls hovered around the body. Plastic boxes were placed on the floor as stepping stones. The man wore earbuds and hummed pop tunes while he shined an ultraviolet flashlight around. The woman had a silver eyebrow hoop and was combing the rug with a dog FURminator.

Terry pointed at a strip of easy-to-peel blue painter's tape. "Don't walk past the stripe. They haven't completed EC yet."

Jack knew that meant evidence collection. "They got here fast for a town with no cops on the payroll."

"They're on loan from Menlo Park PD."

Jack looked at Dexter again and wondered if he'd been jumped from behind or knew the killer well enough to turn his back, never suspecting he was in danger.

"See anything missing?" Terry asked.

Jack inventoried the room. He couldn't remember every piece he'd seen the night of the dinner party but there were no obvious gaps on the shelves. All of the expensive artifacts appeared to have been left untouched. His eyes wandered to the Japanese scroll depicting the samurai and geisha. The secret panel hiding Little Buddha was closed.

"I can't tell. I was only here once before."

"You sure?"

"About the number of times?"

Jack was stalling to buy time so he could keep looking around. If Bobby had been robbing the place, he would have grabbed more than Little Buddha. Stuff would have been knocked to the floor if there had been a struggle. And then there was the air vent. The motor was still running.

"You know what I mean," Terry said.

"The shelves look full to me but what do I know? Maybe he keeps a list somewhere." Jack eyed the floor. "I get it. You're not looking for what's been stolen. You're looking for a murder weapon. You think they hit him with something they grabbed off the shelf."

"What makes you say that?"

Jack could tell the cop wasn't going to give anything away. "I watch TV same as everybody else. The cops need the weapon to make their case. You haven't found one."

Terry started to say something but the baby-faced deputy interrupted. "The coroner's here, Inspector. She's ready whenever you are."

Jack stepped aside to allow her to enter. She was thin and wore a silver tracksuit and pink running shoes. Gray hairs streaked her black hair. Her face looked sleepy. "Dr. Li Soon," she said brusquely. "What do you have?"

Terry gestured to Dexter's corpse. "Him and a whole lot of questions."

9

The sun was clearing the East Bay Hills as Jack took a stool at the bar. The Pier Inn was a classic waterfront dive held together by paint and memories. It teetered on the edge of a wobbly dock hidden in the shadows of the Bay Bridge. The regulars—tugboat crews, hardcore Giants fans, lone eagles, and the like—wouldn't have it any other way. More than one waterfront developer caught scouting the location had taken an involuntary swim.

Wonder Boy brought Jack a mug of coffee and topped it off with a splash of Jameson. The bartender never started a conversation but could always be counted on providing any type of statistic when queried—batting averages, record temperatures, foreign currency rates. Jack never asked Wonder how he obtained all the information nor did he ever question its accuracy. He'd staked his life more than once on the bartender never being wrong.

"The Gs came out of spring training pretty healthy." Jack lifted the mug. "What odds do you give if they go all the way again this year?"

Wonder worked to wrestle his sibilants under control. "S-s-success depends on a formula based on s-s-several factors. First, you multiply s-s-scoring total by pitching s-s-staff ERA and then assign an exponent to s-s-slugging percentage and OBA and then divide by the division's record. You also got to weight the home and away matchups, as well as day and night games."

"The odds, Wonder, the odds."

"S-s-six point three s-s-seven five to four point two nine s-s-six."

"That good, huh. Maybe I'll place a wager at Jimmie Fang's."

Wonder wiped the bar even though its protective coat of resin was spotless. Legend had it the plank was a piece of the *Golden Hind* knocked free when Sir Francis Drake ran aground off Point Reyes. Jack loved the story as much as he loved the bar. He'd downed his first boilermaker, standing at it when he was still in high school, courtesy of his old man, Captain Gavin McCoul, SFFD, deceased.

"I heard about what happened in Woods-s-side last night." Wonder kept polishing.

Jack wasn't surprised the bartender had the story long before Twitter or the *Chronicle* did. His network of insiders and informants was as finely tuned as his statistical recall. "Katie and the wife are old friends. We're the first people she called."

"S-s-so I heard. They s-s-say Terry Dolan is heading the investigation. He s-s-still has it in for you."

Jack blew on the mug and took a sip. The whisky did little to cut the coffee's viscosity. "Luck of the draw. He happened to be in the right place at the wrong time."

"S-s-six thousand to one."

"What's that?"

"The odds a S-s-san Francisco homicide detective would be in Woods-s-side. You take the number of officers, divide by number of days, factor in traffic…"

Jack waved the mug in surrender. "I believe you."

Wonder moved down the bar, leaving Jack to ponder Dexter's murder and Bobby's whereabouts. Coincidences were for Scientologists. Bobby's disappearance had to be tied to Dexter's death but that didn't mean his old schoolmate had mashed in the magnate's brains. Bobby was an unapologetic crook for life from the get-go, and nothing was ever going to change that—not even if he had married someone like Katie. But violence wasn't part of Bobby's DNA. He could talk tough and act as convincingly as a stone-cold killer if a con called for it, but when it came right down to it, he was a lover not a fighter. Jack had seen him backed into a corner plenty of times and he'd never given into panic.

Dexter was dead. Bobby was missing. And Little Buddha? Jack sipped his Irish coffee and wondered where the hell he was.

Jack had no way of knowing if the gold statue was still hiding behind the secret panel or not. If Little Buddha was there then it stood to reason Bobby was in the clear. If the statue wasn't, it didn't mean Bobby killed Dexter either. The trouble was Jack couldn't check to find out. No way he could tell Terry about the statue. Doing that would not only be the same as slapping the cuffs on Bobby, it would give the cop probable cause to arrest him, too. It was Terry's life's ambition to take down Jack ever since Katie threw him over.

The night of the murder Terry ordered Jack out of the library as soon as the coroner arrived. Since there was nothing he could do but wait the cops out, Jack went looking for Katie. She was in the master bedroom trying to calm down Laura. Any hope of going back downstairs to check for Little Buddha were dashed when Terry came upstairs and told them the crime scene team was finished. Laura ran into the bathroom wailing.

"She can't take hearing anything more right now," Katie explained. "It's all too much for her."

Terry locked his blues eyes with Katie's green sparklers. Jack knew the cop was only too happy to have her serving as the go between.

"You need to tell your friend we sealed the murder—" Terry caught himself. "The library. No one goes in or out without my approval."

Katie nodded. "I'll let her know, not that she'd go in there anyway."

"She couldn't even if she wanted." Terry squared his jaw. "I reprogrammed the scanner with my palm print. That door won't open for anybody but me."

Jack steadied his gaze. Now the only way to get in was to drop down the ceiling vent. He was bigger than Bobby and wasn't sure he'd fit.

"What about the rest of the house?" Katie asked.

Terry kept his eyes zeroed in on hers. "What about it?"

"Laura doesn't want to leave. Is it all right if she stays?"

"Alone?"

"I was planning on staying with her."

"I'll have the Sheriff put a cruiser on regular patrol. And I'll be by from time to time, too, conducting investigative work."

Terry's pocket buzzed. He retrieved his phone. "Dolan. Right, I'm on my way." He clicked off and handed a business card to Katie. "In case you lost my number. I've never changed it."

Jack waited until the cop was gone and then said, "You're staying here?"

Katie's eyes widened. "I wouldn't dream of leaving now. Laura needs me."

"That's not what I meant. I wouldn't think she'd want to stay after what happened."

"She says she can't go. Dexter needs her. His spirit won't have any peace until everything is resolved."

Jack blew out air. Laura had always been susceptible to whatever the latest new age huckster was hawking. It had been her idea to follow some self-described guru to Nepal and she'd talked Katie into joining her. Jack and Bobby made the fat phony out as a con the first time they saw him. Part of their motive to get him to shove off had to do with how beautiful Katie and Laura were. And part of it had to do with their sense of professional pride. Amateurs like him gave the trade a bad name.

"Don't tell me you believe Dexter's going to start flying around the mansion moaning and rattling chains until his killer is caught?"

Katie made a face. "Shush"

"Ah, come on, babe. You don't really think he can hear us, do you?"

"It's Laura I'm worried about. She's in a very fragile state of mind right now."

"And that's different than usual, how?"

"We need to be sensitive to her needs. Look, I don't expect you to stay here, too." Katie shook her head. "You need to get back to work. You have a business to run, an app to launch."

"I could commute."

"And increase your carbon footprint? I don't think so." She crossed her arms. "No, as much as I'll miss you, you need to go home. This shouldn't take long. Terry's good at his job. He'll solve this in no time and we can all go back to the way it was."

"Except for Dexter. He'll be moving on to something else, right?"

"You know what I mean." Katie got on her tiptoes and gave him a kiss. "Now, go back to work. I'll see you soon."

Jack finished nursing his fortified coffee and musing on the likelihood of wandering spirits. Wonder Boy ferried over two beers. He placed one in front of Jack and the other in front of the neighboring stool that sat empty.

"Don't tell me you see somebody sitting next to me," Jack said.

Wonder's expression remained the same as it did whenever a regular asked him about pink elephants. "That's for Hark."

The big man clapped Jack on the back and took the stool. He saluted Wonder with the beer. "Thanks, *prodigio,* and thanks for the list of this year's top ten most popular car colors. Sure is coming in handy managing my paint inventory."

The bartending statistician extraordinaire moved off to fill another order. Hark said, "Thought you'd be here. I heard you alibied."

"Is there anybody in this town that doesn't know what went down?"

"Come on, *vato,* you know better than anyone how the real geek squad works. When they're not hacking into the mobile computer terminals of cop cars, they're doing it the old-fashioned way and monitoring their radios. The only thing that isn't out yet is the crime scene photographs. They'll be on Instagram within the hour."

"What's the official word about Katie and me?"

"Not much. Cop log says you're the friends the wife called." Hark sipped his beer and then lowered his voice. "Was it Bobby?"

"It's not his style."

Hark nodded as he thought on it. "I told you Bobby was trouble. Even if he didn't do it, he's a liability for you. Terry's going to make the link sooner rather than later."

"My guess he already has. I'm sure he asked Laura where she'd been that day. Katie would've confirmed it, too."

Hark cocked a brow. "Katie's talking to her ex-boyfriend again?"

"She's staying with Laura. Helping her get through the grieving process. Knowing Katie, she probably has her doing Kundalini and taking oatmeal baths."

"Katie's one thoughtful woman, all due respect." Hark toyed

with his beer. "But that means Terry's going come after you with a whole lot of questions. Ask you about Bobby. More to the point, where he is and if you had anything to do with knocking over the rich dude's antique stash and knocking him off while you were at it."

"More the reason why I got to put a bead on Bobby's whereabouts."

Hark took another swig and wiped his lips with the back of his hand. "He's probably already back in Baja, hiding out in a cave on a beach somewhere. They don't check you going down, only coming up."

"My guess he's still in town. If he snatched Little Buddha, he won't want to be caught with him."

"One way to find out."

"You game to help out?"

"You got to ask?" Hark drained his beer. "I'll sniff around but you got to promise me one thing."

"What's that?"

"When we find him, don't believe anything he tells you."

"Why not? Bobby and I were partners once."

Hark shifted his considerable weight on the stool. "The only person Bobby ever partnered with was himself. Everyone sees that but you on account you have misplaced loyalty tendencies."

"Don't tell me. You got a cousin that designs psychology apps."

Hark grinned. "Yeah, and he's doing pretty good, too. His IPO was killer."

10

"How are we supposed to make any money if you don't even bother to show up?" Moana Akauola jabbed a tin watering can with a curved spout at Jack. Even the overgrown philodendron looked pissed off.

"I'm here now, aren't I?" Jack realized how lame it sounded, but there was no taking it back.

Moana muttered something in Tongan—he was pretty sure it involved a coconut tree and a body orifice. "My family is expecting me to pay for the Heilala Festival feast this year. They already picked out the pigs. Fat ones, too."

"Tell your folks to keep feeding them. We'll be makin' bacon by then." He paused. "How's Do Pray doing?"

Moana pointed the watering can at his cubicle. "See for yourself. He never leaves. Always working. I never even seen him go to the bathroom down the hall."

"And I've never seen anybody code as fast." Jack whistled. "He's got a sixth sense when it comes to identifying and organizing products. Plus the way he plugged in the customer profiling for recommending add-ons is genius. Half the time I don't even need to explain what other functions we want to add.

I've already filed a dozen patent applications. It's no wonder I've attracted trolls. They can sniff out gold in a blizzard."

"You should tell that to Do Pray. He could use a little sweet talk since he hasn't seen a paycheck. Not that I have either."

A pair of bright red Beats covered the programmer's ears. His head was bobbing as his fingers flew and his eyes stayed fixed on a thirty-inch screen swarming with lines of code doing the digital equivalent of a conga line. A pyramid of empty energy drink cans rose on either side of the screen. Crumpled bags of gluten-free yucca chips littered the floor like autumn leaves. Jack watched the maestro at work before tapping him on the shoulder and raising one side of the headphones.

"Michael Tilson Thomas has got nothing on you." He gave him another pat on the shoulder and retreated to his private office.

Jack checked his e-mail but there were no messages from Bobby. He wasn't surprised. No way a pro like Bobby would leave cyber breadcrumbs for the cops to follow. Jack scanned the rest of the names in the in-box, skipping over those he knew were creditors. He spotted two messages from Tingly Meyers.

Though Tingly Meyers sounded like a big law firm, it was anything but. Both names belonged to a sole practitioner who operated out of a sliver of an office above a French Vietnamese restaurant on Belden Place. He was a high-tech version of the personal injury lawyers who advertised on billboards and late night TV. Jack had retained him to defend his patents because of his willingness to take his fee in pre-IPO shares.

Jack opened the first message. *I've resigned you as a client effective immediately.* The second was equally brusque: *All files have been shredded.*

Jack's blood boiled as he hit the speed dial. His suspicion ratcheted up when Tingly's number went straight to voice mail. He nearly broke his phone clicking off.

Moana intercepted him as he sprinted for the door. "You're leaving? You've only been here a few minutes."

"Got a meeting with my lawyer."

"Since when? It's not on the calendar."

"I just made it."

"I make your appointments." She flexed the tattoo on her shoulder. "Is this your way of firing me? That's chickenshit."

"Nobody's firing anybody. I'll be right back."

"Well, if you're going to see that skinny little ambulance chaser, bring back some takeout. We need some lunch around here."

Jack bolted down the hall and hit the sidewalk running. He jaywalked across Market and zigzagged through the Tenderloin, careful not to step on broken bottles and human shit. A panhandling junkie lurched toward him but backed off after Jack glared. So did a hooker who offered to do a pearl necklace for half price. Union Square was jammed with shoppers, but Jack cut through it anyway to save time. A double-decker tourist bus nearly flattened him as he cut across Post. The driver slammed on the brakes and shouted *fuck* into his microphone. The amplified curse echoed across the square.

Belden Place was a narrow, block-long alley running between Bush and Pine in the heart of the city's small but restaurant-rich French Quarter. Cafés lined both sides of the street. Brightly colored awnings covered outdoor tables. Jack skirted diners to reach a stairway that led to Tingly Meyer's second floor office. A man wearing a stained apron was sitting on the bottom step. Van Duong owned the building. His café, Rue du Saigon, occupied the ground floor. He was of indeterminable age but was rumored to have served as a general in the ARVN and later as a CIA spook. Food critics hailed his *bún oc* as deserving of a Michelin star.

Jack gave a bow of respect. "*Xin chào.* How is your son?"

Van waved an unfiltered cigarette. "Getting rich, yes sure."

"The American dream. Still cracking hearts at UCSF?"

"So he texts. He too busy to visit father. His new wife"—he paused to spit—"she always shopping nonstop. New York, Paris, Milan."

"Kids," Jack said. "What you going do?"

Van took a deep drag off his cigarette and exhaled a pall of smoke through both nostrils. "You here for lunch or see lawyer?"

"The latter but I'll pick up something afterward to take back to the office."

"First you can do, not second, yes sure."

"What do you mean?" Jack was suddenly on guard.

"Tingly gone. Not my tenant no longer."

"Since when?"

"Since last night. Yes sure."

Jack felt his pulse blowing through his skin. "What happened?"

"His ship come in. So he say in note." The ash on Van's cigarette curved like his fingernails.

"What ship?"

"Who knows? But it must be big. He stuck envelope under kitchen door full of cash. All back rent he owe." Van smiled. Gold fillings flashed.

Jack's eyebrow arched as he wondered if Tingly had sold him out to the trolls. "Can I go up and look around?"

"You want to rent? I throw in free bowl of pho with spicy shrimp every lunch."

"I'll think about it. Do I need a key?"

"It open. Nothing there. I check already."

Jack squeezed by and climbed the narrow stairs. Three doors fronted the landing. Tingly's office was the one on the left. It had the look of a place cleaned out in a hurry. Jack's eyes started watering from the cloud of garlic, chili, and cinnamon wafting from the kitchen below. He searched the drawers of a battered desk. Nothing. A metal four-drawer filing cabinet was empty, too. All that was left was a white shadow on the wallpaper where Tinsel's diploma from some matchbook law school once hung. Jack blew out air. Tracking down the skinny legal fleagle was going to be a pain.

He turned to leave and spotted an empty Ethernet jack screwed to the baseboard. The lawyer may have left in a rush but there was a chance he hadn't taken down his website yet. Jack took out his phone and typed TinglyMeyers.com. It was still live. He switched over to the Whosis site and looked up the website's host. There was no name, only an IP address. He copied it and then logged onto a site that worked the same as a reverse telephone directory. He pasted the IP and hit search. It was the subdomain of another domain's IP. Jack copied that and went back to Whosis, pasted, and searched.

"Bingo." He snapped his fingers.

Jack found Van Duong in the kitchen overseeing a crew preparing *bún măng vịt* and *bánh chưng*.

"So you take office?" the chef asked. "Two thousand month. Good deal."

"Does it come with free internet?"

"Not free but I give you good deal. Yes sure."

"Like you did for Tingly? I saw yours is the parent domain."

"He very cheap but I give you same deal."

"As cheap as I can get on GoDaddy?"

"Better, yes sure. I give you five e-mail accounts for one price. Good deal. I got waiter moonlight doing tech. He move your site and accounts fast."

Jack peeled two Jacksons from his roll. "What I really need is for you to give me administrator access to Tingly's e-mail account. If his ship came in then he left a lot of flotsam and jetsam in his wake. Either that or he fell to an old San Francisco tradition and got himself shanghaied. One way or the other I need to find him fast."

Skepticism etched new lines in Van's wrinkled face.

"If I don't," Jack added quickly, "the law's going to get involved and you'll get caught up in something you don't want to get caught up in."

The old man ran his finger along the side of his nose. "Make it Mr. Benjamin Franklin and I throw in takeout for you. You like duck noodle soup with fresh cucumber? Yes sure. Special today."

11

There were three rules during phone sex. One, no answering call waiting. Two, no checking e-mail. Three, video selfies were optional. Jack and Katie were playing it by the book, at least according to their respective screens on FaceTime. Occasionally Katie would move her phone around and Jack could catch a glimpse of the guestroom she was bunking in at Laura's mansion. It was done up in earth tones and the pillows piled high on the California King were as puffy as cumulus clouds.

"I wouldn't want a house this big," she was saying. They had been talking for a while, working up to it, saying the kinds of things they would say if they were in bed together and fooling around while catching up on their respective days. "It would be so lonely. Did I tell you I miss you?"

"I'm getting the idea." Jack had the bedroom windows to the loft wide open and the gathering quiet of the streets below signaled the city was settling in for the night, too. "Could you aim your phone a little lower? I want to get a closer look at the thread count in those sheets."

"Really?" She said it with a laugh. Soon Jack's screen filled with a view that was a whole lot better than Egyptian cotton.

"How's Laura doing anyway? Is she having any luck communing with ol' Dex?"

"You really want to talk about ghosts right now? It's a little off-putting if you know what I mean." Her voice was starting to turn throaty.

"Sorry, babe. How about we talk about the Giants instead? You always like listening to the game when we're in the sack at home."

"I do." Her voice caught and Jack could hear a purr and the screen jostled again as she nestled deeper into the linens. "You better get busy, cowboy, if you want to catch up."

"Now I remember. The Gs didn't play tonight. They're on a plane to Atlanta. A long road trip."

"Well, then," she said, her breath quickening, "you're going to have to make it up and call the play-by-play yourself."

"Here goes. It's the bottom of the ninth and the score is tied. Batter up."

In the morning Jack made a double espresso and checked the *Chronicle*. There were no new reports about Dexter's murder. That didn't surprise him. Though a San Francisco homicide detective was leading the investigation, the fact the murder took place outside the city limits bumped it off the home page. It took clicking two buttons and scrolling down a menu to find any mention of it. Even then the report was barely longer than a tweet.

Jack was savoring his espresso when the phone buzzed. "Speak," he answered.

It was Terry Dolan. "You got a minute?"

Jack put down his cup. A call from a cop was never good news. A call from Terry Dolan was off the charts. "Depends. What's up?"

"I'm chasing down some information."

"Aren't we all. What sort?"

"It has to do with the Cotswold investigation. We need to talk."

"Isn't that what we're doing now?"

"I mean face-to-face. It's better that way."

Jack thought about last night. "Not always."

"You don't want to help find your friend's killer?" the cop said.

"With the way launching a start-up works, it means I'm already working for free. I can't afford to take on another job for no pay."

"There's two ways we could do this."

"Spare me the clichés," Jack said. "I'll take *easy*. Got a pencil? My office is on Market. Here's the address. How about three o'clock?"

"How about you get down to the Hall in one hour." It wasn't a question.

"Last time you invited me over to your place, you locked me in a sweat box and tried to pin a murder on me. I'm getting déjà vu all over again."

"One hour," Terry said.

"Have it your way. You want me to bring donuts?"

Terry didn't bite. He clicked off without saying another word.

THE HALL of Justice was on Bryant Street. SFPD's Southern Station was on the first floor. Courtrooms and jail cells occupied the upper floors. Jack pushed through the swinging front doors.

He puckered involuntarily as he passed through the gauntlet of metal detectors even though he wasn't carrying a gun.

It wasn't his first visit to the Hall. That happened when he was a freshman at St. Joseph's. After catching Jack running a three-card monte hustle on the playground, Father Bernardus asked a Mission District beat cop to throw a scare into him. The officer was Terry's dad, Eamon Dolan, better known as "Demon." He'd earned his nickname because of his liberal use of a two-foot police restraint baton called a PR-24, or "Public Relations-24" in cop talk.

Demon hauled Jack out of school, shoved him into the back of his patrol car, and sped off with red lights flashing. It was a quick elevator ride up to the Hall's notorious seventh floor.

"Meet your new classmates, *boyo*," Demon said as he pushed Jack into a narrow hallway lined on either side with locked cells. The cop left him there for two hours.

Jack could still hear the taunts of the caged prisoners and smell the sweat, shit, and semen that roiled like a toxic cloud. But the field trip didn't have quite the effect Demon Eamon and Father Bernardus were hoping for. It taught Jack a valuable lesson about crime instead: Always stay one step ahead of the law.

Jack gave his name to the desk sergeant who buzzed open a connecting door that led into a noisy pen jammed with cubicles. Glass-enclosed offices lined a wall. Terry sat behind a desk in one.

"You get a pay bump to go along with a private office?" Jack said when he entered without knocking.

Terry pointed to a grimy plastic chair. "Take a seat."

Jack sat. "I'm still waiting for my thank-you note."

"What are you talking about?"

"The Huntington murder I handed you last year. The bust made your career. You never said so much as ta."

"The only thing you did was save some time. I'd already made the killer."

"Now, now. Don't forget what the nuns taught us. *Thou shalt not lie.*"

Folk music gave way to rock. Mayors came and went. Earthquakes shook and new sections of bridges had to be built. But some things in San Francisco never changed: bells on cable cars, naked guys running the Bay to Breakers race, and Jack and Terry squaring off. They'd been doing it since kindergarten.

Jack rested an ankle on a knee. "Let's quit wasting each other's time. What do you want?"

Terry pulled a Rumsfeld. "Where is Bobby Ballena?"

Even if Jack hadn't been expecting shock and awe, he still wouldn't have shown surprise. The acting classes he took between stints playing ball at San Francisco State had trained him well. He could sweat on demand, turn on the tears, and even collapse as if struck by a coronary if a con called for it.

"Bobby comes and goes like the wind they call Mariah," he said. "How should I know where he is?"

"Then tell me when was the last time you saw him."

"You already know that. If Laura didn't tell you, Katie would've. No one's got anything to hide."

"I want to hear it from you."

Jack spoke as if reading a shopping list. "I came home from work. Bobby was sitting on my couch, talking to Katie. The three of us went to dinner at Dexter and Laura's. Katie and I went to bed. Bobby slept on our couch. In the morning I got up and went to work. I came home and Bobby was gone. I haven't seen him since."

They stared, willing the other to say something first. Jack wanted to ask Terry why he was so interested in Bobby but that's exactly what Terry wanted him to do. Cops were like con artists;

they asked questions they already knew the answers to as a setup.

The cop blinked first. "So your story is you haven't seen Ballena since he and the dead man's wife took a trip down memory lane. They were lovers once, correct?"

"Bobby and Dexter? I didn't know that." Jack shrugged. "Not that I judge."

"You know who I mean. Ballena met Laura Cotswold in Nepal. They became lovers. They kept it going after they got back, after she got married. They still had it going and now the husband's dead. "

"Lots of people meet in Nepal. Katie and me, for instance. It's where she fell out of love with you and in love with me. You should go there yourself. You might find it life changing. It's very spiritual. Who knows? You might even lose some of that guilt about sex the nuns baked into you."

Jack uncrossed his legs so he could jump out of the plastic chair if Terry came across the desk. It wouldn't be the first time he'd succeeded in baiting him. Luring a cop to cross the line was leverage Jack could always use, maybe not right away but whenever he needed it.

Terry focused on the cuffs of his white dress shirt. "Did Cotswold know about his wife and Ballena?"

"It was no secret. We had dinner at Dexter's. Dexter and Bobby hit it off. Everybody likes him, including husbands. Bobby's charming. It's a fact."

"No, here are the facts. Ballena and his married lover go on a trip together. They go back to her place that night. Maybe it's a couple of minutes later, maybe it's a couple of hours, but the rich husband winds up dead, and Ballena goes missing. And the wife? She can't remember a thing. All she can talk about is ghosts. A jury will find this an open-and-shut case."

Jack shrugged. "I admit I find it strange, too. I've never

believed in ghosts, but listening to my wife describe it? Well, even I'm starting to think the house is haunted." He raised his hands. "Boo."

Terry slapped the desk. "You know exactly what I'm talking about. Ballena's a thief. His sheet's a mile long. He was burglarizing the library. Dexter caught him red-handed. Ballena slugged him with whatever he had in his hand. He took off with the weapon. It's why we can't locate it. Now where is he?"

"My guess? After dropping Laura off, he probably hooked up with another girlfriend who wasn't as strict about marriage. You remember how Bobby was at school. A day without orange juice was a day without sunshine. He'll pull his head from under the sheets one of these days and be as surprised as anybody that Dexter's dead."

Terry attempted another stare down. "Did Ballena ever tell you about his outstanding warrant?"

Jack knew Bobby was riding paper but it wasn't the sort of things friends in the life talked about. The CIA wasn't the only practitioner of plausible deniability. "Can't say that he did."

"He's the prime suspect on a second-story job that was pulled in Marin County a couple of years ago. A wealthy couple living in a big mansion in Ross was hit for a collection of religious artifacts. The wife confessed she was having an affair with Ballena."

Jack didn't let his eyes betray a thing. "What can I say? Bobby has a way with women. Always has, always will. That doesn't make him a burglar, and it certainly doesn't make him a murderer. Your story blaming Bobby for what happened to Dexter doesn't hold water."

He stood and started toward the door. Terry chucked the grenade Jack had been expecting the whole time. "One more thing," the cop said as casually as if asking about the weather. "When was the last time you saw Cotswold?"

Jack kept his back to him. "In his library. You were there. Dexter was on the floor."

"I mean alive, goddamnit."

Jack suppressed a smile. "Earlier that day. I stopped by his office to say hello."

"That's not what Cotswold's secretary says. A Miss Nash. According to her, you stormed in and demanded to see him. When Cotswold finally agreed, you asked for money but he turned you down."

"They don't like to be called *secretaries* anymore. Executive assistants or administrative aides. Besides, what would Miss Nash know? She wasn't in the room."

"She didn't need to be. Cotswold kept a voice activated digital recorder in his office. Miss Nash e-mailed me the file. You sounded pretty angry."

"Listen to it again after you clean out the wax. Disappointed, maybe. Pissed off, nah. Dexter's a VC. He's in the business of investing in start-ups and I have a start-up. I made a pitch but he didn't buy. That's the rule in this business, not the exception. Only one percent ever gets funding. Cy Young winners don't even come close to that kind of strikeout ratio." Jack paused. "I'll spare you the trouble of asking. I didn't kill him, either. If you don't believe me, ask Katie. She'll tell you where I was. In bed making love with her. All. Night. Long."

Jack could see the cop's reflection in the glass door. His expression made the trip to the Hall worth it; it nearly made up for the time Demon had left him in the narrow gauntlet between the cages. Nearly but not entirely.

F og muffled the night and absorbed the lights of the city.
The sky was as pearlescent as the hand-buffed paint job
on Hark's '64 Impala. Purple lights illuminated the dials
on the lowrider's dash and cast an ethereal glow.

"What's with the psychedelic look?" Jack asked from the
shotgun bucket. "I expect to hear 'Voodoo Child' on an eight-
track next."

Hark shrugged as he palmed the chrome chain steering
wheel. "Purple's softer on the eyes and makes night driving
easier. Something I picked up during my tour in the 'Stan." Years
earlier Hark had elected to join the army rather than take a two-
year jolt at Stockton Correctional. "But *vato*, you know the
Sixties were all up in it when it came to music. I got a Santana
mix queued up. You want to listen? I put in a new amp. The
subwoofer will thump your ass."

"*Oye Como Va.*"

They were cruising west on Geary Blvd. toward the Avenues.
The closer to the Pacific they got, the foggier it got. Hark hit the
wipers every other block.

"You sure Bobby's out here?" Jack asked.

"As sure as you can be about a weasel like him. I asked around and heard from a low low customer who does deliveries to this private club we're heading to. He makes good money. Dropped two large at my shop on his whip. A Monte Carlo. We sprayed it metallic candy apple and put in hydraulics. That mother bounces."

"Your friend's positive it was Bobby?"

"That's what he said. Remembers him from the old days. He says Bobby used to be a regular before he lit out to Mexico. Think about it. Now that he's back, it stands to reason he'd be there, it being the kind of club it is."

"And what kind is that?"

"The kind you can get whatever you want as long as you can pay for it. The kind you'll want to put on your app." Hark stopped at a red light at Park Presidio. "You figure out how you're going to charge yet? By subscription, ads, or commissions from the places you list based on whatever the user spends?"

"If I don't find a new lawyer to protect my patents from the trolls putting the squeeze on me, the only thing I'll be charging is hot credit cards to pay the rent and fill the fridge."

"What happened to Tingly Meyers? He's not your brief anymore?"

"Gone. Disappeared without a trace."

"First Bobby goes dark and now him? Maybe I ought to think twice about hanging with you." Hark chuckled.

"My guess is Tingly was either bought off or scared off. I like to think he's living on some South Seas island drinking rum and counting his money."

"By who?"

"I'm still running that down. I got ahold of Tingly's e-mail account and came across a couple of messages that were cloaked in doublespeak but basically the first asked for a special meeting and the next confirmed it."

"Who sent them?"

"The cyber equivalent of John Doe, but I think I know whose interest was being represented by getting Tingly to leave town."

"Anybody I know?"

"Dexter Cotswold."

"The dead dude?"

"One and the same." Jack gave the CliffsNotes version of his various meetings with the little tycoon. "He always sounded a tad too disinterested when he asked about my designs and patents, not to mention my new programmer."

"Bobby part of all this, too?"

Jack shook his head. "Weird timing is my guess. Still, if I get ahold of Bobby, I'm going to ask."

"Then let's get to it."

The light changed and the big man stomped on the gas. The Impala's V-8 roared and the tires smoked. Flames spit from twin chrome tailpipes connected to Flowmasters.

SEA CLIFF WAS WEDGED between the Presidio and Lands End. It ranked among the priciest and most exclusive neighborhoods in San Francisco. Most of the houses were Mediterranean-style with suburban-style manicured lawns and trimmed hedges. The real trophies were the showplaces perched atop a steep bluff that fronted the Pacific. The cost of an unobstructed view of the Golden Gate was measured in the tens of millions.

Hark parked. A three-story Tuscan villa with cream stucco walls and a red-tiled roof occupied the end of a cul-de-sac.

The sound of crashing waves made Jack remember the time his father took the family camping. They got a late start, and Gavin drove through the night while drinking from a flask of Jameson. He finally pulled off the highway and bumped down a dirt road until it petered out. He ordered the kids to roll out their sleeping bags and go to sleep. Jack and his two brothers and sister were no sooner zipped in when the ground beneath them rumbled. The temblor built and built but it was no earthquake. Light shattered the darkness and thunder boomed all around. They were lying right beside a train track.

"Pretty tony address for a private club," Jack said as they approached the entrance.

Hark agreed. "Hiding in plain sight is tried and true. The neighbors think it's a foreign embassy. That explains all the comings and goings. Nobody complains, though. The citizens like all the extra security. It makes them feel safe when they're tucked in their beddy-byes."

"Makes me feel like we may have a problem if Bobby decides he doesn't want to talk to us."

"If he's here he'll talk all right. I guarantee it."

"The place looks like it values discretion. Maybe we should follow their lead."

"I'm down with being polite, 'mano, but Bobby being Bobby, we may not get much of a chance to practice our table manners."

Jack didn't have time to argue. Two men in tight suits stood on either side of the front door. Both were wearing secret service ear buds. The bulges on their right hips would give a tailor fits.

"Good evening, gentlemen," the one with a blond goatee said. "May we help you?"

"Sure, you can get the door," Jack said. Acting entitled seemed a good bet. Private clubs catered to oligarchs who never asked permission for anything.

The man with the goatee kept his voice polite. "Certainly, gentleman. But let's be certain we're at the correct address first. Are we expecting you?"

Hark followed Jack's lead. "I'm expecting you to open the fucking door is what I'm expecting."

"Perhaps you should check with concierge services and let them know who you're making wait out here in the fog." Jack gave it a few beats. "Surely you recognize Geraldo Martinez, former WBA heavyweight champion of the world?"

Hark held up his fists. Each was the size of a frozen capon. He did some fancy footwork and shadowboxed, bringing his right and then his left a whisker away from the blond goatee.

The man jerked his head back. "My apologies, Mr. Martinez. The light out here... well, it's inadequate."

"*No problema*." Hark mimed an uppercut followed by a hook before turning and winking at Jack.

THE FOYER WAS in keeping with the Tuscan exterior. Its walls were painted in a muted palette of umber, cream, and rose. Oriental rugs accented the travertine floor. The furniture was big on red velvet and gilt-edged filigrees.

"Crib is a lot more uptown than I would've taken Bobby for," Hark said as they passed through an arched entryway bookended by white marble statues of nymphs and fauns.

"It is a bit rococo, but Bobby's always been a moth to bling."

"Good way to get your wings singed if you fly too close. How much you think a place like this charges, say, for a half 'n' half?"

"If you have to ask the price, you can't afford the service."

Hark made a face. "Bobby hanging here, means he came into some money. Big time money. If you still think he didn't knock over the rich dude, then maybe you should check out Lasik. All due respect."

"You could be right, but I still want to hear it from him personally."

"It's your party, *'mano*. Let's go find him."

"Looks like somebody already found us," Jack said.

A woman wearing a tight leather suit jacket and matching skirt the color of sapphires approached. The five-inch spiked heels on her black sling backs all but sparked every time they struck travertine.

"Mr. Martinez, welcome to Casa di Sensuale. *Mi scusi*. Please accept my sincere apology for our security detail's lapse in recognition. I am sure you can appreciate their focus on ensuring our clientele's privacy."

Jack couldn't tell what sparkled most, her teeth or the diamond choker around her gazelle-like neck. Solitaires the size of M&M's shined like lighthouse beacons from her ear lobes. Her hair was a raven wave that surged and crested every time she moved her head. The accent made him think of a gondola gliding up a canal.

Hark stuttered as he stared. "Uh, I don't let ego get in the way. I learned that in the ring."

Jack hid a smile. The big man was clearly enjoying his cover —almost as much as he was enjoying the view.

"We are most pleased to welcome a sports celebrity to our establishment," she said with a slight bow. "I trust you will find everything to your satisfaction."

Hark started with the uhs again so Jack stepped in. "I'm Mr. Martinez's manager. The champ would like a tour of the facilities before making a selection. I'm sure you can understand, Ms…"

"Bartoli. Theresa Bartoli. And you are?"

"Jack McCoul. But call me Jack. All my friends do."

She cocked her head and the edges of her lips turned up ever so slightly. Her makeup matched the palette of the walls. "It would be my pleasure to escort you both."

Jack returned the invitation with a smile. "Maybe next time. Is there a lounge, perhaps? Maybe a card room?"

"And what kind of game are you interested in? Hold'em? Blackjack? No limit?"

"I was thinking of solitaire."

Her eyes glinted. "Really? And here I took you for an Up and Down the River player." She smoothed her skirt. It didn't need any smoothing. "Come along, gentlemen. I am sure I can find something to amuse you."

She steered them to a room that was a replica of Harry's Bar in Venice. Jack knew the original from the old days.

"This will do fine," he said. "You kids go have fun."

Hark and his exotic escort left. Jack surveyed the bar. Four men sat a table playing gin. Two more sat at separate tables studying their phones. No one was sitting at the bar so Jack slid onto a high back stool.

The bartender had a Roman nose and wore his hair slicked back. "*Cosa desidera*? What is your pleasure?"

"It's complicated. Grab a cocktail shaker and I'll walk you through it." When the bartender was ready Jack counted the ingredients off with his fingers. "A half cup of crushed ice, two ounces of Cazadores Blanco, one ounce of Don Julio Añejo, one lime cut in half but do not squeeze it, a pinch of sea salt, three liberal dashes of Tabasco sauce, a pinch of pepper, and a teaspoon of cane syrup. Now shake four times, not five, then strain into a tumbler and garnish with a jalapeño."

With each new instruction the bartender's eyes showed recognition. He centered the glass on a cork coaster. "You have exotic tastes."

"And you have excellent skills as a mixologist." Jack toasted him and took a sip. "This ranks among the best I've ever had. The highest honor, of course, goes to its inventor. Bobby Ballena."

"Of course," the bartender said.

"He taught you?" Jack said it with a touch of innocence.

"Many of our clients have special requests. It is my privilege to serve them." He started rinsing out the silver shaker.

"And with the utmost discretion. I admire that." Jack took another sip. "Yeah, Bobby and I go way back. All the way to grade school, in fact. The last time we drank these was in Baja a year ago. Has he been in tonight?"

He slipped the question in casually but the bartender was as skilled at evasiveness as he was blending spirits. "I don't believe I recall that name. But then again our clients rarely provide theirs."

"You'd remember Bobby, all right."

"I serve many clients."

Jack pushed the half-finished drink away. The hot sauce was burning his lips. He never liked the concoction. Bobby only drank them to impress women he picked up in bars. He would show off by instructing a bartender to mix one and then down it in a single gulp, telling his new companion that it made his heart pump faster. He'd grasp her hand and slide it under his shirt and hold it against his chest. It wouldn't be the last throb she'd feel.

The bartender's hand twitched as he finished rinsing the shaker in the sink. The water looked neither hot nor cold.

Jack leaned in. "Bobby told me you make the best drinks in town. It's why this club is his first stop whenever he comes back to San Francisco. He's staying at my loft South of the Slot." He used the original nickname for SoMa, so called for the noisy cable cars that once ran up and down Market Street. "Bobby said you're the guy to talk to about card games. The kind that are a little more sporting than gin rummy."

The bartender glanced up from the sink. "If you are looking for special services, please speak with *Signora* Bartoli. If you would like another drink, I can help you. I do not know your friend, *Signor* Ballena. It's my job not to know anybody."

Jack knew a dead end when he saw it. He pushed away from the bar and made ready to go on a scouting expedition. By now Hark would have done what he was supposed to do—create a diversion to keep everybody's attention so Jack could prowl with ease.

That was when the door to bar bounced off the wall. "It's gulp and go time, *ese*," Hark shouted. "And I mean now."

Jack threw a Jackson on the bar and sprung from the stool.

Shouts and running footsteps echoed behind Hark. For a big man who could fill a doorway, he didn't waste any calories turning around. He threw his elbows back. They caught the security guard with the blond goatee right in the chest and slammed him backward into his partner. Both men hit the travertine floor hard.

"So much for table manners," Jack said as stepped over them.

"You're the one who pinned the heavyweight belt on me. The dude with the goatee called me on it. Said he looked for me on the Internet. I was in the middle of getting better acquainted with some of the talent they got here. I didn't like his insinuation."

"The vocabulary app again?"

"Whatever. If I'm playing the role of title holder, I got a reputation to protect."

"Method actor," Jack said.

They reached the club's front door. Theresa Bartoli barred it. She had a hand on her hip and posed like a runway model. The look would turn a castrated monk.

"Really, Mr. McCoul. I would've expected more from somebody with your reputation. You could have spared us all the histrionics. Next time you need to locate someone as odious as Bobby Ballena, all you have to do is ask." Her left eyebrow imitated a Halloween cat's back. "You know how to do that, don't you, Jack?"

She was a vision, all right, Jack had to hand her that. He tried to come up with a quick retort but all he could do was put his lips together and blow.

13

J ack lay in bed waiting for dawn. He wasn't an early morning person but every time he started to drift off, Bobby Ballena would enter his thoughts. From there it was only a toss and a turn before Inspector Terry Dolan took over. The cop would soon grow weary of looking for Bobby and start rounding up the usual suspects in order to keep the brass happy. It didn't take a sleep apnea expert to know who would be at the top of his list.

The first breath of a new day began blowing away the long night. Jack knew his freedom depended on his ability to anticipate Terry's next move. He figured the cop would be kept busy a while longer building his murder book. That would entail canvassing Dexter's known associates and running down open ends. Everything about Dexter would go into the book—from his personal financial dealings to his peccadilloes and predilections. His marriage to Laura would earn an entire chapter.

That started another round of tossing and turning. What did Jack really know about Laura? The truth was, not much. Though he'd met her the same instant he'd met Katie, he never paid her much mind. Not when they were in Nepal or since. Part of that

had to do with being thunderstruck by Katie, and part of it had
to do with Laura's attraction to men like Bobby and Dexter.
Bobby treated women like disposable gloves; Dexter viewed
them as another metric for measuring his status. Jack had little
respect for a woman who didn't respect herself. It was why he
loved Katie. She was smart and had heart, but above all she had
a mind of her own. It was one of the reasons she'd rejected
Terry's proposal. Too many handcuffs, she said.

The sun started to clear the East Bay Hills and sowed the
retreating clouds with flecks of red and purple. Jack remembered purple was Laura's favorite color. Her flower garden
bloomed with violets, irises, and azaleas. She favored amethyst
earrings, plum mascara, and fuchsia outfits. When Jack asked
Katie what was up with all the purple, she explained that when
Laura was a little girl she had a mood ring that shined like a
bruise every time she wore it. Purple meant she was a romantic
but also moody and mischievous.

Laura still had the ring and treasured it as a childhood
touchstone. She said her parents had been killed when she was
young. A distant aunt and uncle were appointed guardians and
shuttled her off to a succession of boarding schools. She moved
to San Francisco after graduation from one of the Ivies and
bounced from one new age group to the next in search of spiritual transformation. Part of her attraction to the groups was
their universal use of the color purple. All professed it had
healing powers.

Jack recalled how Laura and Katie met. Katie was teaching
yoga at a fitness club and Laura became one of her most loyal
students. She was flexible as a Gumby toy and obsessed with
working out. The two women bonded over a love for natural
foods, sunny beaches, and stylish clothes.

At six the radio alarm triggered. *Morning Edition* wafted
through the loft's speakers. Katie loved waking up to NPR, and

Jack wondered if she was listening to it in Laura's guestroom. That got him thinking about how Laura and Dexter met. It was shortly after Nepal. Bobby had been a no show at the Kathmandu airport the day they were all scheduled to fly back to San Francisco. Laura and Katie wanted to wait for him even if it meant missing the flight, but Jack convinced them otherwise. He knew Bobby was hiding out in a teahouse to avoid having to make a commitment to Laura.

Laura didn't waste any time getting over him. She started attending charity galas. Katie explained it was a common strategy for singles and divorcees looking to hook up. They would bid on items during the fundraising auctions, knowing there were plenty of Type As who would never accept coming in second. After the auction was over, the winner would seek out their closest competitor. Some did it to crow, others because they were naturally attracted to a person who'd gone toe-to-toe with them. An offer of a consolation drink often led to a date and sometimes more. Laura's losing bid at the Asian art museum gala won the biggest prize of all: Dexter Collingswood Edward Cotswold, CH, CBE, FRSA.

Jack's first introduction to Dexter was over dinner at the French Laundry. He pegged the tycoon as an egotist the moment they shook hands. Dexter's grip was hardened by squeezing resistance balls while he barked buy and sell orders on a headset. Jack's assessment was confirmed moments later when Dexter announced he and Laura were engaged. He ordered the sommelier to pour champagne for everyone in the restaurant. Dexter dismissed Jack's attempt to split the bill with a wave of his American Express Black Card, but when Jack stole a peek at the receipt, he saw that the big spender had only tipped ten percent.

The wedding was no less ostentatious and the big-headed billionaire was no less imperial. Dexter dictated everything, from the style of Laura's dress and the music to the toast and cutting of the cake. The entire production was scripted and directed by an Academy Award-winning director, and the action-packed schedule of over-the-top activities came off without a hitch, thanks to a retired general who'd coordinated logistics during the Iraq War.

Despite Dexter's public relations team's best efforts, media coverage of the wedding hardly generated the sort of clips found in treasured wedding albums. For starters there was plenty of criticism aimed at the $3.8 million price tag. And then there were the lawsuits. Dexter chose an old growth redwood forest for the setting. He paid a handsome day use fee to the Park Service. In his quest to recreate Camelot, complete with costumed knights and ladies-in-waiting as servers, he sawed off the lower limbs of a 700-year-old tree, destroyed the nest of an endangered spotted owl, and dammed a stream used by spawning coho salmon. His explained away his misdeeds by quoting Ronald Reagan: *If you've seen one redwood, you've seen them all.* The story went viral and spread horror and anger among environmentally conscious San Franciscans. Dexter treated the cyber equivalent of a tar and feathering with the same aplomb as he wrote off the multimillion-dollar fine on his taxes.

The light outside the loft's windows grew brighter. It was shaping up to be a sunny day. As Jack got out of bed, he wondered if Dexter had put the same sort of planning into his own funeral.

14

S ilicon Valley didn't do death. At least not willingly.
Cynics said it was because there was no money in
attending funerals unless there was ample time set aside
for networking and pitching new ventures. Others opined
mortality was relative, what with cryonics and Facebook pages
that lived forever. Mostly it was a byproduct of a culture
obsessed with the future rather than the past, whether it was
building the fastest chip or chasing after the next Candy Crush.

Jack turned into the entrance to Alta Mesa Cemetery and
followed an oak-shaded drive past the chapel to a field as green
as a Pebble Beach fairway. Orderly rows of granite headstones
were aligned like computer screens sitting on desks in an open-
office floor plan. Buried tech titans included David Packard of
HP fame and William Shockley and Frederick Terman, co-
inventors of the transistor that had launched the computer age.
The Palo Alto graveyard was also rumored to be Steve Jobs's final
resting place but exactly where was a mystery because no
marker could be found. The story was his family didn't want it to
become a shrine like Jim Morrison's grave. That's not to say

rockers were turned away. Ron "Pigpen" McKernan of Grateful Dead fame lay beneath the hallowed sod.

Jack pulled his Prius behind a red Audi coupe with a personalized license plate that read *IPOBALLR*. He was surprised Dexter was being buried in California rather than London's Highgate Cemetery where his family had a marble vault dating back to Henry VIII. Even more surprising was the speed the police released Dexter's body despite an ongoing murder investigation. That meant either the coroner had made a final report on cause and time of death or the cops wanted to use the funeral as a way to get a firsthand look at known associates. Maybe even the perp.

The hearse arrived. It was followed by a black stretch. The liveried limo driver popped out and opened the passenger door. Katie stepped out. She looked fantastic in black. Hell, Jack thought, she looked fantastic in anything, especially when he hadn't seen her for a couple of days. She wore a rakish hat fitted with a black fishnet veil that hung to the top of her lips. He didn't bother to lift it when they kissed.

"Is that the tie I gave you last Christmas?" she asked.

"Yeah. It was still hanging from the headboard from the last time we—"

"Shh." The black netting did little to hide her smile.

Laura slid out of the backseat. She wore all black except for a purple tanzanite necklace with an amethyst pendant in the shape of a heart. "Oh, Jack," she cried. "I can't believe I'm a widow. And at my age, too." She smelled of vanilla vodka.

A Crown Vic pulled up. Terry Dolan was wearing his usual suit and white shirt. He'd put on a somber rep tie with dark stripes.

"My condolences for your loss." The cop said it to the widow but his eyes were on Katie.

Laura grabbed his wrists. "Is there any news?"

"None that I am at liberty to discuss."

"I'm not the only one counting on you. So is Dexter. We may be burying his body today but not his spirit."

A man with carefully coiffed blond hair and dressed in a shiny gray suit approached. His gold cufflinks gleamed when he hugged Laura. "I know you're in a state of shock. We all are but we are here for you. Whatever you need."

When they broke their clench, Laura dabbed her eyes. "I always know I can count on you."

The man turned and introduced himself. "Hello, I'm Winston Cheatham. Too bad we have to meet on such a solemn occasion."

"Winston's firm handles Dexter's legal affairs." Laura's voice choked. "I mean handled. Oh God."

The handkerchief went back to her eyes. The lawyer hugged her. Jack shared one thing in common with Silicon Valley—he hated funerals, too. He'd walked out of his father's.

Laura pulled herself together and raised her chin. "I'm ready now. Winston, dear, would you be so kind?"

"Of course." The lawyer linked his arm through hers and escorted her to the graveside where an Anglican priest and new age swami stood shoulder to shoulder.

"That's what I call covering your bases," Jack said.

Terry shot him a look before following Laura.

Jack touched Katie's shoulder to get her to hold back. "Have you heard from Bobby?"

"No and I'm really worried about him, too," she said. "I can't believe he hasn't called. Do you think he went back to Baja without ever knowing what happened to Dexter?"

Jack hedged. "If he's around he'll turn up and then we can ask him. How are you doing?"

"Tired. I'm doing lots of yoga and swimming—Laura's pool is

huge—but, well, being in mourning from morning til night is exhausting. I can't wait to come home."

"What about right after the funeral?"

Katie's lashes fluttered behind the veil's netting. "Laura still needs me." She put her finger on his lips. "But we can still, you know, FaceTime every night."

"It's not quite the real thing."

"You're spoiled."

"Rotten," he said.

THE HOLY MEN took turns extolling Dexter's virtues and commending his soul to heaven, the hereafter, reincarnation, or whatever their particular branch of the spiritual tree called for. Jack tried not to fidget. He'd endured plenty of religious upbraiding when he was a student at St. Joseph's. Father Bernardus and his cadre of nuns wielded the bible, guilt, and a straightedge ruler with equal force. Jack busied himself by scrutinizing the faces of the mourners. Some appeared to be grieving. Others struggled to restrain themselves from checking their e-mail.

Jack recognized Miss Nash, Dexter's gatekeeper. The woman's icy demeanor had melted. Her face was flushed, her eyes puffy, and her handkerchief wringing wet. She was dressed in all black except for the gold and jade Siamese cat brooch and amber Chinese bracelet. With each prayer or chant she leaned against Capital Dexterity's managing partner, Arjun Chopra. His charcoal suit and black turtleneck made him resemble a vulture. Two younger men in open collar shirts and Tahari blazers stood behind them. Jack guessed they were junior members of the firm.

After the cherry wood coffin with brass accents was lowered

into the hole and the last single stem white rose was tossed on top, the mourners lined up to pay their respects to the widow. The receiving line was little different from a wedding's. Jack didn't join in. He watched as Winston Cheatham and Arjun Chopra spoke to one another. He couldn't hear their words, but it was clear the pair was well-acquainted.

When they finished talking, Cheatham cut in front of Miss Nash who was next in line, gave Laura a hug, whispered in her ear, and left. Miss Nash glowered and then swore. Her cries were guttural. Laura recoiled as if in shock. Chopra tilted his head and the two bookends in blazers responded. They quickly ushered Miss Nash away. Chopra took her place and bowed to Laura. He grasped her hand gently and spoke softly. Laura threw her arms around him and kissed his cheek.

Miss Nash was still fuming as she neared Jack. She stopped and wheeled on him. "I remember you. You were very rude. What are you doing here?"

"Paying my respects to the dearly departed."

"Your presence is an insult to Mr. Cotswold's memory. You call yourself his friend? You're like everyone else. All you wanted to do was use him. You were after his money." She shot an angry look at Laura. "You're no different than that... that—"

Jack cut her off. "Bad form to out grieve the widow no matter how many special bonuses Dex laid on you."

She shrieked. The blazer boys grabbed her by the elbows and quickstepped her toward the line of cars.

Chopra approached. His eyes were hooded, the pupils piercing. "I apologize for Miss Nash. She was Mr. Cotswold's longtime executive assistant, and his death has naturally upset her. I am afraid her emotions may have gotten the best of her. But your comment was insensitive and uncalled for."

Jack shrugged. "I flunked cotillion. What can I say? But tell me, with Dexter out of the picture, do you inherit Miss Nash?"

Chopra stiffened. "We treat all employees with dignity and respect. Miss Nash is a loyal member of our staff. She will always have a home at Capital Dexterity."

"You get a bump in title, too?"

"I do not see how that is any of your business."

Jack leaned in. "Sure it is. Dex asked me to look out for Mrs. Cotswold in case something happened. You know, he being older than her and all. I'm honoring his wishes."

Chopra paused before answering. "Capital Dexterity follows all best business practices. We have a succession plan the same as does every other firm of our size and stature. As it is, I happen to be the senior partner now."

"And how many other partners are there?"

"None at present."

"Laura doesn't automatically take over where ol' Dex left off?"

Chopra looked down his nose. "In the venture capital space, partnerships are earned, not inherited."

"That certainly makes the math easy."

15

Two days after Dexter Cotswold's funeral the Giants were still in the middle of a slump that included a sweep by the Braves and an extra-inning heartbreaker to the Brewers. Jack's luck was no better. He still hadn't found Bobby nor any capital to keep his fledgling business from suffering the same fate as Canvas, Outbox, CarWoo!, and hundreds of other tech flameouts.

"So it's come down to this," he said to himself as he sat in his office, staring at his phone and a cold call list of investors.

Willing himself to start dialing for dollars was bringing back memories of a dark period in his life when he'd been reduced to selling fake Revolutionary War battle re-enactment travel packages to Tea Party members. Grifting was like baseball. There were good seasons and bad. So many factors could make the difference—the quality of the players, the competition, and situational vagaries that were the equivalent of a broken-bat RBI single and windblown walk-off.

Jack picked up the phone, stabbed the list of names at random, and started pressing numbers. The phone rang once, twice, and three times. Before anyone picked up, Moana filled the doorway.

"What are you still doing here?" she said. "You're going be late for lunch. Get a move on. *Wikiwiki.*"

Jack put his hand over the phone. "What lunch?"

"I put it on your calendar. Arch Ventures."

"Never heard of them." Jack clicked off and punched in his calendar. He held it out to Moana. "See? Nothing."

She grabbed it and looked. "Today is this week not next week. Get going. Do Pray and I are counting on you. And if they don't fund us at, at least stick them with the check."

SAN FRANCISCO OPERATED a fleet of historic streetcars that had been collected from around the world. Jack rode a vintage tram from Milan that was painted in Giants orange and black. He got off at the foot of Market Street. If the representatives from Arch were out to show him they were foodies with a fat expense account, they were off to a good start. The chic restaurant they selected was world famous for serving the freshest fish along with the biggest bills. The hostess wore a turquoise sheath as tight as a mermaid's tail. She led Jack to a window table with a view of the gray-green waters of the bay. Two men were already seated but neither was watching the parade of colorful tugs, freighters, and sailboats. One stared at his phone, the other at the menu.

Jack stuck out his hand. "Jack McCoul."

The one with the phone pressed to his ear barely acknowledged Jack's presence. The other glanced up from the menu and scowled. "I'm Tomasz Radic, he's Jeremy Werthing, and you're late." His accent was Slavic.

Jack withdrew his hand. He was on time but didn't argue. He didn't apologize either. He was no stranger to the one-upmanship that was part and parcel of VC meetings. He sized up the pair with the same eye for detail he used when picking out marks for variations of a Thai gem or Spanish prisoner. Tomasz was muscular and wore his hair cut in a hipster undercut. Jeremy looked to be in his late twenties. He was dressed in Silicon chic—jeans, Desert boots, and a zippered hoody. The lenses of his designer black-frame eyeglasses had a gray tint, the kind favored by French movie directors. They cost the equivalent of the month's rent Jack was behind.

"Thanks for your interest in my enterprise," Jack said as he took a seat. "We can start with small talk or go right into an overview and Q and A. What's your pleasure?"

Tomasz scowled again. "You're starting out with a question instead of an answer? Already I'm not impressed."

Jack worked hard to hold onto his smile.

Jeremy put down his phone and carefully wiped the rim of his water glass with a napkin. His Adam's apple didn't bob as he took a sip. He centered the glass back on its doily.

"We hear a dozen pitches a day, Mr. McCoul. Give us the elevator but no more than three floors, please." His eyes were small and his voice as thin as his smile.

Jack sucked in air. "The app's a mobile assistant of a *personal* nature. Say you're on business and a first time visitor to Chengdu. You want a martini and a massage to go with it. The app will tell you where and even book it for you. Looking for a game of poker in Kiev where gambling is illegal? Say the word. You'll not only get a seat at the table, but the app can transfer the funds to cover your bets and collect your winnings. Lonely in Riyadh? Companionship is a click away. Burka or no burka, your choice. The app features location services and a user profile memory." Jack exhaled. "We reached the third. Want to keep going or get off?"

Tomasz shrugged. "It's nothing more than a pimp in a pocket. Lame." He went to work on the breadbasket, slathering a chunk of sourdough with butter, showering it with salt, and then plunging it into a pool of olive oil blackened with droplets of balsamic.

"Even the world's oldest profession can benefit from new technology," Jack said. "We've done focus groups with global business travelers. The positives are in the 90-percent range. Some of the participants wanted to place orders immediately. Others provided suggestions for add-ons. A function that enables data export to your company's expense account reports. Password protection in case, well, you lose your mobile device or your spouse checks it. No one wants any surprises unless that's what you're into and willing to pay for it." He winked. "The app can handle that, too."

Jeremy swabbed his water glass with the napkin again. His tiny eyes darted behind the fancy gray lenses. "Who is your software architect?"

"Are, as in plural. And they're all geniuses," Jack said.

"All right, then. Plural. Name me their previous products."

"That would fall under the classification of trade secrets. I'm sure you can understand."

Jeremy wiped the rim of his water glass before taking another sip. "And I'm sure you can understand we're not about to invest considerable funds without knowing more about what it is we're investing in. More specifically, who it is."

Jack's gut was telling him something, and it wasn't that he was hungry. It had been a while, but he hadn't forgotten the golden rule of always staying in control of the table, even if it meant having to turn it. "Before I do that, how about you tell me about yourselves? The only thing I could find out about your firm was an under construction homepage."

Tomasz brandished the slathered chunk of bread. "Hey, genius. We're the ones with the fuckin' money. Now answer my partner."

Jack got what he wanted. He leaned back in his chair. "You know, boys, my old man was a fireman. Two-fisted when swinging an axe, two-fisted when hoisting a boilermaker, Catholic when he had to be. You know what he used to tell my sister? Let 'em hook up the hose for free, and they won't buy the hydrant."

Tomasz's face tightened. Even the hipster haircut couldn't mask the rough edges of someone who looked like he was more used to a street brawl than Wall Street. Jeremy waved his white napkin limply. "You'll have to excuse my partner's abruptness, but in our world, time is measured in millions made or lost. Technology is a competitive business. We have to move faster than our rivals. Who we are isn't as important as the fact that we have money to invest in your enterprise, perhaps even acquire it, and you have creditors to satisfy." He gave the thin smile again. "And according to our research you have plenty."

Jack caught the malice lurking in Jeremy's rodent-like eyes. He prided his discipline in always being able to walk away from a play when it no longer felt right. It had kept him out of prison and saved his life more than once. He signaled the waitress. "Could you bring us a round of Plinys, please? The colder the better. Thanks."

When she returned with a trio of brown beer bottles, Jack took one and held it up to show his tablemates the plain red label. "This is brewed up on the Russian River and named for Pliny the Elder. He was Ancient Roman. Wrote the world's first encyclopedia. Dedicated his life to the pursuit of truth."

Jack took a long drink of the double India pale ale and savored it. Then he stared hard at his tablemates. "Let's cut the shit, okay Tom and Jerry? You're not VCs no matter how dressed up you get. You're pointers flushing birds for the real hunter. And something tells me he's no angel when it comes to investing. Who do you really represent, the trolls trying to hijack my patents? Or is it some wise guy who thinks he knows what I did for a living once and figured, hey, go convince him to be our front?" He paused, studied the label again, and then studied the men sitting across the table. "So what's his game? Get ahold of my app and tweak it to be a back door for getting to users' personal financial data, or is it a simple case of money laundering and buying a legit start-up to do the wash?"

Tomasz crushed the chunk of bread in his fist until butter slippery with olive oil oozed between his scarred knuckles. "You got some fuckin' mouth on you."

Jeremy quickly placed a hand on Tomasz's forearm. "Yes, we are quite aware of your background. And it is true that Mr. Radic and I represent someone who prefers to remain anonymous. He is as cautious as he is results oriented. He only considers very special types of investments. Our task is to determine if your enterprise is special. More to the point, if you are special."

"*Special*, like did I ride the short bus to school? No, I walked. Saint Joe's in the Mission District to be exact. But my real learning came from the streets. It taught me about people like you and your boss." Jack shook his head. "Hoods in hoodies. My, the times we live in." He got up from the table.

"But you haven't heard our proposition yet," Jeremy said, his tone turning saccharine. "All we're looking for is an open mind. That and a little cooperation. The rewards for both sides will be handsome, I assure you. Surely more than sufficient to meet your creditors' demands."

"Somehow I think the people I owe money will be a lot less

demanding than your boss." He turned for the door. "Don't forget to leave a tip, boys."

As Jack walked away, Jeremy called out. "I suppose I should say, I hope you'll reconsider, but I learned hope is never a strategy. Until next time."

16

J ack had seen a million bucks before. More than once. The first time he'd taken it off a sleazy insurance broker who was fleecing seniors by selling policies that would only pay off in the event of a meteor strike. Jack convinced the mark he was a crooked IRS agent who could save him a bundle in income taxes. The million-dollar bribe came in a dozen cardboard boxes stuffed with used fives, tens, and twenties. Jack swore he'd never accept small denominations again. The next time he conned a mark out of a mil, he demanded crisp Benjamins. The bills came packed in a stylish monogrammed suitcase that could have been mistaken for Katie's overnight bag.

Either way, a million bucks always looked good but stacks of currency had nothing on the sight of Katie bounding out of the Cotswold mansion and greeting him with a jump-in-his-arms smack on the lips.

By the time she finally let go, Jack knew the meaning of *How can you miss me if I never go away?*

"Some outfit," he said as he admired her sizzling pink T-shirt torn in all the right places and the black leggings that were surely painted on.

"It's Laura's." She gave a quick spin. "I just finished an hour of kickboxing and was about to take a dip. The pool is divine. You want to join me?"

"Only in the deep end," he said.

They walked across the entryway. "Nobody home?" he asked.

"Laura went out to lunch. All very mysterious."

They reached the other side of the house and exited through a set of French doors. The backyard was even showier than the front. Jack guessed the mow and blow guys needed three days a week to keep it so spotless. Marble sculptures and potted palms ringed a covered patio set up with wicker furniture. The outdoor kitchen looked industrial strength.

He pointed to a waterfall cascading into an infinity pool. "There a hidden cave behind that?"

Katie's eyes twinkled. "How did you know?"

"Wishful thinking."

She pulled the torn T-shirt over her head and peeled off the leggings. Jack could see she'd been working on her allover tan during her stay in the suburbs. She posed at the edge of the pool before executing a swan dive into the topaz water. It barely caused a ripple, much less a splash. When Katie turned around he held up 10 fingers.

She laughed. "Show me what you got."

Jack kicked off his shoes, unbuttoned his shirt, and stepped out of his jeans and briefs. "A full pike with a two and a half gainer coming up."

He sprinted toward the pool and splashed down in a cannonball instead. By the time Katie rubbed the water from her eyes, he'd surfaced right in front of her and pulled her close.

"Looks like you need a little mouth-to-mouth," he said.

"Don't you wish." And she deftly slipped from his grip and kicked toward the bottom.

Jack took a deep breath, jackknifed, and followed. It was eyes wide open as he chased her underwater across the length of the pool. When he finally caught up to her she was heading for air. They surfaced inside a grotto hidden behind a glistening curtain of falling water.

"Remember that time in the Caymans?" She threw her arms around his neck and pressed her breasts against him. "We had that villa right on the beach. The water was so warm. We swam every night."

"That and some other things every night."

Katie started nibbling his ear. "What's the name of that ghoulish Danish banker who lives there? Hans? Sven? Something like that."

"You mean Anders."

"Talk about a fish out of water." She shuddered. "He reminds me of a frozen cod."

"And we're talking about bankers and fish sticks, why?" He moved his hands behind her and cupped her cheeks.

She nibbled his ear some more and locked her legs around him. "A distraction," she said.

"Why do you want to be distracted?"

"Not me, you." She locked her legs a little tighter and whispered. "The only thing that should be rushing right now is the waterfall."

THEY WERE in Laura's kitchen. Jack wore a towel tied around his waist. Katie had slipped on the torn hot pink T-shirt but not the leggings. She was making sandwiches. He was opening a bottle of Puligny-Montrachet he'd found in the fridge.

"You should have put some sunscreen on before swimming," she said.

"That was the last thing on my mind. It wasn't like the sun was shining inside that grotto. Or anywhere else, for that matter."

"Be serious." She cut the sandwiches in two. "With your skin color you don't want to burn. You're at a higher risk of developing basal cell carcinoma, not to mention what it does to the aging process."

"I thought wrinkles were in now. You know, shows character. Makes a tough guy look distinguished."

"Before you go I'll rub some of my special healing balm on your shoulders. It has safflower oil, rosehips, yarrow, comfrey, and goldenseal. Some licorice root and horsetail, too. All pesticide-free, of course."

He pulled the cork. "That the stuff that smells like pond scum and looks like ear wax?"

"Don't be such a Neanderthal." She handed him a tofu and sprout sandwich on nine grain bread.

"What, no brontosaurus burger?"

They carried their food outside to a teak table with a yellow market umbrella at the edge of the pool.

"So what's the big mystery about Laura's lunch date?" Jack examined the sandwich.

"What do you mean?"

"You said her going out was mysterious."

"Did I?" Katie took a sip of wine.

"Okay, I get it. It was a slip of the tongue and you didn't mean to say it, but you kinda did on purpose because it's bugging you and you wanted me to know it, too. So what's the big mystery?"

"Oh, the usual women stuff. All women have secrets they can only tell each other. Best friends stuff." She avoided his gaze. "Look, there's a hummingbird. Isn't she beautiful? She's sipping the honeysuckle."

Jack put down his sandwich. "Give it up. You know you want to. It'll make you feel better. What's going on with Laura?"

Katie took another sip of wine as if to steel herself. "She was having an affair before Dexter's murder, and she's still having it. There. Are you happy now?"

Tofu and sprouts weren't Jack's favorite meal, not by a long shot, and Katie's confession gave him the perfect excuse to pretend to choke. He spit out a mouthful of the slimy mess.

"You mean Bobby?"

"Bobby? What are you talking about? They broke it off in Kathmandu. Of course it's not Bobby. Bobby's been in Baja for the past year." Her sigh topped the charts in exasperation. "Men. You're so clueless."

Jack looked across the garden. He didn't see any humming-bird but he did spot an old crow perched on the limb of a gnarled oak tree.

"Okay. I get it. I wouldn't notice George Clooney if he was in the shower with you. And, by the way, he has wrinkles, too. But if it's not Bobby Ballena she's fucking then who is it? The Valley has no shortage of possible suitors. Men still outnumber women in tech seven to three. Look at all those solo guys who showed up at Dexter's funeral."

"You don't need to be so crude. Laura's my friend."

"Let me rephrase." He slipped into a Masterpiece Theater accent. "With whom, my dear madam, has Mrs. Cotswold been cuckolding her husband? Dearly departed murdered husband, I should say. And found in the library no less with his cranium violated by what one could only surmise was a candlestick. Colonel Mustard, I presume?"

"This isn't a joke. Poor Laura. She's always been confused about men. It goes back to her childhood. She's never come right out and said it but I think she was abused. My guess is it was her uncle who became her guardian. It explains why her mood ring was always purple."

"And I say when she married dear old Dex that ring turned royal purple. The guy had more money than the Queen. Laura has it made in the shade." He paused. "I thought she loved him."

"She did and she still does. Laura's positively heartsick over Dexter. But you more than anybody know that money isn't everything."

"But it certainly comes in handy sometimes."

"Don't confuse money and love." She grew testy. "Or love and sex. Or money and sex, for that matter."

Jack poked his sandwich with a fork trying to spear the tofu. "Does that mean Dexter was big on the bucks but light on the fucks?"

"I don't know. Maybe. Laura always said he worked all the time. He about lived at his office. Some guys get off on that, you know. Making deals instead of making love. Both are about power."

Jack knew better than to argue feminism with Katie. Because of her looks she'd spent her whole life proving people's assumptions about her were wrong. She'd waltzed through Cal with a four point oh and was headed to med school when she developed her own theory on alternative healing methods. Jack pitied anyone who treated her like a bimbo. Katie was cheerful by nature but sexism and intolerance triggered the temper of a wildcat. She didn't scratch when she was provoked, she went straight for the throat.

"Your boy, Terry?" Jack said. "He's looking to hang Dex's murder on someone. His first choice is Bobby Ballena, given Bobby's not exactly your citizen-of-the-year type. Runner up? Your best friend. If Terry finds out Laura had an affair, that's one thing. But if he finds out she's still having it? So much for giving her a grieving widow pass. You get what I'm saying?"

Katie stuck out her chin. "Why do you think I told you? I'm worried about her. I know she never could have hurt Dexter, but now she's hurting herself. We have to get her to stop seeing this other man. At least until Terry catches the killer."

Jack blew out air. The last thing he wanted to do was get dragged into a soap opera. But he knew he had no choice. This was another skin of the onion he had to peel if he wanted to find out if Bobby was innocent.

"Okay. Who's the guy?"

Katie tossed her hair. "I don't know. Laura never said. But he must live around here."

"What makes you say that?"

"She said Dexter nearly caught them one time. She'd told him she was running down to the Stanford Shopping Center to pick up a dress when she was really going to meet this guy at his house. Dexter showed up at his front door."

"He must have been following her."

"Laura said it was bad timing is all. A coincidence."

"You mean the guy's a neighbor? Dexter goes over to borrow a cup of sugar and guess whose car is parked in the driveway and guess who's parked in his wife?"

"Don't be crude." Smile lines framed the corners of her lips as she said it.

"I'll dig around and see what I can turn up. In the meantime you better have a best friend's chat with your best friend. See if she won't tell you who he is. And while you're at it tell her to cool her heels, or she'll find herself cooling them in county lockup."

Katie beamed. "This is so fun. I love it when we work together."

And then she launched into her tofu and spouts sandwich like a cavewoman taking on a mastodon bone.

17

Laura returned home late that night. Jack watched her turn into the driveway from the front seat of the Prius. He was parked in a turnout listening to KCSM. The station was playing a Bill Evans retrospective. In Jack's book it was a toss up to which was the jazz pianist's purest, the version of "My Foolish Heart" recorded live at the Village Vanguard or "Peace Piece" on the remastered *Best of* disc. He gave it an hour before ducking into the trees that bordered the Cotswold mansion's front yard. The downstairs lights went off. By midnight the windows in the guest room and master bedroom darkened, too.

Jack waited another hour before creeping around back. He'd planned the route to the rooftop during lunch. While Katie was excited about them working as a team, Jack drew the line when it came to B and E. Providing a spouse with ignorance to a crime was the secret to a happy marriage—almost as important as remembering the anniversaries.

He stood on a teak table, scrambled onto the portico, and crossed to the main exterior wall. It was made of limestone blocks and the edges provided finger grabs and toeholds. Jack tucked in the laces of his rubber sole climbing shoes, chalked his fingertips, and played Spiderman.

It was a fairly easy climb until he reached the eave. It over-hung the wall by a good two feet. Jack jammed his left fingers into a crack, reached backward with his right, and felt for the copper gutter. It was do-or-die time. He released his hold on the wall and let go. Five fingers clinging to the metal edge bore his full weight as he dangled in the darkness. There was no time to feel his tendons stretching or listen for the pop of his shoulder. He blinked away the image of splattering on the flagstone patio three stories below and reached with his left. Two holds on the gutter was better but there was still no time to dawdle. He took a deep breath and executed a pull-up. When his chin was level to the roof, he swung his right leg and planted his heel. From there it was a three-point push and roll. He was up and on.

Jack shined his headlamp around. The mansion's roof was tiled in slate and the rake to the ridge angled steeply from where he stood. It was too slippery for a direct approach. Jack spotted a valley gutter running between two roof hips and belly crawled to it. He jammed his hand into the gutter and spread his fingers. It was enough of a hold. He climbed that way to the top and strad-dled the knife-edge ridge.

An aluminum exhaust vent hood shimmered in the beam of his headlamp. His goal was twenty steps away. Jack took another deep breath and stood. He extended his arms, lifted one foot, and froze. It was the tree pose Katie taught in her yoga classes. *Vrksasana*, she called it. When Jack felt his balance point, he brought his foot down. He breathed in, breathed out. He lifted the other foot, paused, and then placed it in front of the other. Slow and steady. Jack kept his outstretched arms still. The key to tightrope walking was not to imitate a bird. Start flapping and it quickly proved that men couldn't fly.

He grabbed hold of the vent hood. It was a hinged boxlike

structure. Jack unhooked one side and swung it open. "Thanks, old chap." Dexter had designed the centrifuge system with regular maintenance in mind. The fan and motor were seated on a metal basket fitted with an electric winch and greased tracks. Jack raised the contraption and swung it out of the way. His headlamp pierced the dark chamber and revealed a ceiling grate two floors below. The colorful pattern of an oriental carpet showed through the grate's openings. It wasn't the same rug Dexter collapsed on after being brained from behind, but it did signal pay dirt.

Jack took the climbing rope from his backpack, looped it around the collar of the vent, and snaked one end through his climbing harness. When all was secure, he stepped into the open mouth of the vent and glided down the rope using a Spiderjack to control his descent. Two easy-to-remove screws held the ceiling grate. Bobby had been right about how to access the library. It was pop the top and drop.

No alarms screamed when Jack's feet touched the floor. His headlamp revealed the contents of the shelves. A pair of jade Foo dogs growled silently. The raised front paw of a porcelain tiger threatened from a perch between a Han dynasty vase and an ivory water buffalo pulling a motionless cart.

Iridescent fingerprints glowed in the light's beam; it was residue from the lab rats' investigation. Plastic flags marked a blood splatter. A purple exam glove lay crumpled in a corner. Jack could hear his own heartbeat; his breathing made the same sound as wavelets washing across the sand. It was all he heard. If Dexter's spirit was restless, it was wandering around in another part of the house.

Jack studied the shelves to make sure he hadn't overlooked a missing artifact when he'd been in the room with Terry Dolan. Whatever had been used to strike Dexter wasn't taken from any of the shelves. There were no gaps. Jack took a deep breath.

There was only one place left to check for a murder weapon. He went to the wall with the Japanese scroll of the samurai and geisha doing the Rocking Horse position and tugged. The secret panel door whooshed open.

"MOTHERFUCKER." Hark slapped the '64 Impala's chrome chain steering wheel. "I told you the dude did it. Bobby commits a crime even when he's dreaming. Sorry, *vato*, but it's the way he is."

"Doesn't mean he did it," Jack said.

Hark smacked the steering wheel again. "What are you talking about? The statue's gone. Who else you think grabbed it? The dead dude's ghost?"

"Bobby pinched Little Buddha, all right. I don't doubt that for a second. It doesn't mean he killed Dexter."

"'*Mano, 'mano*. You said yourself the dead dude's head was like the watermelons that old stoner comic used to hit with a sledgehammer. If the cops get ahold of the statue and put it in the hole in his skull, it's going fit and no way they're going acquit." Hark looked pleased with himself.

Jack shot him a look. "Really? You're doing Johnnie Cochrane now?"

"I been saving that one for the right time."

"Twenty years?"

"So it's a goldie oldie."

Jack shook his head. "Stealing isn't the same as murder. I still don't think Bobby did it. Maybe the murderer brought the weapon with them and that's why the cops can't find it. Maybe I'm overlooking something. Who knows?"

"You can ask Bobby yourself. We're coming up on the joint I told you about."

It was still dark and dawn was a dream away. They had taken Alemany Boulevard south to the old Meatpacking District. An icehouse near the Cow Palace had been turned into a kink club and porn film factory. The authorities didn't seem to care as long as the patrons were consenting and the owners paid their taxes.

"And you're sure Bobby's here," Jack said, turning his gaze from the passenger window. "More sure than when we visited that place out in Sea Cliff?" His thoughts touched briefly on the gorgeous madam, *Signora* Theresa Bartoli.

"My bad. That was a dead end, but this joint's more his style. Rough around the edges, if you know what I mean."

"Who tipped you off this time?"

"I may be retired but there's still street punks who acknowledge my rep. 'Banging has always been about respect. Defending your turf and honoring the people who came up before you." He shrugged. "It was the same way when I was in the man's army. Having each other's back. I don't know how I got out of there alive with only a couple of bullet holes to show for it and the Purple Hearts to go along with them."

"Okay, we'll play it your way when we get there. Remind me, what your way is?"

"Same as was when I was a punk on the streets and a grunt in the 'Stan." Hark made a fist. "Kick ass, take names, and let God sort them out."

THE NEW OWNERS of the Ice House hadn't bothered to change the sign on the outside of the old brick building despite the hot and sweaty action going on inside. The front of the club was devoted to a dimly lit lounge where the patrons favored leather chaps and latex body suits. Tattoos and nipple rings were big. So were dog muzzles and studded collars.

"If I knew you were bringing me to be an S and M parlor I would've worn my old man's boots and bunker coat," Jack said.

Hark nodded. "You definitely don't want to sit down anywhere. You do, you'll have a dry cleaning bill, for sure."

They pushed their way to the bar. A guy wearing a black harness French kissed the air as they passed by. His tongue tack was the size of a lug nut. A topless woman with razor blades dangling from her ears took a paper match and split the base so it looked like a stick figure. She straddled it on her right nipple and split a second match and did the same to her left. She lit the match heads with a third. As the heads of the nipple-riding paper cowboys flamed, she gave Jack a sultry come-hither look.

"Didn't the Girl Scouts teach you not to play with matches?" he said.

"What are you, a pilgrim?" She pinched the flames out and stomped away in thigh-high red leather boots.

"Definitely Bobby's kind of joint," Hark said. He signaled the bartender for a couple of beers. "Bottles. And leave the tops on."

Jack laughed. "Maybe you ought to put a condom on yours to make sure."

"Wouldn't be the first time. Three six-packs of Trojans was standard GI issue for every deployment. Newbies thought maybe the Muslim women weren't so religious after all. Wasn't til their first mission they found out you slip a rubber over the barrel of your M4 to keep the sand out."

"Gives new meaning to shooting a load."

Hark scrunched his face. "Man, that's filthy."

"Pilgrim," Jack said.

Hark slammed the caps off the beers on the edge of the bar. He handed one to Jack and as soon as they clinked, he said, "Hey, there goes Bobby."

Sure enough, Bobby Ballena was across the room and walking quickly toward a hallway. "Let's go," Jack said.

The hallway was gloomier than the barroom. Bobby was nowhere to be seen. Closed doors lined both sides. Jack picked one and twisted the knob. The room was lit in red. A man wearing diapers was strapped to a slowly revolving oversized roulette wheel. A woman dressed in a leather cat outfit cracked an Indiana Jones whip. Jack shut the door.

Hark opened the door directly across the hall. "Sorry." He quickly slammed it.

"What's wrong?" Jack asked.

Hark shuddered as if he'd caught cold. "Two dudes dressed up as nuns. They had beards like Mother Superior back at Saint Joe's."

"Probably members of the Sisters of Perpetual Indulgence working out a new skit. Katie and I never miss their Christmas show. Those boys can sing."

Jack tried the next door. A naked couple faced each other and took turns reading Samuel Beckett out loud. The man glanced up from his book. "Would you care to join us?"

"Hate to spoil the ending for you but Godot's a no show." Jack closed the door and shrugged when Hark gave him a look. "I took a lit class at State."

Hark pushed open the next door. Bobby was seated on a leather couch beside a silver ice bucket with the neck of an open champagne bottle poking out. His smile was the brightest thing shining in the whole damn club.

"What took you so long?" he asked.

18

Hark wouldn't sit on the couch. He wouldn't accept a glass of bubbly either. If his eyes were .45s, Bobby would be spouting blood, not bullshit.

"You boys need to loosen up," Bobby said. "This place has more sweets than a candy store. Three doors down? Twins from Iceland. It's two, two, two mints in one." He flashed the halogen grin.

"Can it," Jack said. "Dexter's dead and Little Buddha's gone. What did you do?"

"What I always do. I made a big score." Bobby licked his finger and touched his hip. "Chhhhh. *Don't stop me, baby, I'm on fire.*"

"And I'm the one going put you out," Hark muttered.

Jack stepped between them. "Did you kill him?"

Bobby put a hand over his heart. "I'm hurt, bro. Truly. Why would I off the old boy? I had him set up as an ATM machine. Do you think Little Buddha was going to be my only withdrawal? Come on, you know me better than that. When have I ever thrown away easy money?"

"If you didn't cave in Dexter's skull, who did?"

"How should I know?" Bobby shrugged. "I reclaimed my property and rode off into the sunset."

"What about Laura?"

"What about her?"

"You spent the day together. You took her back to her place after Napa. You were lovers in Nepal. You were—"

Bobby cut him off with a nasty tone. "And you're starting to sound like a cop. What have you been doing, rubbing shoulders with our old classmate the altar boy?"

"Terry's got you lined up as suspect number one. He's already made a reservation for you at Quentin."

"Then he's going to lose his deposit because he can't pin a murder on me because I didn't do it."

Jack stared at him hard. "Then why have you been hiding out?"

"Who says I have? I've been busy is all."

"Doing what?"

"Doing *it*."

"With who?" Jack said.

"You mean *whom*." Bobby laughed. "No one you'd know."

"Laura?"

"You have to be kidding. I've only been wining and dining her as a way to get close to her husband."

"You're lying."

Bobby leaned forward so his face was inches from Jack's. "Far be it from me to talk out of school, bro, but your wife's best friend? She's got monsters in her closet. Big, nasty ones. They don't even offer the stuff she likes here." He mimed straightening the lapels of a suit coat. "Even I have standards of decency."

Jack knocked the champagne flute from Bobby's hand. Shards of crystal skittered across the floor. "Dexter's murder brought Katie into this whole mess. She's not going to quit on

Laura until the killer's caught. That means I'm in it, too. One thing I don't like is being close to a crime I had nothing to do with." He took a deep breath. "What happened that night? Dexter caught you lifting Little Buddha and didn't leave you a choice?"

"I told you. I grabbed the statue and booked. You can beat the shit out of me, but it's not going to change the truth."

"Then prove it. Describe how you went up and down the vent. If you're lying, I'll know because I made the round trip myself."

"Good for you but I didn't need to play Santa."

"What do you mean?"

"Sure, that was my original plan. I had my go-bag and everything already packed in the trunk of the rented convertible. I dropped Laura off, drove up the block, and waited for the happy couple to go to bed. Then what do you know, a car drives up and parks in front of the house. The mansion's front door opens and the driver hops out and goes inside. It was like he was expected. I give it a bit of time. Maybe he's delivering a pizza or something. But then he runs back out and hauls ass."

"So what?"

"So, he left the front door wide open. Laura may be kinky as hell but I still consider her a friend. I was worried she'd been ripped off or worse. I go inside. I walk around. The door to the library is wide open. I go in. There's Dexter lying on a Turkestan rug. Early 1800s from the look of it. Kim would pay a hundred grand for it easy. Well, he would once the blood stain was washed off."

"You're saying you found Dexter and didn't call the cops?"

"Jack, listen to yourself. There was nothing I could do for him. His eyes were nearly popped out of his head he'd been hit so hard. What am I supposed to do, pass up the opportunity of a lifetime? No way. And you wouldn't either. I go over to the scroll,

open up the magic door, grab Little Buddha, and psshhht, away
I go."

"Could you tell if anything was missing? Something that
may have been used to hit him?"

"It wasn't like I stuck around to take inventory. I grabbed
Little Buddha and split."

"You didn't think about checking on Laura? See if maybe
she'd been hit in the head, too? Might need an ambulance?"

"I didn't need to. As I am heading out of the library, I hear
her coming down the stairs, calling Dexter's name. I hide behind
a couch and then when she passes me, psshhht, I slip out the
front door the same way I came in."

Jack leaned back. He'd made a good living being able to read
people. He could spot a tell on a Greek statue, catch a lie before
it was even told, and sniff out a sleight of hand with his eyes
closed. Bobby had a poker face, all right. Few touch artists were
smoother. He could coax a diamond necklace off a woman's
throat while whispering sweet nothings in her ear and slide off
the matching wedding ring to boot."

"Okay," Jack said. "I believe you."

"Motherfucker," Hark muttered from his place by the door.

Bobby's gave the high wattage smile again. "You should see
Little Buddha. He's shinier than ever."

"Where's he stashed?"

The smile blinked off. Bobby cocked his head warily. "Somewhere safe."

Jack knew better than to press. If Bobby thought he was after
the statue, he'd disappear. That would make it harder to ID the
killer. "What about the driver who showed up at Laura's? Could
you recognize him?"

"I was too far away and it was dark. Rich guy, though."

"What makes you say that?"

"He was driving a Tesla. Black. Only rich geeks spend a

hundred grand for a battery-operated car." Bobby's smile returned. "Boys and their toys."

"Who opened the front door, Dexter or Laura?"

"Could've been either one. I couldn't tell. I was too far away."

"Sounds like the driver whacked Dexter," Hark said.

"Maybe," Jack said. "Or maybe he was already whacked."

Bobby pulled the champagne bottle out of the ice bucket and drank straight from neck. "The more suspects the merrier. It takes the heat off me."

"Don't get too comfortable," Jack said. "If you think confession was tough at Saint Joe's, you don't want Terry to get you in the box."

19

K atie pulled Jack close and he responded. Her arms wrapped around him and she caressed his back, his hips, and his legs. They were naked, and she smothered his face with kisses as she hugged harder. His lips opened and her tongue snaked in. He kissed back but something was different. The taste. It was strange. He tried to remember what they had eaten for dinner. Where had they gone? A new restaurant? Had they cooked at home? And then there was her body. It felt, well, unfamiliar, the curves all wrong. He pushed away and looked into her eyes. But they were not green. And then he touched her hair, but it was long and black.

"What the hell?" he said. But the words stayed trapped in his head. He fought to push away, but the woman was holding him even closer, tighter. Crushing him to her breast, smothering him, clutching him around the neck, the shoulders, the waist, and the legs. Her hands were everywhere, and it was as if she had as many arms as an octopus. He struggled for breath, but she squeezed harder until bright lights started shooting and a black tunnel called. He worked his hands between his chest and hers and shoved—shoved and thrashed with all his might. And then he heard his own shouts and awoke drenched in sweat with the sheets wrapped tight around him.

"Benzai-ten," he shouted. And the specter of the Japanese goddess faded away.

The bronze statue paperweight on Dexter's desk. He couldn't remember seeing it when he dropped down from the ceiling and searched the library.

Now that he was awake, he lay in bed and started sorting through what he knew and what he didn't about Dexter's death. Learning the identity of the mystery visitor was key. Tracking down a Tesla wouldn't be too hard even if it were the latest must-have among the Silicon Valley set. Katie's story about how Laura's secret lover probably lived nearby echoed. And what about the missing eight-armed statue? Who had given it to Dexter and where was it now? By the time the sky outside the bedroom window blued and the sunrise faded into memory, he was no closer to the truth then when he began.

If he couldn't sleep he might as well get sweaty, so he flung off the comforter and dressed in shorts, running shoes, and a San Francisco State sweatshirt. On the way out he grabbed an orange ball cap with the Giants logo stitched in black.

The early morning endorphin junkies were already chasing their fix as Jack hit the Embarcadero. He quickly fell into a steady pace for the half marathon to Fort Point and back. The first ferry delivering commuters from Marin County was still chugging across the bay as he passed the clock tower. The tourists hadn't descended on Pier 39 yet, and the only activity at Fisherman's Wharf was a sidewalk vendor icing down a tub of Dungeness crabs. At Aquatic Park a pod of swimmers stroked for the tip of the breakwater. They were members of the Dolphin Club and never missed their early morning dip no matter the weather. Knowing many were in their '70s spurred Jack to pick up the pace.

Freelance fitness instructors were setting up on the Marina Green. One guy cordoned off an area with rows of Pilates balls and resistance bands. A youngish Schwarzenegger look-alike lined up free weights and staked out a sign that said "Get Guns like Gaga Here." A skinny guy with a shaved head and wearing a G-string was doing downward dog on a pink yoga mat. Food trucks jockeyed for the best parking spots alongside the Green. One offered breakfast burritos, another Blue Bottle coffee. Jack fought temptation and kept pounding.

He'd fallen into a good rhythm with his arms and legs pumping in synch and his heart rate and breathing holding steady. The wide gravel path leading into the Presidio was surprisingly empty. He ran past the great marsh at Crissy Field and followed the shoreline west. A Chinese freighter riding a rising tide made Jack smile. A year before he'd played three-card monte with shipping containers as part of a scheme to rescue Katie from a madman.

A *V* of pelicans kept pace as he ran. Two orange towers strung with graceful cables rose ahead. He never grew tired of the majestic sight. The Golden Gate Bridge was his lodestone. It always brought him back, no matter how far he roamed or how dark his thoughts. He checked his watch and noted his record pace. When he reached the trail's terminus at Fort Point, a wave crashed against the seawall and showered him with salty spray. A foghorn blared and seagulls screeched but Jack didn't stop to acknowledge the ersatz welcoming committee. He spun on his heels and raced for home.

The trail back through the Presidio was still free of runners, though two Segways riding side by side were heading toward him. Jack guessed it was a pair of tourists that hadn't read the rental rules about riding in single file. As the machines approached the riders moved to either side of the path leaving Jack no choice but to run between them. He was about to warn them they could get a ticket for traveling abreast when the machines suddenly swerved right at him. One struck a glancing blow and sent him caroming off the other. He lost his footing and took a header onto the gravel.

As Jack started to pick himself up one of the riders rolled close and blocked his movement. The other circled around and pinned him from behind.

Tomasz Radic sneered from his perch behind the handle-bars. "Don't move or I'll break your fuckin' legs."

The thug with the hipster undercut underscored the threat by leaning forward. The shift in weight caused his machine to advance. One of the fat wheels pressed against Jack's shin. "Snap, crackle, pop."

Jack rolled on his back and pressed the sole of his running shoe against the Segway's LeanSteer. The pressure triggered the onboard computer to lock the wheels.

"They make these things idiotproof," Jack said. "Guess we know where you rank on the IQ test, huh, Tom?"

Tomasz's face twisted with rage. "I'm going to flatten you."

"With what, this stand-up vacuum cleaner?"

Jack sat up but kept his foot on the LeanSteer blocking the Segway's advance. He looked over his shoulder. Jeremy Werthing was astride the second two-wheeler. "If you guys wanted to buy me lunch again, all you had to do was call my office. Would've saved you the cost of renting these toys." He dusted off his palms and started picking the gravel out of the strawberry on his knee.

"You didn't seem to comprehend the seriousness of our previous conversation," Jeremy said. "Or the seriousness of our intention."

Jack picked out a few more pebbles. "And you think pushing

me down on the blacktop is going to get me to cry uncle? Grow up."

Jeremy's eyes darted behind the gray lenses of his designer sunglasses. "Don't underestimate our perseverance or our practices."

"Let me guess. You've been using a thesaurus app." Jack studied his knee. Blood ran down his shin and pooled in his sock. "That'll make a friend of mine happy."

The smoky glasses darkened as Jeremy's pupils widened. "You speak very glibly for a man in your present predicament. I'm not sure how much longer my colleague can exercise self-control."

"Yeah, not fuckin' long," Tomasz growled. "You're roadkill."

"You're the ones who seem to have trouble comprehending. Tell your boss I'm not interested in giving my app away. Who is he, anyway?"

Jeremy's teeth showed. "Someone you should be very cautious about."

Jack picked out the last shard of gravel. "Caution's my middle name. It's why I never talk business with the hired help. You do know who you're working for, don't you? Have you met him or did he hire you online?"

"You're not going to talk to nobody because I'm going to bury you in the dunes." Tomasz started to step off his two-wheeler.

Jack flung the handful of gravel into his eyes and kicked the LeanSteer. The machine toppled over and took Tomasz down with it. Jack kicked him in the face and then spun and grabbed Jeremy's wrists and yanked him off his Segway.

"Don't hurt me," Jeremy cried.

Jack could see his reflection in Jeremy's sunglasses. The look on his face would've scared him, too. He tightened his grip, put his hips into it like he was back in the batter's box, and swung for the bleachers. When he let go Jeremy sailed through the air and crashed on top of Tomasz.

Legs and arms and the LeanSteer went akimbo. Jeremy's sunglasses lay on the gravel. Jack stepped on them and ground his foot. "Jeez, Jer'. You look like what the cat dragged in."

He didn't feel the scrape on his knee the rest of the run home.

20

N otices for unpaid bills covered Jack's desk like drifts of dunes. Polite e-mails had given way to pink slips from collection agencies threatening legal action. He pushed them aside to make room for his tablet and started Googling the latest stats on Tesla. The figures for over thirty thousand car sales a year plus the corresponding share price were stunning. "If I'd only bought in at the IPO, I wouldn't have to worry about the leg breakers," he muttered.

Another few clicks took him to blackpearl.bf. The anonymous Burkina Faso TLD was a notorious bazaar for illegal transactions. Black Pearl was the Silk Road for hackers. Jack typed in a request for a list of all Tesla registrations in Woodside. If the mystery driver who ran in and out of the Cotswold mansion the night of the murder was indeed Laura's lover and if Katie's story about Dexter almost catching them in flagrante was true, then chances were he lived within honking distance.

While Jack waited for some hacker in some far corner of the globe to respond to his cyber classified, he ran through what he knew so far. Dexter Cotswold was a workaholic, egomaniac, and fabulously successful. At least that's the image he portrayed. Jack had spent too much time on the other side of a con to believe everything a person projected, especially when it came to money.

Laura was a New Age nympho, a trophy bride with a kinky side and a rich lover. Had the lover bashed Dexter's brains in or had Laura? Maybe they did it together.

Bobby and Little Buddha were loose ends. But loose ends caught in the middle of a murder investigation never escaped the attention of a homicide cop who wore starched shirts and had it in for Jack.

And Katie? If he didn't do something about the murder quick, she could be collateral damage.

Something else nagged him. Jack trusted his instincts, and while he was sure Dexter had been behind the run on his app, just because he was dead didn't mean the board had been swept clean. In the cutthroat game of tech, there were always others eager to pick up the pieces. In this case it had to be Dexter's managing partner and now the firm's only partner, Arjun Chopra. Jack had been able to survive by seeing the connections and never trusting coincidences. Players that suddenly appeared on the stage in the middle of a con were never impromptu actors. And wasn't the tech business the biggest con of all? People were making fortunes convincing others they couldn't live without the latest gizmo.

The tablet flashed with an incoming message. The sender's name was Skrlt Pmprnl.

Regards yr Black Pearl ad. How much?

Jack typed back, *200 US + 24 hr turnaround*

HaHaHa, the hacker responded. *Get real*

How much u want

1K US

Jack checked his anger. *U Get real. $500 LBFO*

He watched the screen. Minutes passed. It was all part of the game. Hackers loved to play chicken. Jack typed, *Others bidding. Going once, going...*

His screened flashed. *Deal. 24 hrs.*

Jack tried to picture Skrlt Pmprnl. It could be anybody—a pimply kid sitting in the nearest coffee shop or a loner hunched in a dingy basement apartment half a world away. They were as invisible as the Net that linked them.

He switched gears and started thinking about Tomasz and Jeremy. The pair had come out of nowhere and in the middle of the action, too. Why now? Who did they work for? More importantly, what did their boss really want?

The phone interrupted his ruminations. Caller ID said it was Katie. The fear in her voice bolted him straight up.

"Terry's arrested Laura. He says she murdered Dexter. I tried to get him to stop but he told me he was doing his job. He's taken her away."

Jack felt Katie's pain more than he heard it. "It's probably nothing. The brass is on Terry's ass to deliver a suspect. He's gasping and grasping because he's got nothing. Do you know where he took her? It's got to be either the cop station in Menlo Park or county lockup in Redwood City."

"I didn't ask. Should I have? Laura was hysterical. I was trying to calm her down." Katie took a breath. "Terry wouldn't let me go with her. He handcuffed her and put her in the backseat like a common criminal. I can't believe he's being so mean."

"He's trying to scare her into saying something." Jack maintained his calm tone. "I'll make some calls."

"You have to do more than make calls. You have to find out where he took her and go get her. She's got no one else. We're all she has."

Jack swore to himself. Not being in control was a player's worst nightmare. "Okay, babe. I got this one. Come on home. There's nothing you can do down there. As soon as I find out where she's at, I'll let you know. I'll get a lawyer working on springing her right away."

"Who?"

"A guy I know."

"Not that unctuous little Tingly Meyers?"

"Tingly doesn't do criminal law. And anyway, he seems to have retired. The guy I'm talking about is the best there is when it comes to this sort of thing."

"Then call him as quick as you can. Please? Laura won't survive a minute in jail."

"I'm on it. Trust me."

"I still don't understand why Terry is acting like this. I tried talking to him, but he wouldn't listen." She caught her breath. "I can't believe I ever loved him."

Jack could say something that would bury Terry forever, right then and there, but he didn't. As much as he wanted the Katie's ex-lover out of their lives for good, deep down he knew he was a by-the-book cop. Terry wouldn't have arrested Laura unless he'd found something incriminating, and Jack needed to make sure it wasn't something that could pull him down, too.

21

Cicero Broadshank ordered his handmade suits from Sam's in Hong Kong. They came in two sizes: 54S and 58S. The only time he was able to squeeze into a 54 was following his annual 10-day rehab at a fat farm in Tecate. They went right back on the hanger within a week of his return to San Francisco and all of the city's culinary delights. The lawyer preferred tropical weight wool in midnight black with wide chalk stripes accented by a yellow silk tie and matching pocket hankie. The black wasn't intended to minimize his weight nor were the pinstripes meant to make him look taller. His attire was part of his courtroom signature, as memorable as his flowing white mane, red-faced summations, and obvious disdain for police officers who bent the rules.

Jack found the corpulent counselor wedged behind a table at the Flower Market Café. He was eyeing a stack of pancakes topped with sliced bananas and powdered sugar as if considering a generous settlement offer. A pink cloth napkin was tucked between his spread collar and third chin.

"What brings you to this fine dining establishment on such a glorious day," Broadshank bellowed. "Don't tell me you're being arraigned at my fair Iron Lady?"

The lawyer took a proprietary view of the gray-walled Hall of Justice located across the street. Its courtrooms had been his stage for more than thirty years and the site of countless hard-fought and hard-won verdicts that had netted him millions. The underworld considered Cicero Broadshank the next best thing to a Get Out of Jail Free card.

Jack frowned at the heaping platter of carbohydrates. "I hope you've doubled up on your statins."

"Now, now. I've divorced four wives already. I don't need a fifth." He dug into the restaurant's signature specialty. The Flower Market Café was not only the closest restaurant to the Hall, it was also one of the city's hidden gems—its food as fresh and colorful as the blooming plants sold at the historic whole-sale flower mart next door.

Jack signaled the waitress for coffee and waved off the prof-fered menu. "I need your help, CB. More to the point, a friend needs your help. And right away."

"When someone asks me to *help* a friend, what they really mean is for *free*." The lawyer sucked a sliver of banana off the tines of his fork. "You know I absolutely abhor four-letter words."

"Dexter Cotswold," Jack said. "As in Capital Dexterity Dexter Cotswold."

Broadshank took his eyes off the plate for only a moment. "You have me confused. From what I hear, the only person who can help him is Saint Peter." His belly laugh jiggled the table.

"I neglected to add an important three-letter word." Jack took a sip of coffee and savored it as he played the moment out. "*Mrs.* She's at the Hall. Terry Dolan brought her in. He's charging her with murder one."

Jack had never seen Broadshank walk away from a full plate

before, much less run. He was half way across the restaurant shouting into his phone by the time Jack got up from the table. Money and fame were the only things that proved more irresistible than food.

"Wait a sec, CB," Jack called as he caught up to him on the front steps of the Hall. "You agree to represent her, no questions asked?"

Broadshank's voice rose to its famous courtroom pitch. "When a woman's constitutional rights are at the mercy of a law enforcement system infamous for its high-handed attitude toward the law—no, infamous for running roughshod over—neither patience nor trepidation is a virtue I, for one, am willing to entertain." He sucked in air before delivering his close. "Justice will not wait. It cannot wait. It shall not wait. It is my duty to obey and serve without delay."

"Meaning in the time it took you to cross the street your receptionist was able to secure a retainer."

The lawyer tut-tutted. "I never concern myself with the business of law, only the law itself."

Jack didn't contradict him even though it was common knowledge that Cicero Broadshank, Esq. was without equal when it came to wresting sizeable deposits from the most dangerous and desperate of clients no matter the hour, the charge, or the evidence stacked against them.

The lawyer led the way. He threaded his ample frame through the metal detector without ruffling a shoulder pad. Once cleared he barreled straight toward the police station tucked in the corner. Broadshank rapped the bulletproof glass with his UC Hastings College of Law class ring. "Open the door immediately. My client is being detained unlawfully. I have witnesses who will testify that she was never Mirandized."

The same desk sergeant who'd buzzed in Jack the other day scowled. His face was chiseled by years of hearing every plea in the book. "Who's the scumbag this time, Broadass? Another drug dealer? Maybe a gangbanger?"

The lawyer drew himself up to his full five foot six. "Everyone, and I mean everyone, is entitled to the law. My client is Mrs. Dexter Cotswold of..." he snapped his fingers.

"Woodside," Jack said.

The desk sergeant hawked at a dented metal trashcan and missed. "Here at the Hall, Cotswold is as common as Brown or Sanchez. I need a first name."

All three of the lawyer's chins jutted. "Keep it up, Sergeant, and I'll have you charged with discrimination. The department is still reeling from the last seven figure settlement I won for a client who suffered at the hands of a racial profiling."

"It's Laura," Jack said. "Laura Cotswold."

"Did you hear that? Laura with an *L*. Must I spell it for you? Now open this door posthaste." The lawyer held up his phone. "You have two seconds, or I will transmit a complaint to Police Chief Lau and Judges Hoyos and Naftolin naming you complicit in an obstruction of justice charge."

The desk sergeant gave in and triggered the automatic door. Broadshank charged through it faster than a rodeo bull coming out of the chute. He kept his phone pointed in front of him.

"Attention, everyone. Be advised I am video recording my entrance for evidentiary purposes. This action is permissible under California Civil Code Section 11.43, subsection 5595.6, parentheses *a*, end parentheses."

The spiel sounded like total bullshit to Jack but none of the cops looking up from their desks appeared willing to challenge Broadshank. He reached the far side without interference. Interrogation rooms lined the wall. He turned the phone around and took a selfie.

"My name is Cicero Broadshank, Esquire, Managing Partner of Broadshank, Hicklin, and Wong, LLP. I hereby duly charge

Inspector Terrance Dolan with unlawful detention of Mrs. Laura Cotswold of Woodside, California. The aforementioned is my client, and as such is protected by attorney-client privilege. I submit the following facts as basis for my claim: One, Inspector Dolan arrested Mrs. Cotswold in San Mateo County, which is outside of his jurisdiction; two, the aforementioned Inspector neglected to deliver a Miranda warning to Mrs. Cotswold; three, the aforementioned Inspector circumvented due process by interrogating Mrs. Cotswold without presence of counsel; four..." He paused and looked pointedly at a camera mounted on the station's wall.

The door to the middle interrogation room flew open. Terry's glare could melt wax. "Broadshank and McCoul. Criminalist and criminal, and no way to tell them apart."

Broadshank waved his phone. "I'll remember that slander in the complaint I'm filing against you. Now, out of my way, Inspector. Your conversation with my client is not only over, it is inadmissible *in toto*."

The fat lawyer pushed his way past. Terry's face reddened. Jack couldn't help himself. "In case you forgot your Latin, that means *fuck you*."

LAURA'S MAKEUP had more streaks than the Joker's. Puddles of mascara caked her high cheekbones and rivulets of eyeliner ran to her chin.

"Jack," she cried, making it multiple syllables. "What's happening to me? I don't understand a thing. I want to go home."

Broadshank plucked a hankie the color of an ear of corn from his breast pocket and handed it to his newest client. "My name is Cicero Broadshank, Esquire. Your late husband's corporate counsel has retained me as co-counsel, given my expertise in these matters. I'm authorized to serve on your behalf. From this moment no words are to pass your lips to anyone but me."

Laura keened. "Why am I in this awful place? Why am I tied up?" She raised her hands to show the cuffs and the loop of chain that ran through a ring bolted to the table.

Broadshank patted her wrist. "Questions that deserve answers, my dear Mrs. Cotswold, but all in good time. The first order of business is to get you out of here."

"I shouldn't even be here. I didn't kill my husband." Her sobs triggered another flow of mascara. "You have to believe me. I've been trying to tell them, but they won't listen. I told them I—"

"Not another word," Broadshank said with force. "The authorities breach rights to privacy as a matter of course. From here on I will do all the talking. I must instruct you again to say absolutely nothing without my approval. Not even a nod or a blink. Do I make myself perfectly clear?"

Broadshank motioned for Jack to join him at the other end of the room. He turned his back to the two-way mirror and spoke in a sidebar whisper. "I must go and work on obtaining a release. It may take time to convince the right judge, so I must warn you I may not be able to accomplish that by four o'clock. You know what that means."

"The witching hour," Jack said.

Suspects still in custody were transferred upstairs and either temporarily placed in Jail One pending release or booked and locked up in Jail Two, Four, or Five, depending on their gender and crime. Jack figured Laura's mood ring would turn from purple to black in a heartbeat if she was given an orange jumpsuit and thrown in with the general inmate population.

"Can I stay with her until you get back?" he asked.

Broadshank's brow rose. "Given your disdain for the authorities, that's most generous of you. I'll inform them you are my associate and thus part of Mrs. Cotswold's legal team." The lawyer examined his watch. "I'll try to keep you updated on my progress, but if I'm not back in time, don't resist when they come to take her upstairs. The last thing she needs is any complications. And the last thing I need are two clients in lockup."

The lawyer left. Jack took a seat opposite Laura. It was the first time he'd ever been on that side of the interrogation table. He held his fingers to his lips to make sure she understood. Then he pulled a deck of cards from his jacket pocket, winked at the two-way mirror, and started showing off his repertoire of false shuffles, snap changes, sleights, and vanishes.

22

Katie was in the gym, smacking the hell out of a speed bag. She wore a sleeveless T knotted above her belly button and 10-ounce boxing gloves emblazoned with the pink ribbon. Perspiration beaded her shoulder blades. A wisp of hair escaped the tie at the back of her neck and teased her right eye. Every so often she would let fly a roundhouse kick at a 100-pound heavy bag dangling from a rope. It all but groaned from the blow.

Jack learned early on never to interrupt her when she was working out. "It's all about staying centered and maintaining the proper aura," Katie had said. Jack had translated that to mean *working shit out*. And from the look of it, she was definitely dealing with a heavy load.

Katie launched a furious final combination that nearly tore the speed bag from its hanger and finished off with a double kick to the heavy bag that sent it careening into the wall. She neatly spun out of the way when it came sweeping back. As she did, her eyes met Jack's. He draped a snow-white terry cloth gym towel around her shoulders and held out a water bottle with a straw.

"How's my million dollar baby?"

She took a sip then raised her boxing gloves so he could untie the laces. "Much better now. Anger is so toxic. It can really pollute your body chemistry if you don't purge it."

Jack nodded at the heavy bag. "Just be glad you don't have to pay *him* worker's comp."

Katie's name was listed as sole proprietor of the residents only gym, but Jack was her silent partner. He'd funded it with the finder's fee a Chinatown Triad gave him for helping them out of a jam. Member dues now covered the lease and the fitness instructors' salaries. Sometimes there was even enough money left over to pay Katie for leading yoga classes.

"You know I'm not angry with you," she said as Jack tugged off her gloves. "It's not your fault Laura had to spend last night in jail. The person I am mad at is whoever killed Dexter and who's putting her through all this."

"CB worked hard to get her released, but the clock ran out, and they had to take her up to booking and holding," Jack said. "He says there may be a case for wrongful imprisonment since Terry convinced the San Mateo County DA to use a technicality to transfer jurisdiction to San Francisco PD. Even if that doesn't work and the San Francisco DA goes forward with an arraignment, CB will argue to have her released on her own recognizance. If worse comes to worse and the judge rejects OR, well, Laura has plenty of bucks to pay for bail no matter how steep."

Katie's cheeks were red as apples from the workout. "How long will it take before she can come home?"

"Forty-eight hours max. The judge will set a prelim. That's a hearing where they determine whether or not there's a case. Usually that's ten days later, but there's a lot CB can do to delay it."

"And all that time people will be gossiping and wondering if she really did it." Katie blew at the loose wisp of hair. "We have to find out who killed Dexter right away so Laura can get on her with her life and Dexter can move on to the next."

"That's easier said than done, babe. And I'm not even talking about the ghost part."

"Don't be negative. We have to think positive."

"I'm trying to manage expectations here."

"And I thought you would've *managed* to find some leads by now. What's taking so long?"

Katie's upper lip was crowned with perspiration. As much as he wanted to, Jack restrained himself from reaching out and brushing it off.

"Well, I'm chasing some things down but—"

"Laura's counting on us. We have to get cracking. I'll go take a shower and meet you upstairs. Okay?" Katie didn't wait for a response. She trotted off, shadowboxing as she went.

Jack watched her go and then glanced at the heavy bag. "You heard her, you big lug. Stop hanging around and get back to work."

SUN SPARKLES DAPPLED the gray-green waters of San Francisco Bay. Jack never tired of the view from his loft. It was as ever changing as the city he loved. He sipped an espresso as he stared out the bayside windows and tried to figure out what he was going to do next. The list of Tesla owners Skrlt Pmprnl had submitted was unwelcome news. The tiny town of Woodside had one of the largest concentrations of registrations in the world. It was as if every household had one parked in the garage. Running down the owners would take too long. Jack pinged the hacker back and asked for a digital map of the addresses arranged by concentric circles around the Cotswold mansion with overlaying screens populated by name, age, occupation, and club memberships. Chances were good that Laura and her secret lover had another connection beside proximity.

The last of the espresso grew cold as he watched a red and white Coast Guard helicopter buzz by. A black-stacked Crowley tug towing a barge piled high with riprap plowed south toward Candlestick Point. His phone buzzed.

"Speak," he answered.

"I'm afraid something's come up." Cicero Broadshank's usual thunderous voice was nearly drowned out by the background sound of cutlery and conversation. "The proverbial wheels of justice have run into a roadblock."

"Meaning?"

"Mrs. Cotswold must remain incarcerated for the foreseeable future."

"Since when couldn't you get to a judge?"

"The bench is not the problem. And neither are my powers of persuasion. The trouble is the client. In all my years at the bar I have yet to witness this sort of behavior. She has disregarded my advice and admonishments absolutely."

Jack walked over to the kitchen island and put his cup down. "What did she do?"

"It would be quicker to say what she hasn't done."

"Laura's only been in the joint twenty-four hours. That's hardly enough time to get a tattoo, much less brew a batch of pruno and marry her cellie. Don't tell me she tried to hang herself and ended up in psych."

"Worse. She confessed to murder."

Everything went catawampus. The loft's floor buckled. The windows tilted. The Bay Bridge swayed before Jack's eyes. At first he thought it was an earthquake.

He took a deep breath. "Was it the statue? Is that what she used?"

"What are you talking about? What statue?"

The lawyer's confusion allowed Jack to catch himself. "Sorry, figure of speech. I meant whatever she says she used to hit Dexter in the head with. Did she say why she killed him?"

"No, no, no. Not her husband." Broadshank took a deep breath. "She still claims innocence to that. Mrs. Cotswold confessed to a different crime altogether. She told the police she'd been molested by her father, and as a result was complicit in his death. Her mother's, too."

Jack felt the loft list again. "What are you talking about?"

"Laura didn't confess to mariticide, she confessed to parricide. Or at least conspiracy thereof."

"Are you shitting me? What are we going to do now?"

Broadshank paused. Jack could hear a knife and fork scraping china and then the lawyer chewing. "I already called the firm that retained me as co-counsel and apprised them of this turn of events—all under attorney-client privilege, of course—and advised that I would need to expand the original scope of my services if I'm to continue leading the defense. They need to confer with their client before issuing guidance on next steps."

"Who's the client now that Dexter's dead?"

"That would be Capital Dexterity's senior partner."

"Arjun Chopra."

"Quite right. I'm impressed you know that." Broadshank paused. "Perhaps I shouldn't ask why you do. I've never met Mr. Chopra personally or had occasion to speak with him but his reputation precedes him. Evidently, he's very exacting, but I shall have no trouble meeting his expectations."

Jack worked to keep ahead of the changing circumstances. "Laura's lucky Chopra came to her aid."

"While Mr. Chopra initially may have acted out of fidelity to his late partner, if criminal defense has taught me anything, it is that loyalty only goes so far when murder is involved. I suspect

Mr. Chopra's motivation now is driven more by a desire to insulate Capital Dexterity from negative publicity. Venture capitalists aren't as big as risk takers as you might think, especially when it comes to scandals involving partners and their wives."

"Okay, assuming Chopra greenlights you to continue, what then?"

"To start, I'll need to gather all the information I can find about the circumstances prompting Mrs. Cotswold's confession. That in itself will prove challenging since the events took place twenty years ago. Right now all anyone has to go on is her claim. And that includes the police." The lawyer drank noisily. Jack assumed it was a lunchtime Chardonnay.

"Then there's the added problem of her not residing in California at the time she alleges the molestation and murder occurred. I will need to obtain copies of the official coroner's exam, police reports documenting the crime, the alleged molestation, and any other documentation I might need. That will be extremely challenging because if she actually had been tried and convicted for parricide, her record will either be locked or expunged, depending on the jurisdiction since she was a juvenile at the time. The San Francisco District Attorney will be doing the same, and she won't be pleased since it will consume a considerable amount of her department's resources. I have no doubt she will welcome this development as warmly as embracing a suspect with Ebola."

"You said Laura has to stay in jail. Can't you spring her?"

"I certainly won't give up trying—I have plenty of legal remedies at my disposal—but the confession does add a degree of complication." Broadshank took another swallow. "The DA may assume the confession is either a ruse aimed at delaying the original murder charge or it's an elaborate scheme to justify the spousal homicide. An unorthodox defense strategy, mind you, but not at all without possibility."

"What are you talking about?"

"There could be an argument made that Mrs. Cotswold suffered post-traumatic stress disorder as a result of being molested and that is to blame for her murdering her parents as well as her husband."

Jack sucked in air. "PTSD."

"I could find subject matter experts to call to the stand."

"This sounds like it will take a lot of time. Katie's anxious to get Laura released. When do you think you'll hear back from Chopra?"

"It wouldn't be him directly. All conversations must go through the attorneys."

"Full employment act, huh?"

Broadshank mustered a tone of moral offense. "I'm hurt by your perpetuation of such baseless stereotyping."

"Sorry. Let me restate. When will Chopra's mouthpiece get back to you?"

"Like any adept counselor would he demurred by committing to a specific time, but I hazard a guess it won't be long. His firm is top-notch, one of the most respected and successful around. In addition to representing all the leading technology and private equity companies, they specialize in helping launch start-ups. Speed is part of their firm's DNA."

"What's the name of the firm?"

"Marcus and Cheatham."

Jack stiffened. He'd seen the name in a footnote on a brief filed by the lawyers who were representing the trolls going after his patents. His memory turned to Dexter's funeral and the carefully coiffed lawyer with gold cufflinks introduced by Laura. The name hadn't register at the time.

"Are you dealing with Winston Cheatham or another lawyer at the firm?"

"Credit is due, Jack. You are more perceptive about the legal profession than I thought. Winston's an excellent attorney. Very smart. Very successful. He graduated top of his class at Stanford Law."

"Very smooth, too. I've met him. I'll give him a call and let him know Katie and I appreciate him helping Laura out by keeping you on the case."

Broadshank tut-tutted. "That's very well meaning, but I must insist you refrain from doing so. As I said earlier, all communication must be made between the counselors themselves."

"I'll take it under advisement." Jack hung up and counted all the way to three before dialing 411.

23

A bronze plaque depicting an owl and a full moon rising greeted Jack as he opened the front door to the Bohemian Club. Its inscription warned Weaving Spiders Come Not Here. He recalled the line from an acting class at SF State. It was from *A Midsummer's Night Dream*; he'd played Puck. Tricksters and jesters were his favorite Shakespearean characters. The Fool, Touchstone, Feste, and Speed all relied on disguises and wits to unmask and upend the entitled.

"Let's see if anyone inside is spinning a web of deceit," he said as he entered the private bastion for men only near Union Square.

An old duff with floppy white eyebrows guarded the front desk. Jack told him he was a guest of Winston Cheatham. A liver-spotted hand pointed him to a doorway across the dark-paneled lobby. It led to a comfortable lounge. Cheatham was holding forth at the bar. A group of nattily dressed men clutching drinks formed a semicircle. All wore grins and their faces were flushed from booze.

"I'm reviewing a twenty-four-year-old client's draft submittal for his newest start-up," Cheatham was saying. "Checking the packet for omissions and conflicts was strictly pro forma since he cleared two hundred million on his last venture and Goldman had already told me they were all in. The client's in my office, playing Clash of Clans while I peruse his personal financial statement. I spot an automatic debit to another personal checking account for forty-five dollars on the first of every month. Considering his net worth is nine figures, the miniscule payment stands out like a postdated prenup. I ask him what it's for and who is it going to." Cheatham paused before delivering the punch line. "He pays his father back for his cell phone. He's still on the family plan."

Everyone laughed heartily. One man slapped his thigh. "If I was the kid's old man I'd say, 'Junior, keep the forty-five and give me a wireless company, dammit.' "

There was more laughter.

Jack tapped the lawyer. "Excuse me. Jack McCoul."

Cheatham turned around. "Of course. I recognize you from the funeral. A terrible thing. A tragedy for everyone. My secretary said you wanted to discuss something about Mrs. Cotswold. She said it was urgent. How may I help you?"

"It's about the case. I need some legal advice."

Cheatham held out his martini glass like it was a stop sign. "I'm afraid you've wasted your time. There's nothing I can tell you. To begin with I'm not directly involved—I'm only serving as an intermediary as a favor to a valued client. Furthermore, everything about the case is attorney-client privileged. I'm sure you can understand." He took a sip and didn't offer to order Jack a drink.

"So Cicero Broadshank told me. I'm the one Laura called the night of the murder. I'm also the one who alerted CB to her arrest."

"He gave you sound advice. You'd be wise to follow it."

"There's been a development. I'm not sure how to handle it."

Annoyance crossed the lawyer's face. His skin was otherwise free of wrinkles, his brow waxed so it didn't meet above his nose. "I'm sorry but are you operating in a formal capacity? What line of business are you in?"

"I have a mobile app start-up, and if the number of patent trolls going after it are any metric, I'd say I have a hit on my hands." Jack waited and watched for a tell. If the lawyer had any direct connection to the law firm representing the trolls, he didn't show it. Jack tried again. "Maybe Dexter mentioned it to you? He was considering investing in it. That is, before he was murdered."

"I never discuss private conversations," Cheatham said indignantly.

"Of course not."

"I thought you said you had something to share about the case. Mrs. Cotswold?"

"I do."

"Then what is it?"

"Is there a place we can talk privately?"

Cheatham showed a flash of impatience. He turned to his fellow club members. "Why don't you all go up to dinner and I'll join you shortly. David, order a bottle of the Screaming Eagle. And make sure it's properly decanted. Last time it wasn't."

"This way Mr. McCoul."

A broad stairway took them to the basement level. Jack followed the lawyer into a cavernous room decorated with murals reminiscent of a Parisian cabaret at the turn of the century. He half expected Toulouse Lautrec to be sipping absinthe in the corner and sketching cancan dancers.

Cheatham took a seat at a long table. His gold cufflinks gleamed as he made a show of checking his Rolex. "I have five minutes."

"Does attorney-client privilege extend between us?"

Cheatham sighed. "Mr. McCoul. Jack. May I call you Jack? It's important for you to understand I'm a corporate lawyer. My specialty is intellectual property, finance, contracts, mergers and acquisitions, that sort of thing. I'm hardly qualified to offer counsel on a criminal matter much less take a statement. I must tell you again it's highly inappropriate for you to be speaking about Mrs. Cotswold's case with anybody but Mr. Broadshank."

"I understand but something happened, and I felt it best to talk to another lawyer first."

He sighed again. "Your wife is Laura's friend, excuse me, Mrs. Cotswold. They've known each other a long time. Tell her the best thing she can do—both of you can do—is let the legal process take its course."

"If you think Katie put me up to this, you're wrong. She doesn't know a thing about it."

"Be that as it may, I'm afraid there is still nothing I can do for you." Cheatham pushed away from the table.

"There's a witness," Jack said. "He's an acquaintance."

The lawyer paused. "Have you told Mr. Broadshank?"

"Not yet. I wasn't sure if I should. If I tell CB, won't he have to tell the prosecutor before he has a chance to talk to the witness? That might scare him off. That's why I came to you first. I figured it was the safest thing to do. You know, attorney-client privilege. If you say I should tell CB then I will. If you say I shouldn't then I won't."

Cheatham studied him. He spoke slowly. "Does Laura, Mrs. Cotswold, know about this?"

Jack shook his head.

"Have you told anyone else?"

"Only you."

"Not the police?"

"No."

"How do you know this person is telling the truth?"

"I've known him a pretty long time."

"And what exactly did he tell you?"

"He said he was at the house the night of the murder because, well, let's say he was there under unusual circumstances. He told me Dexter and Laura weren't the only ones there. He said he saw what happened."

"And exactly what did he see happen?"

"A car coming and going. The driver. Dexter dead."

"Did he see the actual murder?"

"No."

"Can he identify the driver?"

"No. It was dark."

"What about the car? A license plate, perhaps?"

Jack shrugged.

"It's not much of a testimony."

"I know this guy. If he says he saw something then he saw something all right. He's holding back until he gets some guarantees. Until then he's not going to talk."

"What sort of guarantees? Money?"

"A guarantee the cops won't turn it around on him."

"I may not be a criminal defense attorney but I do know this: unless there's hard evidence to corroborate what your friend told you, it doesn't mean a thing. Criminal cases often have people making false statements or testifying to things they thought they saw, but it was what they *wanted* to see. The police and prosecutors are skilled at determining fact from fiction. More than likely your friend's testimony will be inadmissible." He paused. "What did you say his name was?"

"I didn't."

"Forget I asked. It's better that I don't know. His statement is unlikely to help unless it can be verified and corroborated. In fact it could very likely damage Laura's defense. We certainly wouldn't want that."

"Of course not. But if he can prove she didn't do it, isn't it worth the risk?"

Cheatham shook his head. "Law, no matter if it's corporate or criminal, is about managing risk. I'm sure you've heard the old saw that trial lawyers never ask a question they don't know the answer to. What you've told me is filled with too many unknowns." He positioned the chair back at the table. "I tell you what. I'll invoke attorney-client privilege between us for the time being. Let me do a little research. If it turns out this could be a help not a hindrance to the defense team, I'll let Broadshank know and he can take it from there."

"Thanks. That's a big relief."

"Not a problem. We all want to help. In the meantime it's best if you don't say anything to anybody until you hear from me."

"Of course."

"Now I really must be going." Cheatham turned to leave but stopped midway. "You mentioned your business and a patent dispute? IP law is something I do know plenty about. My professional advice is to settle. Litigation is much too costly. You could wind up losing all of your assets trying to protect something that may not pay off anyway."

"Thanks," Jack said. "I'll keep that in mind."

24

B uster's was one of the few joints South of the Slot that
adapted to changing tastes and times in order to
survive the rapacious real estate speculation trans-
forming the district's aging warehouses into million-dollar-plus
condos. The transformation of the corner hangout morphed
from a ship worker's bar to a Hells Angels clubhouse to a gay
bathhouse and leather bar to a nightclub showcasing home-
grown talent. No matter the guise, Buster's stuck to a tried and
true recipe customers could always count on—good drinks,
good times, and no questions asked.

Jack and Katie sat side by side at a pool table whose top
looked like it had been involved in a knife fight. Bay Bridge Beat
was on stage, and their hearty mix of hard-driving blues and
horn accompanied favorites kept the cramped dance floor
hopping. Jack told her about Laura's confession over tapas and a
pitcher of Big Daddy IPA. The news didn't shock Katie as much
as make her more determined than ever to prove her friend's
innocence.

"Laura is the real victim," she said. "She needs understanding and therapy, not to mention twenty years' worth of

apologies from a society that doesn't do nearly enough to stop sexual predators."

Jack nodded even though he could still hear Broadshank's ruminations that Laura's story could be an elaborate ruse. He leaned in close to make himself heard over the wails of the lead guitar. Katie's perfume was intoxicating. "Did Laura ever mention a man named Arjun Chopra?"

"I don't think so. I would've remembered a name like that because of Deepak. His meditation app is very popular." Katie cocked her head. "Why?"

"I've met him a couple of times now. He was Dexter's business partner. He signed off on the company's legal firm to retain CB for Laura's defense."

Katie took a sip of the IPA. "That makes it even more surprising Laura never mentioned him."

"Why's that?"

"She's always been jealous of Dexter's coworkers because he spent so much time at the office. Laura has nicknames for them. She calls Miss Nash *Bisnatch*. That was Dexter's executive assistant. Laura says she treated her like a gold digger." Katie made a face. "Women stereotyping women is very undermining to the cause."

Jack skated his glass around. "What's your women's intuition say about Laura never mentioning Arjun Chopra to you?"

Katie peered over her glass. "If you want to hide something you never point to it, do you?"

A guest singer with black mascara and a hairstyle reminiscent of Amy Winehouse broke into a decent cover of Bonnie Raitt's "Something to Talk About." She had a solid voice but Jack was hearing another song altogether. It was "Hell's Kitchen" by the rapper DJ Khaled. The verse that played over and over in his head was *Omission's usually an admission to guilt, hari-kari yourself all the way to the hilt.*

Katie's intuition was never wrong, but Jack was having a hard time buying that fun loving Laura Cotswold could be attracted to somebody as humorless as Arjun Chopra appeared to be. Then again Jack knew a thing or two about deception. Maybe Chopra was only uncool when it came to business. Maybe he had a wild side. Maybe he even drove a Tesla.

Katie grabbed his harm. "Look, there's Hark."

The big man ambled over. His grin spread as wide as the gothic letters blued on his neck as Katie offered her cheek. He obliged with a kiss and then winked at Jack. "All due respect."

"I hope you have your dancing shoes on. This band is rocking it," Katie said.

"I've been working on some moves."

Jack faked scorn. "Don't tell me you've been sneaking into the gym and taking Katie's Zumba class again?"

"It beats gobbling blood pressure pills. You get to our age, you got to work on your cardio. You should give it a try."

Hark ordered a pitcher of Big Daddy from a passing waitress. She was wearing skintight black jeans and a whole lot of attitude. His eyes never left her backside as she snaked through the crowd.

Katie touched his arm. "Uh-huh. She's not your type."

"You sure?"

"Trust me. You need someone with more substance."

Hark grinned. "Are we talking physical or mental?"

"Personality trumps everything," she said. Katie turned to Jack. "I still don't know why you haven't introduced him to Moana. They're perfect for each other."

"Babe, as much as you like playing matchmaker, let Hark be. You're embarrassing him."

Katie sighed. "Men. Leave everything to you and the species would go the way of the dodo."

Hark kept grinning. "Who says I'm embarrassed? Tell me more about this Moana."

"She's Jack's office manager." Katie smiled. "Incredibly resourceful. Incredibly beautiful."

"Incredibly mouthy," Jack muttered.

"You've been holding back on me, *ese*?" Hark slapped his chest. "How come you don't have my back when it comes to matters of the heart?"

"I do. That's why I didn't introduce you."

"It's the least you could do, seeing how you made out." Hark gestured at Katie.

"Okay but don't say I didn't warn you. Moana smokes cigars and can crack a coconut with her teeth."

Hark's grin grew even wider. "I'm in love already. Hook me up."

It was two in the morning by the time they rolled out of Buster's. When Katie wasn't dancing with Hark, she had Jack out on the floor. His moves were barely perceptible, a bit of slightly clenched fists slowly rolling in front of his chest, a slight twist to the hips. No foot work at all. He was but an anchor for Katie as she flowed around him as effortlessly as water, always in synch with the music's shifting currents and rhythm.

"You sure you don't want a lift?" Hark said. "My whip's right around the corner."

Katie shook her head before Jack could accept. "We'll walk. It's a beautiful night out. Look at that moon streaked with fingers of clouds."

"Catch you lovebirds later then."

Jack and Katie linked arms for the stroll home. The darkened streets were quiet. It was one of the few areas South of the

Slot where the old buildings hadn't given way to modern apartments for the new generation of technocrats.

"Can you imagine living anywhere else?" Katie leaned her head against Jack's shoulder.

"Here in the Slot?"

"Anywhere in the city. I know you'll always be partial to the Mission since you grew up there and, sure, I miss Pac Heights at times but I mean anywhere in San Francisco. It's... it's home. It's where I want to be. It's where I want to raise our family."

Jack caught himself from stumbling. They had never talked about having kids before. It wasn't part of his game plan. No way he would've considered children when he was on the grift, and to think about them now, well, he'd always wanted the flexibility to be able to reach back to his old life in case he needed to.

"Are you trying to tell me something, babe?" He heard the thickness in his voice.

She turned her face and nipped his shoulder. "I'm not pregnant if that's what you're worried about. I meant when the time comes. We are going to have a family someday. You know that. When the time is right."

Jack stifled a comment and tightened his arm around her. They reached the shadowy intersection of Bryant and Third. He was careful to look both ways before stepping off the curb despite the late hour and absence of traffic.

They were midway across when he heard the whine of a speeding car. *A drunk,* Jack tried telling himself, but his instincts screamed different. Out of the corner of his eye, he saw the car switch lanes as it bore down. Jack scooped up Katie and dashed for the opposite curb. It was going to be close, and he weighed the risk of hurling her out of the way. How many bones would she break when she landed? How many would he break when the front bumper struck him?

There was no time for answers. He ran faster—ran like he

was trying to score from third on a suicide squeeze. Katie was screaming and the car's engine was roaring as it closed in. Jack lowered his head and braced for the impact that would be nothing like bowling over a catcher blocking home plate. And then came another roar. Deeper, louder, and familiar. Jack looked over his shoulder as thunder boomed and flames shot from the twin chrome Flowmasters on an ass-dragging '64 Chevy Impala. He kept running and reached the curb as the lowrider painted the color of a Golden Gate sunset screamed down Bryant and swerved into the intersection to execute a fishtail that slapped the oncoming car.

Rubber squealed. Metal crunched. Glass shattered. The collision spun the other car 180 degrees. The Impala screeched to a stop. Hark was out from behind the steering wheel fast for a man his size.

"Down, *vato*!" he yelled.

A hole in the back windshield of the other car exploded as an automatic weapon inside let loose.

Hark pulled his Beretta M9 from beneath his untucked flannel shirt and returned fire. The rounds pinged off the trunk of the car and blew out more glass. Tires screeched again and the assailants raced away.

"You better run, motherfuckers," Hark shouted. "You shoot like you drive. Candy ass."

Jack crouched on the sidewalk with his arms tight around Katie. Any joy from the night of dancing and drinking was long gone. All that remained was the cold fury of a straight edge razor.

Hark came over, his eyes still scanning the street. "You okay?"

Jack nodded. "You?"

Hark glanced at his beloved car. "Nothing a little Bondo and touch-up paint can't fix."

That's when Jack spotted the singed hole in the shoulder of Hark's flannel shirt. "What about that?"

Hark scowled at the wound. "Like I said, nothing a little Bondo and touch-up paint can't fix."

Sirens sounded in the distance. The big man shoved the 9mm he'd brought home from Afghanistan back in his waistband. "We can stay and talk to the cops, or I can chase after those *cabrones*. There were two. A driver and a shooter."

Jack pictured Tomasz Radic and Jeremy Werthing. "They got a head start on you."

Hark spit. "And I got a four twenty-seven under the hood. My ride's low but it ain't slow. I'll put out an APB on the low low net. If that piece of shit stays on the road, some *hermano* will spot it for sure."

Jack gritted his teeth. "Okay but just tail them and find out where they're going. I want to talk to them myself."

Hark glanced at Katie "That goes without saying, but you know if they start shooting again, I got to shoot back. It's about respect."

He sped off with another twin salute from his chrome tail pipes. As much as Jack wanted to go with him, he wanted to get Katie home safe and sound before the cops showed up. The last thing he needed was Terry Dolan riding in on a white horse.

STEAM CURLED from the bathtub as it filled. Jack finished helping Katie undress. She was having trouble with the buttons. Her fingers were still shaking.

"You're home safe, babe," he said and cupped her chin. "Come on now, a warm bath, a brandy, and a good night's sleep. You'll feel better in the morning."

"It's already morning and who said anything about being

scared?" Her voice was defiant. "I'm mad is all. Who do you think it was?"

Jack had made a vow never to lie to Katie, and he always stuck to his word. It wasn't easy, so sometimes it was best to say nothing at all. This was one of those times. He preoccupied himself by lighting the candles they kept stationed around the tub.

Katie rushed to fill the silence. "Maybe it was one of those random drive-bys you hear about where they shoot at the wrong people." When Jack still didn't reply she stuck out her chin. "Then it has to do with Dexter. Someone must have found out we were asking questions, and they're trying to scare us off. We have to call Terry and let him know what happened."

The tub was full. Jack turned the water off. "No way."

"Why not?"

"Because Hark shot back. Because we left the scene of a crime."

Katie shivered. "What are we going to do?"

"First off, you're going to get in the tub and get warm. And then I'm going to pour you a glass of brandy and turn down the bed. Whatever needs to be done can wait."

"But you are going to find out who it was, aren't you? We need to know if they're connected to Dexter's murder. It could help free Laura."

Jack gritted his teeth again. "I'm going to find them, all right. Count on it."

"And then what will you do?"

"Whatever it takes."

"Promise me you won't do anything silly. I couldn't stand it if something happened to you. I'd be worse off than Laura."

"You wouldn't be in jail."

"You know what I mean."

"We could always play *Ghost*."

"That's not funny. You always try to make light of serious things. This is serious. Promise me you're only going to find out who they are and turn it over to Terry." Her voice started to crack. "Promise?"

Jack averted his eyes knowing she would see in them what he would do when he found the pair. "You're getting cold. You should get in while the water's still hot."

Katie stopped talking and slid into the tub. Jack went to the kitchen as soon as she gave into the warm embrace and closed her eyes. He poured a full glass of Irish and slugged it down. Then he poured brandy into a goblet and carried it to the bedroom and set it on her nightstand. Next he turned down the bed. As he pulled back the duvet, a shiny yellow metal figure with an enlightened smile and a blemish on its butt stared back.

It sure as hell wasn't Goldilocks.

25

D o Pray could write code as fast as BLAS running on Big Blue, but his speech was more like the processor that chugged inside a 1981 Kaypro.

"I'm not following you here," Jack told him after trying to sort through the coder's drawl. "Are you saying everything you've written so far and what I've patented is for shit?"

"No sir. It's like I been trying to show you on my screen. We got a big problem needs fixing, and I want your permission to fix it." The young programmer pointed at the screen. "See this line of code here? It's a mite I wrote."

"A mite." Jack said it like it was a bad taste he was trying to spit.

"That's right. We have them in Lous'ana. Little itty-bitty bugs that stick to anything alive. They're too small to see but you sure can feel them when they bite."

Jack blew out air. "Are we developing an app here or are we suddenly in the insect business? Because I feel like a bug on a windshield. I don't get what you're driving at."

Do Pray let his head bob for a few seconds as he gathered his thoughts. "Let me try again. See, back home we got all sorts of insects on account it's mostly swamp. The biggest and hungriest is the praying mantis. It eats anything. Bugs and frogs and scorpions, even hummingbirds. It eats its own mate, too. A black widow has nothing on a praying mantis."

"The code is buggy, that what you're telling me?"

"No. I'm trying to explain the fix I wrote. See, after the female praying mantis mates, she kills the daddy and lays a thousand eggs on him, and then the eggs hatch and the babies eat him. Well, somebody planted a praying mantis in our network, and she's laying a thousand eggs. When those eggs hatch, they'll chomp straight through our data."

Jack smacked his forehead. "You mean the praying mantis, the bug, is hacking us. Stealing our data. It's hijacking the code you've been writing for my app. How did they get in?"

Do Pray beamed. "Now you understand."

"Can you stop it?"

"The mite can. That's why I wrote it. See, most people think the only thing big enough to take on a praying mantis is an owl or a snake. But a mantis has five eyes and can turn its head nearly all the way round and sees anything coming. But what's hard for a mantis to see is a tiny little mite. Now the mite might be small but it's got a big appetite. It sucks blood and when it does, it injects poison."

"You mean a tick. That's what we call them here. Ticks."

"We got ticks too but mites are mightier. They lay their eggs on top of the praying mantis eggs, and theirs hatch first, and they eat the mantis eggs right up. A mite can also sneak up right behind the momma mantis's head where she can't get to it and start sucking blood and spitting poison." Now he was grinning.

"So you wrote code for a mite and it will destroy the mantis the hackers planted and eat the mantis eggs before they can hatch, too. Good. No, better than good. It's great." Jack clapped him on the back. "Any way to tell where the mantis came from? I need to know who's trying to rip us off."

"I'm already working on it."

"Good job. What do you call it?"

Do Pray's teeth lit up the room. "A stinkbug. See, a stinkbug is a favorite food of the praying mantis. They love stinkbug. I'm going to stick a stinkbug out there and whoever's spying on us won't be able to say no. They'll send another praying mantis after it. But when it sinks its teeth into my stinkbug thinking it's the juiciest piece of code they're trying to steal the stink will roll right back in the hole it came through. I'll be able to track it back to where it come from."

"And then what?"

"If it's all right with you, I'll send a third bug into that hole."

"And what will that do?"

Do Pray's long fingers clicked keys. The screen switched from lines of code to a digital image of a spiderlike insect with a bulging red abdomen and scythe-like mandibles. "We got these all over Lous'ana. It's called an assassin bug. They bite fearsome. It's the pit bull of bugs. The assassin bug I wrote will tear a hole right through their system, and they won't be able to launch another bug attack for a long time."

"Perfect," Jack said. "Sic it on the hackers, and if it works you've earned yourself another hundred thousand shares."

JACK SAT ALONE in his office and hit the speed dial on his phone again. Hark still didn't pick up, so he sent him another text. He spun his chair around and stared down at Market Street. The same homeless man from the other day was sleeping on a grimy sheet of cardboard. A pair of pigeons pecked a dried splotch of vomit on the sidewalk. Trolley bells rang from a streetcar rolling toward the Embarcadero.

The fastest way to locate Tomasz and Jeremy rested with Hark. But dealing with them was only half of it. What Jack really wanted to know was who was pulling their strings. He ruled out the usual suspects who trafficked in heavy. If it had been a Chinatown gang, he would've heard about it from the Fangs; they still owed him for helping them recover a boatload of computer chips. Drug cartels? Since when were they into software apps? There was always the Russian mob, of course. Their stronghold was in the Outer Sunset, and while it was true that intimidation, protection and software scams had long been their stock in trade, this didn't bear their usual style. Grigor Dragonov and his boys would've only taken *no* from Jack once. And then they wouldn't have come after him on Segways or a speeding sedan. More like an armored SUV with a .50-caliber machine gun mounted on the roof and rocket launchers strapped to the sides. It had to be somebody else. Someone new. Someone who'd heeded the call of *thar's gold in them thar silicon chips* and came to California with good old-fashioned claim jumping in mind.

Hark would come through. Jack was sure of it. All he had to do was wait to hear from his friend. Patience and self-assurance had always been Jack's strong suit. It was part and parcel of the grift. He knew plenty of swindlers who wound up stacking time because they gave in too fast to greed or fear or, worse, self-doubt. They weren't called confidence games for nothing.

The phone rang. Jack answered without checking caller ID. "What did you find out?"

"Now that's a novel way of saying *hello*," Cicero Broadshank replied.

"My bad. I was expecting someone else. What's up?"

"I wanted to provide you with an update on the Cotswold

case. I petitioned the judge to speed up the preliminary hearing, and I'm cautiously optimistic I will prevail with regards to securing her release on bond. Of course, we may have to grant concessions on electronic monitoring and psychiatric supervision, but I expect to receive a decision any moment."

"Finally some good news. Katie will be glad to hear that. Any developments regarding what happened to her father and mother?"

"Nothing conclusive. I'm still awaiting reports from the field as is the District Attorney."

"Let me know if there's anything I can do to help."

"Certainly, but all seems to be in hand. I'll keep you posted."

"One other thing. Have you heard anything from Winston Cheatham?"

"No. Why do you ask?"

"I wanted to make sure Arjun Chopra hadn't changed his mind about backing Laura's defense."

Broadshank sucked in his breath. It had the howl of an offshore wind. "Perish the thought."

26

Late afternoon rolled around and Jack decided to do some digging on his own before the trail of the speeding car grew any colder. He checked on Do Pray on his way out. The young man was bobbing under his Beats and his fingers flew faster than usual.

"It's coming together real good," he said. "Nobody is going to be able to fight off my mites, and nobody is going to be able to resist my stink bug, and nobody is going to stop my assassin bug. Nobody."

"Let me know when you've launched it. If the hackers gets hold of our code they'll not only steal it, but they'll alter what's in our database."

Jack figured it was all tied to the patent trolls. They were planting evidence to prove infringement. It wouldn't be the first time trollers resorted to dirty tricks to make a case or extort a payoff.

"Leave it to me," Do Pray said, bobbing as he typed.

Jack paused at the front door to talk to Moana. "The kid's worth his weight in gold. Keep him fed and fueled. Our fortunes are riding on him."

"They're also riding on you bringing in some money," she shot back. "You never told me what happened with those investors from Arch Ventures you had lunch with."

"I'm hoping to see them again real soon."

"When you do, put the squeeze on them. And I mean squeeze their *laho* until they cough—cough up a check, that is."

"I'm going to squeeze them, all right. Count on it."

JACK JAYWALKED EVERY STREET, dodging Muni buses and delivery trucks. He reached the Pier in record time. Wonder Boy greeted him with a mug of Anchor Summer Lager and a shot of Jameson.

"Giants are in S-S-San Diego tonight," the statistics-minded mixologist said. "They hit more homers at Petco Park than any other s-s-stadium. S-s-slugging percentage is .125 higher there."

"The boys own the Pad's, that's for sure." Jack savored the pale golden beer. "Seen Hark?"

Wonder shook his head. "Not s-s-since last time you were here."

"I'm trying to get a bead on a couple of mutts masquerading as tech investors. One's called Jeremy Werthing, the other Tomasz Radic." He gave a short description. "They're running point for whoever is hiding behind a front calling itself Arch Ventures. Heard anything?"

Wonder shook his head again. He took the rag draped over his shoulder and started rubbing an invisible watermark on the polished bar. "You want me to put the word out?"

Jack contemplated the tiny bubbles swimming in his beer. Information was the currency of the street. Only a few brokers were worth paying for it. The rest dealt in lies, rumors, and half-truths that usually caused more problems than they solved. Wonder was the exception. He kept a thousand phone numbers in his head. Twice that many e-mail addresses. He knew the movements of every snitch, tattler, and tipster in town and could pinpoint their location according to the time of day.

"Do it. But keep the sense of urgency light on the Richter scale. The last thing I need is a stampede of bogus intel."

Wonder nodded. "I'll s-s-sift and s-s-sort it myself."

He moved down the bar, leaving Jack to study his glass of lager. The color made him think of Little Buddha. Finding the statue was a surprise. And the telltale mark on the bottom confirmed it was the real deal. Only one person was capable of putting him there. Breaking into the loft was a doodle for someone with Bobby Ballena's talents. Why he stashed the figurine there wasn't the only question that needed answering. If the gold effigy was the murder weapon, Jack sure didn't want to be caught with it. But he couldn't let go of Little Buddha either. Never relinquish leverage was among Jack's top ten rules in grifting.

He downed the shot and was making ready to shove off when the bar turned silent except for the squawks of gulls. Hearing the winged scavengers meant someone had opened the door. Jack turned to see who. He shouldn't have been surprised but he was.

Terry Dolan cut a path through the crowd. Most of the patrons averted their faces. Some put their drinks down and quietly slipped out the door as the detective took the stool next to Jack's.

"You're easy enough to find," the cop said.

"I didn't know I was lost." Jack paused. "Buy you a drink?"

"I'm on duty," Terry said stiffly.

"That's your problem. You're always on duty. You've been on duty ever since your parents walked you down to Saint Joe's on the first day of school. Doesn't it get tiring always bearing the cross?"

If the jab hit home, Terry didn't show it. He fired back one of his own. "Funny you should mention our alma mater. A patrol squad picked up an old schoolmate today."

"Lots of kids went to Saint Joe's when we were getting our knuckles rapped. Can't say I've made it to all the reunions."

"You know this one. He was caught rotten."

"Why Inspector Dolan, is that a hint of brogue I hear? Sounds to me you're channeling your old man." Jack was stalling and he knew Terry knew it. He pictured Bobby in an orange jumpsuit.

"At least my father was by the book. More than I can say about yours."

Jack didn't take the bait nor did he list all the police brutality charges Demon Eamon had racked up during his years on the beat. It was true about his father. Jack once discovered a stash of soot-stained loot in the garage. When he realized it had come from burning buildings, he asked his dad about it. Gavin responded with a right to the jaw and a left to the gut and told him to mind his own fookin' business. From that moment on Jack vowed he would out crook him.

"Okay," Jack said. "I'll bite so I can get home. Katie's waiting for me. It's champagne and chocolates night. Who's the unlucky alum?"

"Geraldo Martinez," Terry said. "He got pulled over for a busted taillight early this morning."

Jack kept his cool. "Sounds like Hark's the victim of a classic case of DWB."

"Race had nothing to do with it," Terry said quickly. "He was behind the wheel of a moving vehicle with a code violation. When the officers inspected the vehicle for other violations, they discovered several bullet holes in it."

"So do half the cars parked in the Mission. You know how it is. Punks saddle up for a joyride on a Saturday night and think they're cowboys by firing their six-shooters into the air. They're too dumb to know what goes up must come down."

Terry kept his voice official. "The bullet holes gave the officers probable cause to search the inside of the vehicle. They found a gun."

Jack forced a laugh. "Let me guess. A Beretta M9, right? It's a souvenir from Hark's days serving his country. You know he earned two purple hearts over there, right? It's registered. You got nothing."

The cop twisted his stool to face Jack. Their jaws were inches away. "They also noticed a hole in Hark's shirt. They took a closer look and found a wound in his shoulder."

"So maybe he cut himself shaving."

Terry forced a laugh. "You expect me to believe that?"

"Swimmers buzz their scalps. Cyclists wax their legs. Maybe he's trying out for the Olympics. San Francisco's got a bid to bring them here."

Terry's smile evaporated. "Hark's busted. He's already in lockup on the seventh floor. And I'm going to bust you, too. We got a video from a traffic surveillance camera on Third Street. It shows a lowrider smashing into a sedan and a gunfight. If you look close enough, you can see a couple huddled on the far sidewalk. Do you want to explain that?"

"Sounds like a case of road rage. Did you get a license plate? How about any faces you can ID?"

Terry stayed silent.

"I didn't think so. Fender benders happen every night. And plenty of people sleep on the sidewalks, too. The city hasn't done shit to solve the homeless problem. You don't have anything on Hark. And you don't have anything on me, either. If you did you wouldn't have dared come down here without backup."

Terry slammed his palm down. "I know it was Hark. I know you were there. Tell me who was driving the other car."

"How should I know?"

"You know, all right. The same as I know it was you and Katie on the sidewalk. What kind of man endangers his wife like that? Puts her in the middle of a shootout. I'm going to put you away for good, and when I do, she'll finally come around and thank me for it."

"You want Katie to thank you? Then stop harassing Hark and me and go find who really killed Dexter. You do your job right and Katie will thank you plenty." He stood and twirled the stool before leaving. "She might even send you a Hallmark card, don't you know?"

27

Twilight settling over the city kissed the steel and granite skins of the skyscrapers with subtle shades of pink and indigo. The dwindling impatience of car horns signaled the thinning of the evening commute, and two short farewell blasts from the stack of a Golden Gate Ferry heralded the martini departure for Sausalito.

Jack called Cicero Broadshank as he walked home. The lawyer explained he was ensconced at Alioto's for happy hour but could give him sixty seconds while he waited for a platter of oysters. Jack told him about Hark. Broadshank agreed to represent him and sounded confident the big man would quickly be cleared of all charges, given the flimsy cause for arrest.

"And Jack," the lawyer said. "Please don't go down to the Iron Lady and make a scene. Not only will it not help your friend, but it could have disastrous consequences for Mrs. Cotswold."

"Does that mean your cautious optimism of getting her released is growing more cautious?"

"Perhaps."

"Still no word from Cheatham?"

"Why do you keep asking?"

"No reason."

Jack signed off and kept walking. He wondered if Hark had discovered anything. Had the cops picked him up before or after he tailed the shooters? If he did know something, then why hadn't he sent word? Being in jail was no excuse. Getting hold of an illegal phone in the blocks was as easy as copping a pack of smokes or a tag of rock—all smuggled aboard the chocolate caboose. Of course someone with Hark's street smarts would know better than to hold a jailhouse phone too close to his lips, and he'd use plenty of soap and water after dialing, too.

Up ahead two people were walking Jack's way. There was something about their lurching gait that made him tense. He checked the traffic, ready to dart across the street at the slightest threat. But he relaxed the closer they got. It was only a pair of young men not quite accustomed to navigating city sidewalks in high heels and tight skirts.

"I told you we should've gotten an Uber from BART," one whined. "These Dolces are killing me."

"You mean the knock-offs you bought at the Pleasanton mall," the other hissed back.

Jack told them they were headed in the wrong direction if they were going to The Endup. "But don't sweat it," he said. "You both look fabulous."

He hadn't taken another step when his phone buzzed. No caller ID. *Finally,* he thought. *Hark.*

"Speak," he said.

"For a moment there I thought maybe you had switched sides. Those two are cute." Bobby Ballena laughed.

Jack swiveled his head so fast his neck hurt. "Where are you?"

Bobby laughed again. "It's what I've always told you, bro. You got to think bigger. Much bigger. Try top of the world."

Jack peered up. Across the street rose Contempo Towers,

fifty-eight floors sheathed in translucent blue glass that comprised the most expensive per square foot residential real estate in San Francisco. When construction was completed, the Contempo's residents raised the entire South of Market's income tax base by two thousand percent.

"You're hiding out up there?"

"Don't sound so surprised. You know I was born to live here."

Jack kept his opinion to himself. "What floor?"

"The penthouse, naturally. I'm looking at you through a Celestron Astromaster. I can see you haven't shaved in a couple of days."

"We need to talk."

"Why I called. Come on up and dance among the stars."

Jack ignored the irritating laugh. "How do I get past security?"

"I'll call down. Tell them you're a guest of Ms. Halliday."

"Halliday. As in Kiki Halliday the queen of San Francisco society."

"She's an old friend." Bobby paused. "And Jack, don't forget to use the doormat."

His cackle rang in Jack's ears the entire elevator ride up.

BOBBY WAS POSED against the floor-to-ceiling windows with the lights of downtown serving as a glittering backdrop. He wore a white dinner jacket over a black T-shirt, designer jeans, and black Italian loafers—no socks. The only thing bigger and shinier than his grin was the cut crystal tumbler in his hand. Jack had to admit he did look like he was to the manor born.

"Where's the mistress of the house?" Jack asked.

Bobby waved a hand. "Don't you read? It's opening night at the opera. Kiki's is chairing this year's gala."

"You looked like you're dressed to go."

"I'm not big on fat ladies singing. Kiki and I plan to have our own private after party right up here."

Jack nodded. He'd already guessed Bobby was a self-imposed prisoner. He walked closer and held out his hand, indicating he wanted a sip of whatever it was Bobby was drinking.

Bobby obliged. "Twenty-seven-year-old Caol Ila. Not bad for a warm-up."

Jack sipped the whisky and then set the glass down carefully on the end table. Without saying a word, he slapped Bobby hard across the face. His backhand was equally as vicious. Bobby landed on the couch.

"The first is for dragging me into your shit," Jack said. "And the second is for dragging in Katie. You don't even want to think about what Hark's going to do to you."

Two bright red blotches marred Bobby's Baja tan. He rubbed his cheeks and then worked his jaw to make sure it wasn't unhinged. Next he reached over to the end table, dipped his finger into the tumbler of single malt, and rubbed his teeth.

"So this is the thanks I get." He shook his curls. "*Señor Negativo*."

Jack made a fist. "You expect gratitude? Leaving Little Buddha in my bed? You're fucking *Señor Loco*."

Bobby shrugged. "You know how much he's worth. I gave him to you to show good faith. I trust you and you need to trust me. Like I told you, I had nothing to do with the Cotswold murder. Sure, I jacked the statue. And I planned on jacking a whole lot more. It's what I do. It's what you'd do, too, if you hadn't gone all Holy Roller." His eyes narrowed. "Maybe it's not religion you found, maybe it's nerves you lost."

Jack showed his fist. "I ought to throw you off the balcony. See if you find religion on the way down. You'll have fifty-eight floors to search for it."

Bobby sat up and straightened the drape on his white dinner jacket. He crossed his legs and showed the gecko tattoo above his ankle. "You're not going to do that. Just like you're not going to turn me over to Terry Dolan. And you will get Hark to stand down."

"You know better than to con a con. Tell me what you know. If Little Buddha's not the murder weapon, then why did you park him at my place?"

Bobby reached into his breast pocket and extracted a phone. He tapped an app, scrolled, clicked, and then sat back and watched Jack's face.

Jack's phone buzzed. He opened the incoming instant messenger. Photos were attached. Photos of Little Buddha positioned on Jack's kitchen counter, on his desk next to a photo of Katie, seated on the couch, on the toilet seat, and finally in his bed.

"They're in the cloud, bro. All set with a delayed send. All addressed to Terry Dolan. The only thing that can stop them from going out into the world is me." Bobby picked up the whisky and downed it. "It is more shameful to distrust your friends than to be deceived by them." He said it in the same phony Confucian accent he had used on Dexter Cotswold the day they'd met.

Jack tried reading Bobby's face but it was a blank slate. "What do you want?"

"I already told you. Trust. There's only one person in town who could have found me. You. Terry couldn't find a bitch in heat using a pack of bloodhounds. I need to know I'm going to be safe up here. That you won't sell me out to protect you and yours."

"You have to ask?" Jack flexed his fists.

"Things are different now. You've changed since Kathmandu. I saw it when you and Katie sailed down to Baja after that chip scam last year. You're not the same Jack McCoul I used to run with. I know that now. It was a mistake using you and Katie to get to Laura and her husband, but what choice did I have? It's karma. What's done is done." He made a show of dusting off his palms.

Hark's warning was echoing loud in Jack's ears. *Don't listen to him. Never trust him.* "Why haven't you hightailed it back to Baja?"

"On what? I need money, and it's all locked up in Little Buddha. I'm too hot to fence him, and I can't be found with him either." Bobby took a breath. "I need you to sell him for me. You need to get hold of Kim and broker a deal. You complete the fence and wire the proceeds to my account in the Caymans. I'll give you five percent for your troubles. No, make it ten. And don't look so surprised. You're not the only one with a frosty banker stuck on a sunny island."

"What about Laura?"

"What about her?"

"Aren't you forgetting something? Her husband's dead. She's in jail."

Bobby jiggled his foot. "Not my problem. I had nothing to do with it. I told you once, I told you twice, she's one sick chick. She probably did him."

"I don't buy that," Jack said.

"That's Katie talking there. You've lost your edge. You're not seeing things straight anymore."

Jack hesitated. He knew he had little choice but to string Bobby along. The photos of Little Buddha were too much leverage hanging over his head. "Make it twenty percent and I'll see what I can do."

Bobby clapped his hands and flashed his teeth. "There it is. That's exactly what I was hoping to hear. The old Jack is back." He raised his fist to bump knuckles.

Jack ignored it and headed for the elevator. Bobby had only gotten part of it right. Jack had changed but he hadn't lost his edge. One thing that would never vary was how he approached the game. He only played according to his rules, and he always played to win.

28

Hark slouched in the passenger seat of the Prius the following night. He didn't hurt and he wasn't tired. He was worried about the kind of hit his rep would take if another low low spotted him.

"All I'm saying is if you're going drive this POS, at least you can let me pimp it. It's embarrassing. It's in serious need of chrome. Some 20-inch rims and fat pipes for starters. Listen to the engine. It's got no voice. Sounds like my *abuelita's* cat when you pet him."

"Talk to Katie," Jack said as he steered through Hospital Curve and then down the Bayshore. "She uses the mileage app more than she does Instagram. If the car drops below forty MPG, she's on the horn complaining to the dealer."

"Next you're going tell me she's all up for self-driving cars." The big man shuddered. "What's the world coming to?"

Jack glanced at him. "How's the shoulder?"

"I've had mosquito bites stung more."

"Tough guy."

Hark shrugged. "The cap barely nicked me. Only reason

cops put a bandage on it while I was in the can was because they were worried about taking a brutality hit. Your lawyer had them running scared." He scrunched his forehead. "If I had to change the dressing, you think that receptionist of yours would lend a hand if I give her a call?"

"Moana? You'd be lucky if you wouldn't need stitches afterward."

"Definitely my kind of woman. Like always, Katie knows what she's talking about." Hark leaned forward and touched the screen to pump up the volume to Hendrix's version of "All Along the Watchtower" streaming from Jack's phone. "Goldie oldie," he said.

They crossed under the 280 split. The ghost of Candlestick loomed on their left. Jack checked the side mirror and changed lanes. "You haven't said anything about Bobby Ballena. I thought you'd want to go after him first before showing me where you tailed the shooters."

Hark's head bobbed to the music. "Bobby's just being Bobby. He's always been that way. I'm not the one who's surprised here."

"One night in jail and you're all peace, love, and understanding?"

"Time, *vato*, it's relative."

Jack rolled his eyes. "Dr. Einstein, I presume?"

"That's where the stuff Katie teaches comes in handy, all due respect. You get thrown in the can where there's no vibes but bad vibes, so you got to find a way to rise above. It's how I got through the 'Stan. That and my *'manos* having my back, and me making sure I always had a couple extra clips."

"Roger that."

They were on the low stretch of highway that ran right alongside the flat dark waters of the bay. Katie always said it would be the first to flood when the sea rose because of climate change. The bald silhouette of San Bruno Mountain rose ominously on the right.

"This the exit coming up?" Jack asked.

Hark turned down the music. "Go up and over and follow it back toward the water."

The flyover delivered them onto Oyster Point, a flat swath of oyster beds that had been turned into a landfill and then converted to an office park on the north side of SFO's runways. A twisty blue metal sculpture representing a double helix welcomed them. It sported a sign that read South San Francisco - The Birthplace of Biotechnology. Nondescript two- and three-story buildings lined both sides of the wide boulevard. Most were surrounded by parking lots. Some featured loading docks. Landscaping was limited to raggedy beds of ice plant studded by lone Monterey pines with scoliotic trunks that attested to the strength and constancy of the winds that howled off the bay.

The bigger buildings sported names and logos. "Some pretty big blue chip outfits down here," Hark said. "You'd think they spring for a few flowers to dress up the place. Where do people eat? I don't see nothing more than a Starbucks and 7-Eleven."

"At the company-owned cafeterias," Jack said. "It's the same down in Silicon Valley. Keep 'em on the farm and they got nothing else to do but plow fields and milk cows."

"If I ever get tired running my body shop, I could buy a food truck, load it up with my *abuelita's* burritos and come down here and make a killing."

"You'd do pretty good as long as you didn't eat all the inventory," Jack said with a grin.

"She can cook, true that. I never saw you turn down seconds." They drove another block and then Hark said, "Up there on the right."

Jack slowed as they passed in front of a concrete tiltup set back from the street. It was behind an eight-foot-high wrought iron fence. A guardhouse anchored a mechanical gate. A guard sat inside, watching TV.

"The shooters pulled into the driveway and didn't need to honk. They called ahead," Hark said. "The guard didn't give a shit their car was shot to shit."

"Looks like Tom and Jerry found a hole to crawl into."

"Who are they?"

Jack told him. "No way they hold the deed to this property. Somebody else does. Somebody with a lot of money and a lot of juice. My guess is this building can lead me to him."

"Looks like the driveway goes around to the back. Maybe they're still here."

"Only one way to find out."

The boulevard split 100 yards past the building. The left was signed toward a marina. They kept to the right and merged onto DNA Way.

"All these roads loop back and forth," Jack said. "They're laid out like a double helix, too." He checked the GPS and slowed in front of a two-story building that was still under construction. A For Lease sign was staked out front. "Lucky us. I make this place right behind our target."

He turned in and drove around back. The parking lot was empty. They got out. A chain link fence topped with three strands of barbwire separated the two adjoining properties.

Hark grinned. "The building we want has a fence around it like a redneck's mullet. Wrought iron business in the front, party in the back." He glanced at the Prius. "Don't suppose it comes with bolt cutters?"

"Not even a tire iron."

"You're kidding me."

"Doesn't have a spare."

Hark winced. "People don't drop nails on roads no more?"

"Guess we'll have to do it the old fashioned way."

"Your ride doesn't have the muscle to pull this fence down."

"I mean one of us boosts the other up and over."

"You know I took a bullet in the shoulder for you already."

"You told me it was a scratch."

"Yeah and if I get caught up in that wire, it's going have a lot more to go with it."

"I was thinking you'd do the boosting and I'd do the up and overing."

Hark leaned against the chain link and made a stirrup with his hands. "Talk about the brown man's burden."

Jack lifted his foot. "A regular Rudyard Kipling, aren't you?"

THE GROUNDS WERE PAVED and poorly lit by a couple of floodlights mounted high on the rear wall of the building. Jack kept to the shadows. No shot-up car was parked in the lot. No cars at all, for that matter. His phone vibrated with a text. Hark had driven back around to the front and let him know the guard was still watching TV.

The rear of the building had a loading dock. Jack hopped up and checked the overhead doors. They were shut tight and fastened from the inside. He followed the dock around to the right. There were no doors or windows on that side of the building. He did a U-turn and went back to the side that fronted the driveway. Stepping out from behind the building would put him in direct line of sight of the guardhouse.

He texted Hark: *Need a diversion.*

A minute later the familiar beep-beep-beeping of the Prius' horn sounded, followed by the high-pitched whine of the car's security alarm. He pictured Hark pulling up in front of the gate and jumping out and waving his arms around like a madman.

Jack moved fast. He kept close to the wall and followed the

driveway toward the front of the building. Halfway there he found a side door. Fire codes required emergency exits. The door was made of reinforced metal. The handle was equipped with a special lock that provided access to firefighters. Jack pulled out a key ring that held the only memento he kept of his dad, who'd met a fiery end in a Noe Valley four alarm. Practicality, not sentimentality, drove Jack to hold onto the special key.

He inserted the blade into the lock, pulled it out, made a couple of tweaks to its adjustable teeth, and tried again. It only took him three times to find the right combination. "Thanks, Da," he whispered as the handle turned.

Jack closed the door behind him in a second. If it was alarmed, the trip was either delayed or silent. He shined a penlight around. The building's interior was as plain vanilla as the outside. The warehouse had no wares. The only thing inside was covered by a blue tarp. He peeled it back and found the shot-up car. Cold fury washed through his veins again. The backseat was littered with glass. Shredded headrests showed how close Hark had come to nailing the driver and shooter. The license plates were gone but Jack found a barcode sticker on the driver side doorjamb. He pointed his camera, zoomed in, and shot.

There was nothing else in the warehouse. Jack went up front. A door led to an empty reception area. He climbed the stairs to the second floor. The suites of offices above the reception area were empty, too.

He opened a maintenance closet at the end of the hallway. It contained a bucket and mop, some half used plastic jugs of cleaner, and a flat of toilet paper rolls. He turned the flat upside down. A label from an industrial maintenance supply house was stuck to the bottom. He photographed it.

His phone buzzed with an incoming text: *Guard on the move.* Jack started moving, too. He took the stairs two at a time. He sprinted to the loading dock doors at the rear of the building. They were the kind that rolled up and down on rubber wheels. Heavy-duty slide bolt latches held the doors shut. He chose one, threw the slides back, and hoisted it up a couple of feet. The screech grated his fillings and echoed through the empty warehouse. Jack dropped and rolled underneath. The door slammed back down. The noise wasn't as loud as the deep-throated growl of the Rottweiler standing over him. Slobber flecked Jack's face, and the beam of a powerful flashlight made him squint.

"Freeze, motherfucker." The owner of the voice tried to match the menace in the dog's snarl.

"Nice doggie," Jack said. "Attaboy. Attaboy." He adjusted his eyes to the bright light. A man in a rent-a-cop uniform held a thick leather leash in one hand and the flashlight in the other. "This isn't what it seems."

"No?" the guard said. "Then what is it?"

"A case of a mistaken address. My GPS steered me wrong. I was looking for Alakazam Genetics. The side door was open. I peeked in and it slammed shut behind me. This was the only way I could get out."

"Save the bullshit. I already called the cops." He gave the leash a shake and the dog barked.

"Good. They'll be able to straighten this out. Now how about you make Rover here sit while I get up."

"His name's Terminator. I give the command and he'll bite your fucking head off."

Jack knew the 120 pounds of pure muscle could do it. But the guard only had two hands and both were holding onto something. He was also standing close to the edge of the loading dock.

"How about I buy you and Terminator steaks? I got a wallet with five large in my back pocket. It's yours if you let me walk."

"It's mine even if I don't let you walk." The guard laughed

through his nose. The sound made Jack's fillings hurt again. "Hand it over."

"Okay. Let me up and I'll give it to you."

"Fat chance. You stay on the ground."

"Then how am I supposed to give you my wallet?"

"Roll on your side and use one hand. Do it slowly or I feed you to Terminator." The guard snorted again.

Jack went for fear in his voice. "Back him off a little bit first. I don't want him to get the wrong idea."

The guard thought about it and then yanked on the leash. He had to take a step back to get enough leverage to budge the muscular hound. Jack was hoping for that. He scissor kicked the guard's legs and knocked him off his feet. The guard fell backward and tumbled off the edge of the loading dock. His weight yanked Terminator with him.

Jack jumped and ran. He leaped off the dock and headed straight for the front gate. All the roadwork he put in jogging to the Golden Gate Bridge and back came into play—arms pumped, lungs bellowed, legs moved like pistons. He could hear the big dog right behind him, its nails clicking on the pavement, its jowls flapping. The beast didn't waste precious air on baying or barking. Rottweilers were bred to pull heavy carts piled with butchered meat, herd cattle, and guard their owners. Slowing down was not part of their DNA.

The lights of the guardhouse shined like a beacon. Jack headed straight for it. He hoped the door would be open and he could slam the brute outside. No such luck. Terminator closed in. Jack had one chance and one chance only to evade the powerful jaws. He whipped off his jacket and threw it at the dog's head. Without losing a step he sprung for the gate, twisting his body as he flew. His legs were nearly parallel to the ground as he pushed off the wrought iron bars and used the momentum like a gymnast performing a vault. He flipped up and over the top, clearing the pointed metal stakes by less than an inch.

Jack hit the ground and rolled as Terminator smashed into the gate. The hound's howls easily drowned out the purr of the Prius as Hark swooped in.

"I'll be baaack," Jack said to the guard dog.

29

The way Jack saw it, whoever invented romance knew what they were doing. What else could explain makeup sex? Its heat always surpassed the argument that spawned it, a spontaneous combustion that came when no one wanted to admit they were wrong at the same time they wanted to forgive and be forgiven.

The bedroom was testament to how stormy Jack and Katie's disagreement had been and how tumultuous the reconciliation. The duvet lay tossed in a corner. The mattress was askew on the box springs. A bedside lampshade had been knocked off. A painting of a San Francisco street car entering the Twin Peaks Tunnel hung as crooked as if an earthquake had struck.

Jack propped on one elbow and looked at Katie. She was sitting with her back against the headboard.

"That was the absolute best," she gasped, her breath sounding as windblown as her hair looked. "The thing you did with the—"

"Takes two to tango." He wrestled with his own breathing.

She took another gulp of air. "I always wanted to visit Argentina and now I have."

Jack started humming the theme song from *Evita*.

Katie's emotions flashed between war and peace. Passion simmered in her eyes along with a pout and a glower. "This doesn't mean I'm not still mad at you. What you said about Laura was cruel."

Jack was about to say what Katie had said about him wasn't exactly out of the Miss Manners playbook but he swallowed the words. The argument had started when she came home from visiting Laura in jail and launched a broadside attack against anybody with a swinging dick. A crazy man killed Dexter. Terry Dolan arrested Laura to get back at Katie. The prison guards were sadists. Cicero Broadshank was a shyster.

And then she'd turned her sights on Jack. "And look at you," she railed. "You've been sitting around all day while poor Laura is locked behind bars. They only let her take a shower every other day, and the towel is the size of a washcloth. If you don't care about her, you don't care about me."

"I've been working my ass off," Jack fired back. "While you're blaming everyone, don't forget to add your girlfriend to the list. I talked to CB a little while ago. He got the reports back. Laura's father? His head was bashed in with a golf trophy. Sound familiar? Her mother was so undone, she downed a bottle of sleeping pills and slipped into the bath for the kind of wet dream you never wake up from. That fancy boarding school Laura says she went to? Try Nut House High. She majored in Thorazine and electroshock."

Jack knew he was throwing a Molotov cocktail, but he couldn't stop himself. In the ensuing conflagration, every word became fuel and nothing was off limits as the flames grew higher—his life as a crook, her policeman lover, their differing tastes on everything from the way she decorated the loft to him not hanging up his clothes, from her stuffy Pacific Heights parents to his abusive father. The only things they could agree on were the Giants and sex. And since the Giants were on the road, sex had to save the day.

Jack slid off the bed. "I got a bottle of Schramsberg chilling in the fridge. How about a water break between rounds?"

She found the only pillow left on the bed and chucked it at him. "Don't think this means I forgive you."

Jack fetched glasses and the champagne. When he returned Katie had already been to the bathroom and back. Her face was washed but her hair remained tousled. She patted the spot on the sheets next to her. He poured two glasses and joined her. They sat with their legs outstretched and backs against the headboard, hips and shoulders touching.

The champagne was crisp and cold. "I'm sorry I said what I said that got you so pissed off," he said.

"And I'm sorry what I said about you. I know you're trying your best. We can't forget we're a team. We can never lose sight of that."

He rested his hand on her thigh. Katie sipped her wine and then said, "It broke my heart to see Laura like that. She seemed like a lost little girl. We had to talk through a thick sheet of glass and use telephones."

Jack kept his lips busy on the champagne to keep from saying anything. He knew he was equally to blame for the fight. He was already defensive when Katie got home because he'd come up empty trying to run down the contact number of the industrial supply house in Burlingame and the bar code sticker in the shot-up car's doorjamb.

The sticker was the kind rental car agencies used. It had taken him three calls before he found the right company. Jack pretended to be a cop. His story was he needed to trace down the renter because the car had been found abandoned and they had to make sure it was a simple case of an unreported GTA and not a carjacking with an injured victim laying somewhere. The agency's records showed it had been rented via an internet-based travel company from a Wilhelm Mertz using a credit card from Germany and an international driver's license. Jack knew both would turn out to be phonies. He also knew it would be a waste of time trying to find anyone who could describe the renters. They would have bypassed the rental car counter at SFO and used the get-in-and-go aisle.

Jack didn't have any better luck with his call to the industrial supply house. He gave the receptionist a line about being the owner of the building in Oyster Point and wanting to resume service. One lie led to another and all he got for his story was the name of a company associated with the corresponding account number. It proved to be a dead end. No address. Nobody's name. Nobody's contact information. A search on the property tax records was equally futile.

Katie set her glass on the floor, rolled on her side, and started kissing the green shamrock inked on Jack's shoulder. "You know arguing is a sign of trust. It's why we're so good for each other. We trust each other no matter what the other person does or says."

"We're better than good," he said. "We're damn good."

She hooked her leg over his hip while she continued to nibble his shoulder. "And the fact that you trust me means a lot because I know you don't trust many people."

"I trust most people will lie and cheat and steal if given the chance. There's only a couple of people I trust with my life."

"Hark," she said.

"And you," he said.

They lay in silence letting the touch of their skin do the talking. After a while she said, "Ready for another trip south of the border?"

"How about the Mideast this time?"

She was rubbing her leg back and forth now. "What kind of dance do they do there?"

"The whirling dervish."

"Sounds exotic. How does it go?"

"Like this." And he pulled her on top and started her spinning.

KATIE WAS ASLEEP. The city was, too. But not the Net. Jack sat at the dining table and resumed chasing down the company name the supply house had given him. The trail kept running into dead ends. One holding company fronted another. All were businesses with voice mail and post office boxes in corporate tax havens such as the Netherlands, Luxembourg, Singapore, and Hong Kong.

Jack sent a message to the hacker he'd found on Black Pearl. Seconds later his tablet flashed with an incoming. Skrlt Pmprnl accepted the new assignment to find a name to go along with the Oyster Point building. There was a PS: *Waz Tesla list + map ok?*

The list had been huge and no names jumped out. Most were registered to companies or trusts or fictitious businesses, a common way for a high net worth to write off their fancy rides as a business expense. The map showing proximity to the Cotswold mansion wasn't any help either. Jack typed *2 many 2 chase*. He was about to hit send when he remembered what Henri LeConte taught him about the power of WAG. Jack added his own PS: *How $$ 2 cross-reference Tesla list w/Oyster Point bldg?*

A couple of seconds passed and the screen flashed: *50% upcharge.*

Deal.

He pushed away from the table, made an espresso, and

waited to see if his wild ass guess would bear fruit. It was still hours before dawn, but he knew going back to sleep was impossible no matter how much Katie and the bed beckoned. He drank the shot while standing in front of the window. Mist haloed the streets lights. A garbage truck rumbled somewhere below. Jack stared in the direction of the Contempo Towers. It was only a few wing beats away as the pigeon flew. He knew time was running out. Bobby would discover that Jack hadn't reached out to Old Kents and Sunglasses yet. A photo of Little Buddha would soon arrive. His phone would ring, too. The message wouldn't be civil.

A flash reflected in the window signaled an incoming from Skrlt Pmprnl. *U wont find me,* it read.

Paranoia went along with the usual personality traits of hackers—arrogance, vindictiveness, sociopathy—but the speed of this about-face threw Jack.

Wouldnt try, he typed back. *Wazup?*

U b wasting time ::poof::

Dont poof. Wazup?

U looking 4 wrong peeps

OK who r right ones

I found right peeps They wrong

WDYM wrong?

I mean bad

Jack realized English may not be Skrlt Pmprnl's native language. Either that or the hacker was laying down a smokescreen to mask his or her identity and whereabouts. He typed *Why + how they bad?*

The hacker responded. *Very bad*

They own the building? Own a Tesla?

Yes Yes

Jack's pulse quickened. *Who r they?*

Bad people Very bad ::poof::

Don't go GDI What @ $$ IOU?
Keep it ::poof::
OK 2x ur $$
Not worth it
3x?

Jack watched the screen. Nothing flashed. *Bye bye, Skrlt Pmprnl. I should've let you name your price*, he thought. He kept staring, willing an incoming flash.

Finally, the tablet complied. *I name then ::poof::*
OK
Whydah
Wot that?

Jack waited for an answer but there was none. He had no idea if Skrlt Pmprnl had disconnected. His last shot was to challenge what all hackers had in common: big egos. He Googled Whydah and then typed *BFD every1 kno that pirate ship. U suck.*

A minute passed and then the screen flashed. *And U dead man typing*
AYFKMWTS?
Not fucking kidding This shit real
Prove it

A minute passed. And then another message came. *Whydah name of shell company connex 2 holding company owns building + Tesla*
So why u scared?
Not scared Smart
Wot @ Whydah so bad?
Whydah peeps find me I dead, Find U U dead
What about Whydah? I pay 10x

The screen stayed lifeless. Finally it flashed. *Whydah connex 2 Mumbai mafia*

Jack felt the room tilt and the floor roll again. He rubbed his fingertips together and then typed. *Arjun Chopra = Capital Dexterity = Whydah = Mumbai mafia?*

No answer. The screen stayed static. Jack waited. He started counting. He reached one hundred and then he got his answer. *U didn't get it from me Now ::poof:: Forever*

Wait Need more 411 Will pay whatever U want

Jack stared at the screen for an hour. He resent his last message twice. He logged onto blackpearl.bf and submitted a request even though he knew he'd never hear back. Skrlt Pmprnl was gone, vanished forever into the ether of the Net with the press of the delete key.

30

The morning was unseasonably cool. Sea smoke billowed over the Pacific. Jack was driving across the Golden Gate Bridge toward Marin. Despite the damp he had the windows down so he could hear the Point Bonita Lighthouse foghorn. Its rhythmic baritone was as reassuring as his own heartbeat.

Traffic was light compared to the inbound lanes that were crowded with commuters driving nuts to butts. Though he'd joined the nine-to-five life Jack was glad he'd picked an office he could walk to. But for how much longer was anybody's guess. Katie surprised him with her talk about kids. His life in the life trained him to always think a couple of moves ahead and he was pretty sure a baby would start him on a path searching for good schools and a neighborhood where bad guys didn't try to run over people while firing an AK47 out the rear window.

The first exit after the bridge led him down the eucalyptus-studded headlands, past Fort Baker, and into Sausalito. He turned into a parking lot at the edge of town. The stalls were filled with vehicles as eclectic as the owners who dwelled in the adjacent houseboats. A vintage Mercedes Benz sported a bumper sticker proudly proclaiming it ran on BioWillie. A Blue Bird school bus was a rolling psychedelic poster from the '60s complete with a Keseyian goal of "Further" hand lettered above the windshield. The usual assortment of Beamers, hybrids, and Volvo wagons surrounded a bug-like burgundy Citroen with a blue disabled parking permit hanging from the rearview mirror.

The owner of the French classic lived in a brown shingle cottage built atop an old gravel barge moored at the end of the furthest dock. The houseboat had blue trimmed windows and matching flower boxes filled with geraniums. A white standard poodle with a gray muzzle guarded the front door. When he gave a hoarse growl, Jack unwrapped a bagel and handed it over. The dog's teeth were nearly ground to the gums but he took the offering with a wag of his stumpy tail, plopped down on the redwood deck, and began licking the cream cheese.

Jack gave a warning rap on the front door before pushing it open. "Anybody home?"

Henri LeConte was sitting in a wheelchair pulled up to the galley table. "I can still answer the door, you know." He thumped the armrests. "Don't forget this is only temporary."

"I know." They were both lying. Henri had graduated from walker to wheelchair two months before. "I also know I shouldn't feed Chagall lox and bagels, but I do."

The forger's scowl shaped into a smile. "Still the rebel. The coffee's fresh and so am I every time my new nurse drops by."

Jack poured a cup and ferried it to the table. "You'd better be careful. She's likely to roll you right off the dock if you don't behave yourself."

Henri was dressed as dapper as always but it was clear he'd lost weight. His silk ascot hung as loose as a bib on a broomstick. "*Au contraire.* She'd push me off if I didn't misbehave. She's quite voracious this one. A Mozambican beauty."

The coffee was dark, thick, and very sweet. "Katie sends her love. She feels bad she hasn't stopped by recently but she's been preoccupied."

"And there's nothing wrong with my eyesight either. I still read all the blogs and papers. Her friend Laura is in quite a fix." Henri's navy blue beret dipped as he hunched over his demitasse and picked it up with both hands. The coffee sloshed onto the saucer as he brought the cup to his lips. There was a time when his fingers were the quietest in the business. He once duplicated a Matisse that fooled a roomful of museum experts. "A young wife accused of murdering an older rich husband is hardly unique but murder always comes with unexpected complications."

"Nothing wrong with your intuition either."

"While I appreciate your visits, I enjoy them infinitely better when you come with problems to solve rather than nag me about my health. What do you have for me?"

"I'd never dream about trying to pull something without conferring with you first." Jack took a moment to savor the coffee. "What can you tell me about the Mumbai mafia?"

Henri's pencil moustache formed a *V*. "*Ooh*. That takes me back and not to the fondest of memories, mind you." He paused. "You've encountered one or more of their members? In that case you might want to pour a glass of pastis. It will make what I have to tell you easier to digest."

THE WAY HENRI TOLD IT, Bollywood fabricated the story about the Mumbai mafia getting its start as a Robin Hood-like band of slumdogs robbing from the British Raj to give to the poor. The origin of Indian organized crime was no different than that of Sicily, Moscow, or Chicago. Ruthless dons figured out a way to monetize human frailty and divided India's largest city into territories for control of prostitution, extortion, and drug dealing. For decades the Mumbai gangs were largely ignored by officials in exchange for payoffs and a pledge to keep their criminal activities confined to the ghetto. But everything changed when India's economy evolved from heavy industry into engineering, technology, and call centers. The torrent of new money spawned a new generation of mobsters who had no patience for the old ways of doing business. Trust and mutual respect went out the window. So did a few of the old dons. A decade-long bloody turf war resulted. Mumbai's ruling class screamed for protection as it spilled into the wealthier neighborhoods and the bodies piled up. The police were forced to crack down. Shootouts and arrests had a Darwinian effect. The gangsters who survived were stronger, smarter, and crueler than their predecessors.

"The mafia shape shifted into corporate enterprises complete with boards and shareholders," Henri said as the ice in his glass of pastis turned the anise-flavored liquor milky. "Some bet big on real estate. It was a smart move. Bombay—*excusez-moi*, I still think of it by its colonial name—is the wealthiest city in India. Square foot rates for apartments and commercial buildings may not come close to San Francisco or Hong Kong but they still rank among the highest in the world."

"The guy I've run into is a big shot in Silicon Valley venture capital. A black hat I hired connected him to a mob back home."

Henri shrugged. "Technology has erased territorial borders everywhere, even those of organized crime. What's his name?"

"Arjun Chopra. The firm is Capital Dexterity. He's in charge now."

"Ah, now I understand why you're here. Katie's friend. What's the situation you find yourself in?"

Jack gave a quick rundown. "So you see there are plenty of loose ends. There's Dexter's murder. There's Laura in jail. There's Bobby and Little Buddha. And then there's Chopra maybe picking up where Dexter left off regarding my patents. I don't know why he's bothering going after them. Capital Dexterity is a very successful firm. From everything I can tell they don't have a track record of patent trolling, but here they are represented by one of the biggest law firms in the valley who does connect to the trolls going after me and mine. The lawyer, Winston Cheatham, was Dexter's corporate lawyer and now he represents Chopra. He's also the one who retained CB to handle Laura's defense."

"Perhaps everyone see something in your application that you do not." Henri rubbed his sunken cheeks. "I've always said don't underestimate yourself. Confidence games require confidence, even those run by Fortune 500 companies."

"But no one will really know how good the app will work or how much of a market it'll command until it's up and running."

"What about these other players that showed up out of nowhere, the Tom and Jerry characters you described?"

"They seemed random at first but what are the odds two different criminally minded parties would be going after my app?"

Henri tut-tutted. "Just because you've never seen a black swan doesn't mean it doesn't exist."

"True but I tracked these mutts to an office building down in Oyster Point that's connected to a shell company that when you run it out eventually connects back to Chopra. Or at least his car."

"Dot to dot. I admit that's rather compelling evidence. Job number one must be figuring out the best way to deal with them as they pose the most immediate threat to you and Katie. You must also be sure to keep Bobby Ballena on the sidelines. He's the wild card in all of this and could prove disruptive in any sort of play we might devise. Of course from what you say about his obsession with the golden Buddha, taking care of him will be easy. What does the statue look like?"

Jack described it right down to the blemish on the Buddha's butt.

Henri listened intently and then picked up his drink with both hands and brought it shakily to his lips. "That sounds like a beautifully crafted artifact. Solid gold, you say?"

Jack nodded.

Henri seemed lost in thought. After a bit, he said, "Dealing with Arjun Chopra is the more difficult task. I can't say his name rings a bell, but then again it's been quite some time since I had anything to do with the Bombay criminal element. It was not a pleasant experience."

"Do you want to tell me about it?"

The old forger gave a painful grimace as he shifted his weight in the wheelchair. "It all started with love. It's always been my Achilles' heel."

"Who was she?"

"An Indian dancer of incredible grace and beauty and even more incredible ability when performing the *Bharatanatyam*." His eyes turned the color of the pastis as they clouded with memory. "This was decades ago, mind you. I was at the peak of my craft. That particular year I was working as the artist-in-residence on a luxury cruise ship that sailed between Singapore and Bombay. I taught watercolor classes to wealthy passengers and sold my work in the onboard gallery. On shore excursions I would lead tours to museums and so forth. It was a pleasant and profitable way to pass the season."

"And meet wealthy marks for future transactions, I'd wager."

Henri tipped his head in Jack's direction. "We must always be on the lookout for the next opportunity. It's what we do."

"Did," Jack said. "Don't forget, we're retired."

"Perhaps." The ice cubes clinked as he took another sip.

"Madhuri, that was her name, was working on the ship as a member of a dance revue. We fell in love. It was magical. At night we would have the deck to ourselves. It would be awash in moonlight as we steamed across the Bay of Bengal." He sighed. "The liner's final port of call was our last as well. Bombay was her home and she was eager to show it off while showing me off to her family."

Jack could see the memories rack his old friend's bony frame. "Madhuri's family made me feel most welcome and it was an incredible homecoming for her. There were lots of relatives and food and music and dancing and laughter. For the first time in my life, I could see myself settling down. Bombay was exotic. Madhuri was exotic. And I was hopelessly in love. But then I met her brother. There's always a black sheep, isn't there?" A scratching sound came from the front door. "Chagall wants in. Can you let him?"

The old poodle made a beeline for the wheelchair and put his head in his master's lap. Henri scratched behind the dog's ears. "His name was Rajan and he was the sort of little brother that gives little brothers everywhere a bad name. A real rotter. Spoiled, petulant, mean, and not very bright. He also had a gambling problem—the problem being he never won. Madhuri was blind as protective big sisters are prone to be, but I sized him up the instant we met."

Henri paused to wet his lips. "Rajan took me aside one night and confided that he'd gotten in deep to a loan shark. If he didn't make good, his entire family would be held responsible for his debts. It's the way it was there. Probably still is. When I told him there was little I could do, Rajan played his trump card. He said the loan shark would seize Madhuri as payment and turn her into a sex slave. I had no choice. I had to act to save her."

Jack gave a knowing nod. "You pulled a gold brick."

Henri raised his hands in surrender. "You were always my

best student. I told Rajan I had acquired a stolen painting by the late Indian master Abanindranath Tagore. It would easily fetch a million on the legitimate market. I offered to give it to the loan shark in exchange for Rajan's debt plus Madhuri's freedom and fifty thousand dollars of walking away money."

Jack had helped Henri pull the same type of grift plenty of times. "The trick to selling a gold brick is to always wrap it in something personal. That way the mark sells himself on the reason why you're so eager to unload it. When the loan shark agreed you went out and painted one. You've always enjoyed the challenge of duplicating a masterpiece."

Henri accepted the compliment with a bow. "I admire Tagore's style. He was the father of Indian modern art. Everything went according to my plan with one exception."

"Rajan," Jack said.

"Precisely. I thought his love for his sister would equal my love for her but his love for money proved greater. He did not deliver the painting as agreed upon but sold it to a fence who represented a private collector. Rajan took his payment and immediately fled India."

"The buyer discovered it was a fake."

Henri nodded. "Rather quickly at that. The consequences were akin to a collision of comets. The buyer turned out to be the don of a Mumbai mafia family while the loan shark worked for yet another. Both wanted revenge. It was the first time the two rival mobs could agree on anything. They tracked Rajan down to a suite at the Four Seasons in Bali, hacked him into pieces, and shipped them home in a box. The parents were forced to sell everything to pay off his debt. In the end they were reduced to living in the worst of Bombay's slums and fighting over scraps."

Henri gulped the rest of his pastis. "Madhuri turned herself over to the loan shark in exchange for sparing her parents' lives and mine. I flew home to San Francisco to make as much money as I could so I could buy her freedom. I wasn't home a month before I learned the loan shark had sold her. One evening her new owner smashed her ankles with a hammer in a fit of pique because she refused to perform the *Bharatanatyam* for him. She escaped and hobbled to the Mithi River and threw herself in. The casts on her broken feet took her straight to the bottom."

Henri slumped in his wheelchair. The story hung over the room as thick as sea smoke. Jack reached over and put a hand on his mentor's shoulder. They sat in silence. The old artful dodger finally looked up.

"You see, *mon fils*, there are always consequences, especially when it comes to matters of the heart." He took a deep breath and motioned for Jack to refill their glasses. "But sometimes you're left with no choice. If this Chopra fellow is really the sort of man you believe him to be, then we need to find a way to stop him in such a way that not all of Bombay will come after you and those you love."

31

Katie wouldn't take no for an answer. It wasn't the first time nor would it be the last. No matter how hard Jack tried telling her going to jail with him was a bad idea, she insisted nothing would stop her

"Laura's my best friend. She can't survive there much longer. I need to tell her we still love her."

Katie said all this while peeling off an orange sleeveless crop and black stretchy shorts she'd worn doing morning yoga. While Jack was glad to see she was rocking the Giants' team colors, he didn't want her to accompany him because talking to Laura alone was part of the play he'd cooked up with Henri's help.

"But, babe, look what happened last time you visited her. You said anger is toxic so why pollute yourself? Wait until she's out on bail. CB says it won't be much longer."

They were talking in the bathroom. Katie reached into the limestone-tiled shower and turned the faucet. "Then how come you're not waiting until she's free?"

"I need to ask her some stuff that could prove helpful in identifying the murderer."

"Does Terry know?" She held her hand under the water to test the temperature. The water beaded on her skin and made it glisten.

Normally Jack would be ripping off his clothes to join her, but time was running out. "The cops are doing their investigation and I'm doing mine. If I come up with something, I'll let him know."

Katie stepped into the shower. "If Laura knows anything, she'll be more comfortable saying it if I'm there. She trusts me. Wait a sec, I won't be long." She threw back her head and aimed the spray at her chest.

Jack gave up. Trying to convince her was pointless and ducking out while she was in the shower would trigger a tsunami. If Katie was hell-bent on going, there was nothing he could do to stop her. He'd either have to bait the hook while she was in the visitors room with him or manufacture another opportunity to talk to Laura alone.

His phone buzzed. "Speak," he answered gruffer than usual.

"I feel like a sixteen-year-old waiting for someone to ask me to the prom. Why haven't you called?" Bobby Ballena was going for cute, but the undercurrent of his tone was anything but.

Jack carried the phone into the living room. "Why so stressed? What's going on?"

"What's going on is I need my money, bro, and you're not getting it for me."

"You know these things take time. Never mix speed with need."

"And I say I don't have a lot of choice. You know I'm here on a limited time basis. I can't wait any longer."

"Is Kiki kicking you out?" Jack was stalling; he'd already decided he couldn't let go of Little Buddha. While the statue may not be the murder weapon, it was certainly one helluva bargaining chip. Another golden rule to grifting: never give up something for nothing.

"Her kids are coming home for a long weekend. I need a change in venue," Bobby said.

"So go back to Baja. I'll ask Anders to set up a Cayman wire transfer once Kim makes payment."

"Stop bullshitting me. You haven't even talked to him. I know because I did. He'll broker the statue on my behalf. All you got to do is hand it over to him."

"Where is he, still in Thailand?"

"He'll be wherever he needs to be to do the deal."

"You know Kim wouldn't set foot in the U.S. even if Costco had a deal on cartons of Kents and cases of Ray-Bans. And I don't have time to jump on a plane, fly across the Pacific, and ride in the back of a tuk-tuk to go meet him. Besides, if I booked a ticket out of the country, Terry would be at the airport waiting for me. We're both on the No-Fly List by now."

"Figuring out how to get Kim the statue is your problem not mine," Bobby shouted. "Do it or so help me those photos go viral."

Jack squeezed the phone. His words came out as tight. "We've known each other a long time. Been in and out of scrapes together since Saint Joe's. But if you know one thing about me, it's how I react to threats. You don't want to go down that road, don't you know?"

Moments passed before Bobby responded. "Relax. Don't get your Irish up. But you got to help me. Kiki's kids are coming home and I got to split."

"You can't come here." Jack said it quickly to head off the inevitable. "Terry shows up all the time. He makes it look like it has to do with the case, but it's really an excuse to see Katie."

"All the more reason why you got to get me my money, and right now it's all sitting in your place wearing a golden grin. You got to sell Little Buddha. You got to do it before the cops find me. If you don't, I'm dead."

"How long until Kiki's family shows?"

"Tomorrow. They're flying home from school somewhere back east."

"Hold tight. I'll call you back."

Jack hung up before Bobby could respond. It was perfect timing. Katie walked out of the bedroom. She was wearing tight jeans and a V-neck cashmere sweater. "I'm ready," she said.

"Great but you might want to put on something a little less... a little more bulky."

"Why? This is very comfortable."

"You don't want to give the guards a reason to give you an extra pat down."

LAURA LOOKED LIKE SHIT. Her complexion was as wan as the cinderblock walls in the visitors room. The only purple she had on was a bruise on her cheek to go along with a freshly split lip.

Katie's gasp fogged the window that separated them. "Oh my God. What have they done to you?"

Jack and Katie were sharing a phone. Laura clutched a handset on the far side of the glass. Other visitors were doing the same. Grandmothers held kids on their laps so they could wave to their mommies. Sullen boyfriends sat like they'd rather be getting a tooth drilled than listen to their imprisoned girlfriends. Every visitor looked relieved they weren't the ones wearing the new black.

When Laura didn't answer, Katie asked if she'd received the care package she'd dropped off. "The shampoo has soy moisturizer and the skin cream is PABA free. I packed that natural spearmint toothpaste you like, too."

Either Laura didn't get them or she was too scared to use the shower. Dirty laundry showed more life than her hair.

"I don't know how much longer I can take it," she finally said. Her voice sounded as if someone had their hands around her throat. "Some of the people here should be locked up in an asylum. One girl, she... I think she wants to kill me."

"The lawyer says you'll be out in no time." Katie put her hand over the mouthpiece and whispered to Jack. "Go on, tell her. Give her reason to hope."

"Katie's right," he said. "Cicero Broadshank is doing everything he can."

"He's certainly taking his sweet time." Laura's face finally showed some color.

Jack registered the quick temper. "The slowdown's because you told the cops about your parents. That complicated everything."

Laura's eyelids fluttered. "That was all a huge misunderstanding. I was only trying to help."

"You mean you didn't kill your father?"

"I can't believe you're bringing that up. I've spent my entire life working to get over what he did to me."

Katie shushed at Jack. He put his hand on her knee to signal the conversation was leading right where he wanted it to. "It's not like the cops can put what you said back in the bottle. They have to investigate it. It's what cops do."

"Why? They asked me about my past so I told them. I should get points for telling the truth, not recrimination." She turned her hard stare on Katie. "I thought Terry was your friend. Look what he did to me."

Katie started to apologize but Jack launched right in. "Terry's a cop. What did you expect? He has to make sure what you told him about your dad has no bearing on what happened to

Dexter." Jack counted to three. "On account they both died from blows to the head."

He put it out there and watched for Laura's eyelids to flutter. He could feel the air move despite the inch-thick glass.

"The only thing there is for Terry to know is I underwent a serious trauma when I was a child and received extensive therapy because of it." Laura's chin started quivering. "I have nothing to be ashamed of. I was a victim. What happened does not define me as a woman. I've moved on with my life. I'm in charge, not my father. I'm all about positive energy now. I have a very positive aura. I can't believe you don't understand that. I thought I had friends I could count on."

"You do and you can," Katie said. She moved her head away from the phone and exaggerated mouthing the words as if Laura could only read lips.

"Katie's right," Jack said. "Everybody's working hard to get you out. Katie, me, the lawyers." He let it sit. "Dexter's partner is especially concerned. He's the one who ordered Winston Cheatham to retain CB and give him whatever he needs."

"That's because Winston and Arjun believe in me."

Jack gave a nod of encouragement. "I talked with Chopra at the funeral. He seemed plenty worried about you."

"He did?"

"Yeah. You haven't talked to him?"

"Not since I've been in here." Laura hesitated. "I mean, it's hard for me to make calls and the only person permitted to call me is Mr. Broadshank."

Jack let it hang there. Saying nothing often proved better than asking a question. Laura leaned forward until her face was nearly pressed against the glass. "So what did Arjun say about me?"

"He knew Katie was staying with you, so he asked how you were holding up. He seemed to know a lot about you: your travels to Nepal, moving here, how you met Dexter, how you were decorating the house."

"Well, we've had plenty of occasions to talk to one another over the past year or so since he joined the firm. You know, at social and business gatherings."

Katie tensed beside him. Jack knew her intuition was in high gear now because Laura had never mentioned Chopra to her.

"Did you talk to anybody else about me? Laura asked.

"No, only Chopra."

"Oh." She seemed disappointed. After a while she said, "What else did Arjun say?"

"He knew Dexter and I had spoken about my start-up, and that Dexter was considering investing in it. Chopra said the firm might still be interested. He told me he'd send someone around to talk to me about it and sure enough he did. A couple of guys. I still need to thank him for doing that."

"That's Arjun. He's very thoughtful."

"I'm sure he is, but I got to say, the guys he sent weren't cut from the same cloth."

"What do you mean?"

"They were pretty heavy-handed. Chopra should give them some customer relations training."

"Maybe you mistook their eagerness for bad manners. Everyone who works in tech is in a hurry."

"I understood them all right."

"I'm sure they weren't following Arjun's instructions. He's very proper. It's his upbringing."

"I'm sure." Jack kept his hand on Katie's knee. It was time to throw the changeup. "By the way I spoke with Bobby. He's worried about you, too."

"You did? Where is he? I haven't heard a peep from him."

"Since the night Dexter died?" Jack didn't wait for an answer.

"Me either. I figured he'd gone back to Baja and was out of the loop."

"That explains it," Laura said.

"No, Bobby's been here the whole time. He's hiding."

"Whatever on earth for?"

"He's scared. The night he dropped you off, he'd had a lot to drink. No sooner does he pull out of your driveway then he veers off the road and, wham, hits a tree. It knocks him out. Air bag goes off and everything. When he comes to he starts to pull onto the road but the next things he knows a car comes up from behind him and speeds past. Nearly peels the paint off his car. Bobby hits the gas instead of the brakes and, bam, he clocks the tree again. Out he goes. He comes to again only this time there's police cars screaming toward him. Bobby thinks he's about to get popped for a DUI but the cops go past. He drives away and spends the night at a friend's. Come morning Dexter's murder is all over the news. Bobby freaks. He figures the cops might get the wrong idea and try to pin the murder on him. You know, when they find out he spent the day with his ex-girlfriend and that night her husband is killed. Bobby's been laying low ever since, waiting for everything to be solved."

Jack released his grip on Katie's knee. She took the cue. "Oh my God. Maybe the speeding car was the murderer's. This could be the clue we've been hoping for."

Laura sat motionless. "What kind of car was it?"

"Bobby said it was a Tesla. A black one."

"How can he be so sure? You said he'd hit his head." Laura's words rushed out faster than the electric sedan's ability to go from zero to sixty.

"Bobby has a thing about them. He's always ragging me for driving a Prius. He calls it a poor man's Tesla."

Laura's lids did an up and down. "Where's he hiding?"

Jack shook his head. "He didn't say."

"Well, if you talk to him again, tell him I said to say hello and I'm thinking about him."

"Sure thing. And likewise if you talk to Arjun Chopra. Tell him thanks for me. Not only for helping you out by hiring CB but for wanting to invest in my start-up and sending those two guys around. Their names are Tomasz and Jeremy."

"I'm not exactly sure when I'll be able to do that. You know, because of the phone thing here."

A deep voice barked over the PA system, announcing visiting hours were over. Laura hung up without saying good-bye. They watched as she exited through a gray metal door without so much as a wave.

32

Bella Luna was wedged between a laundromat and corner grocery on Green Street. The North Beach restaurant's specialty was handmade *tagliolini alla frantoiana*; its wine list featured a selection of hard-to-find Brunellos from small vineyards clustered on the hills surrounding Montalcino. The owner's daughter was working as the hostess when Katie and Jack came in for lunch. Gina greeted them with kisses on the cheeks before leading them to their favorite table by the window.

"I've missed you at my Zumba class," Katie said. "How are you feeling?"

Gina cradled her belly. "Little Marco Polo doesn't like bouncing around anymore. He's already telling his mamas what's on his mind."

Katie placed her palm above Gina's. "I feel a kick. He'll be at your breast in no time."

Gina smiled. "I know. I keep telling my wife she'll have to make room."

Katie laughed. Gina left them with menus. Jack had a feeling which way the conversation was going to go, but Katie surprised him by launching right into a debrief of their jail-house visit.

"You didn't want to ask Laura anything, you wanted to tell her things."

"Right."

"Is any of what you said true?"

"More or less."

"You spoke to Bobby? Have you seen him?"

"Yup and yup."

"Stop playing Clint Eastwood. I admit, Laura certainly knows a lot about Arjun." She made a face. "Not that she ever mentioned him to me before. So much for girl talk. Do you think he's the mystery lover?"

"I do."

"Does he own a black Tesla?"

"As the night."

"I thought Laura was going to break the phone when you told her about the car. It meant something when she asked if Bobby could describe it, not if he saw it go in and come out of her driveway, didn't it?"

"I'd say she telegraphed she knew the car had been there."

"But that doesn't prove Arjun killed Dexter."

"No but he's hit a three-bagger. There's not a cop on the force who doesn't think means, motive, and opportunity translates to guilty. Including Terry."

"Quit acting so cute. We're talking about Laura here. Even if Arjun was there it doesn't mean she knew about it. Laura could have been asleep and he could have dropped by to talk business with Dexter."

"At midnight?"

"You know everyone in tech works crazy hours."

"So what you're saying is maybe when they're talking busi-ness, Dexter accuses Chopra of giving the business to his wife.

One thing leads to another and Dex winds up on the floor and Arjun pulls a *Fast and Furious*."

"Even if he is the murderer, it still doesn't prove Laura knew anything about it."

"She never told Terry that Chopra was there. She's still holding back."

"Maybe she didn't know. Maybe he came after."

"That's a lot of maybes."

Katie's eyes flashed. "You haven't told Terry about Chopra, either."

Jack let the comment sit. "But what if it was the other way around? Say Laura told Dex she was sleeping with Arjun or maybe Dex told her he knew she was. Either way, Dex ends up on the floor and the only person left standing is Laura."

"But that wouldn't explain Arjun stopping by and then speeding off."

"What if Laura called her boyfriend to help tidy up the mess she made. He takes one look and realizes it's going to take more than Comet and a sponge. Plus he starts rethinking his relationship. If she did that to Dex, well, so much for ever getting into an argument with her. Maybe Chopra eighty-sixed himself."

Katie rattled the menu at him. "You have a devious mind."

"Come on, babe. You're thinking it yourself. I felt you tense when Laura started asking questions about him. It was like grade school. She was dying to know what the cute boy in class was saying about her."

"There was always more than one cute boy," she said.

The waiter ferried over water glasses and a bottle of Pelegrino. When he asked if they were ready to order, Katie ticked off dishes without hesitation: bruschetta to start, followed by gnocchi alla Florentine as her *primo* and gamberi al diavolo as her *secondo*. "We'll split a Caesar, and I'll have the tiramisu for dessert."

"Glad to see our little outing to the doll house didn't dampen your appetite," Jack said.

She threw a breadstick at him. Jack winked at the waiter. "I'm on a liquid diet. A bowl of minestrone and a bottle of the 2007 Altesino."

When they were alone again Katie leaned in. "Tell the truth. Do you know for certain Laura had something to do with Dexter's death?"

"All I know is what Bobby told me. He saw the Tesla coming and going, and he saw Laura wide awake."

"How could he know that? I thought you said he was in his car."

"I may have taken some literary license with timing and setting, but Bobby says he went inside after the Tesla split. He saw Dexter's body and then he saw Laura."

"What was he doing there?"

"He went back to get something. For what isn't important. What is is what he saw."

"Laura didn't see him?"

"No. He says whoever was in the car left the front door wide open. Bobby went inside. He found Dexter. He heard somebody and thought it could be the murderer coming back so he hid. It turns out it was Laura. He didn't know if she was in on it or not, so he split. He was scared."

"But Bobby's a witness. He can identify Arjun Chopra."

Jack waved a finger. "No, he can allege he saw a Tesla. He didn't see the driver. He didn't see the murder. Without corroboration, the prosecutor will say he made it up to protect Laura or he's the murderer himself."

"Then we're going to have to find out who was driving the car and what he did when he went inside."

"I'm working on that, but Terry wouldn't have arrested Laura if he hadn't found something pretty incriminating. By now he knows what happened to Laura's parents and why she ended up in the rubber room. Let's face it, your ex-boyfriend may have been dumb enough to lose you but he's not that stupid when it comes to police work."

Katie peered over her pert nose. "You may have been smart enough to find me, but don't forget you have to be even smarter if you want to keep me."

The waiter came back with the wine and poured a taste. Jack nodded his approval. When their glasses were filled, he raised his toward Katie's and said, "Whatever happens, no matter what we find out, we don't let it take us down with it, okay?" They clinked on it.

The food came. Katie devoured everything with gusto. After she polished off the tiramisu, she wiped the chocolate from her lips and said, "You told all that stuff to Laura on purpose. You want her to call Arjun and tell him what you said."

"Newton's Third Law. For every action there is an equal and opposite reaction." It was the driving force of every con he'd ever run.

"In other words, he'll do something that could give himself away."

"That's the plan."

"But isn't that dangerous?"

"For him, yeah. It's what I'm counting on."

"But what about for us?"

Jack finished the Brunello. "I won't let that happen."

IT WAS a gentle spring afternoon and the temperature was up and the wind down. Jack and Katie held hands as they strolled Columbus toward Fisherman's Wharf. The sun-dappled bay sparkled like diamonds tossed on a pool table. Seagulls squawked and sea lions barked from their haulouts on the docks at Pier 39.

Katie was quiet and Jack wondered if she was thinking about Gina and what it would be like to carry a little Marco Polo of her own. They were taking the long way home so they could shop for dinner. Popeye sold the catch of the day from the stern of his forty-foot Monk berthed alongside the wharf. His bread loaf biceps were the product of retrieving nets and crab pots. Few people knew fish better, and he'd as soon as cut off his leg than sell anything that wasn't an hour past swimming in the sea. Popeye launched into the merits of broiling handline caught halibut with tarragon and fennel-seed butter when Jack's phone buzzed. He wandered off to take the call.

"Speak," he answered.

It was Moana. "You're not a very good role model for the staff when it comes to work habits. Where are you?"

"You've been reading those HR blogs again, haven't you?"

"Someone has to be in charge of personnel issues around here. You know the kind of worker's comp lawsuits I keep you from getting?"

"You mean you're stopping yourself from suing me? Thanks."

"You wish. But that's not the reason I called. Do Pray's been trying to reach you. He says he's made some kind of break-through. By the way, you might want to congratulate him, considering what you're not paying him."

"Put him on and I'll tell him now."

A crowd was gathering at the end of the wharf where a fishing boat was docked. A cop car with flashing lights but no siren eased onto the wharf and headed toward it. An EMT meat wagon followed right behind. Jack couldn't resist. He talked as he walked.

"That you, Do Pray?"

"Yes, sir. I wanted to let you know the mantis is dead and the assassin bug is on his way."

"Can you tell how much of our code they hacked?"

"They got some but not so it amounts to anything special," the young programmer said. "The mantis never saw my mite coming. I set out the stinkbug and sure enough the hacker couldn't say no and sent another mantis. By then my assassin bug was waiting and watching. He saw where the new mantis came from." Do Pray took a breath.

"Who sent it?"

"Well, that's where I still need to do some work. See, the assassin bug tracked it to a big server farm and then had to chase it down a rabbit hole. The server's linked to a terminal that's a slave."

"Can your bug track the slave to the master computer?"

"Should be able to."

"How long will that take?"

"Depends on how many traps they set but I don't think long."

The cop car and meat wagon stopped. The cops got out. One cop hailed the skipper of the fishing boat. The other bellowed at the crowd to stand back. The EMT techs pulled red duffel bags from their rig.

"Once you find the master can you put an address to it?" Jack asked.

"Piece of king cake. See, my assassin bug's equipped with a transmitter. Once he lands on the slave he's going to start doing what he does best. Munch, munch. Every time he munches, what he's munching is going to ask the master to send in help to try and squash him. The commands going back and forth will give away the master's position. It's like scratching a real bug bite. You wind up making it itch a whole lot worse."

"Good work. Keep me posted. As soon as you find out anything no matter how small, let me know."

Jack clicked off and joined the crowd at the end of the wharf. There were several tourists taking selfies and a couple dressed in matching track suits the color of butternut squash. A deckhand operating a boom winch hoisted a bulging net from the boat's deck. A cop was gesturing like he was directing traffic in a busy intersection. The deckhand maneuvered the net until it was dangling right over the dock. That's when the winch gave way and the net spilled open. A ton of herring whooshed onto the wharf in a slippery, silvery wave. A dead man surfed on top.

"My God," the woman in the track suit gasped.

Her companion dropped his ice cream cone and said, "Forget about going to that fancy seafood restaurant tonight."

A man wearing boots and a Dallas Cowboys jacket shrugged. "Ah, hell. It's just a jumper. Dozens go off the Golden Gate every night. What do you expect in a town where everybody's a fag?"

The cops pushed the crowd back, and one of the EMT techs slipped on the slurry of fish.

Another car arrived. Inspector Terry Dolan slid out behind the wheel of a black Crown Vic.

Jack nodded at the detective's spit-shine oxfords. "Hope you got a pair of hip waders in the trunk."

Terry pushed past without acknowledging him.

One of the uniformed cops saluted. "Inspector. You want us to string up the tape?"

"Keep the onlookers back for now. Let's see what we got." Terry pulled a pair of purple latex gloves from his pocket.

Always the Boy Scout, Jack thought. He glanced back at Popeye's. Katie was probably finishing up with her purchase. He didn't want her to see this. Nobody needed to see this. The bigot in the football jersey was probably right about it being a bridge jumper. Most of the time the bodies were never found. Outgoing tides either held them down in the Potato Patch, or they were carried out to sea and into the jaws of a great white shark patrolling the waters between the mouth of the bay and the Farallon Islands.

Jack turned to leave. He hadn't taken three steps when Terry shouted, "Halt! McCoul, get back here."

Jack stayed put. "Make up your mind. Stay or come? You sound like a dog owner."

"Now. That's an order."

Jack was careful not to step on any of the herring. It wasn't easy.

Terry pointed a purple finger at the body. "Recognize him?"

It took a moment because the skin was white as ocean foam. A second smile had been carved in the throat.

"Yeah, it's Tingly Meyers."

"Your lawyer," Terry said.

Jack checked his surprise. "Up until a few days ago."

"The word I got is you'd been looking for him."

"No secret there. He was representing me in a patent fight. My name is all over the claims he filed in court. When he sent me an e-mail saying he was resigning my account, I went to his office to ask why."

"You spoke to his landlord, searched his office."

"That's right. Van Duong told me Tingly left a note saying his ship had come in. He'd cleared out. I went upstairs to see for myself. I wanted to make sure any files regarding my case were properly secured."

"When did you see Meyers next?"

"I didn't."

"You sure you want to stick with that?"

"Why wouldn't I? *The truth shall set you free.*" Jack glanced at the body and then back at Terry. "What are you thinking, the ship he talked about was actually a real one? I snuck aboard and pushed him overboard while he was shaving? Get real."

"What were you really looking for in his office, copies of his invoices to you so you could rip them up? How much did you owe him?"

"Not a dime. Tingly worked on commission. He doesn't get paid unless there's a settlement. My suit's still open. That's a fact."

Terry peeled off his gloves. "Here are the facts as far as I'm concerned. Fact, you can't keep up with your start-up's burn rate. Fact, you tried to wrestle money out of Dexter Cotswold, but he turned you down. Fact, right after that he wound up dead. And here's your lawyer. Fact, now he's dead, too."

"And I've got a fact for you. Now you got two murders on your book. You better find the real killers and quit hassling innocent civilians if you want to keep that shiny inspector shield clipped to your belt."

Terry pressed in close. "If you're so innocent then tell me why a car tried to run you and Katie down, the men inside shooting your friend Hark? Who are they? And don't lie. I had the video enhanced. I can make you out plain as day."

"Really? I haven't seen it yet. Put it on YouTube and send me the link."

"Still the class clown. You don't know what you're up against."

Jack didn't answer.

Terry poked him in the chest. "You're out of your depth. This isn't one of your scams. Tell me what you know and maybe I can keep you from winding up like your lawyer here."

"I'll think about it."

"Think harder. Don't do it for yourself. Do it for Katie."

"Katie has nothing to do with this."

"Sure she does. It's her friend in jail. It's her friend's husband who's dead. And it's you who's putting her life in danger."

Jack batted away Terry's finger. "And I said she's not involved in any of this. None of it."

"If that's true then why was she visiting Laura earlier today?"

"You said it yourself, they're friends. It's what friends do." A flock of seagulls circled the wharf. "Of course you got to have friends in the first place to know that."

"You were there, too. What did you talk to Laura about?"

"The Giants. They don't let 'em watch the games in jail."

Jack wasn't surprised Terry knew about their visit; he'd been counting on it. If Terry was the sort of cop Jack knew him to be, he'd listen to the jailhouse visit tape and zero in what Jack said about the Tesla and late night visit the night of the murder. It would move Chopra to the top of the list of suspects. Terry would contact him, maybe even bring him in for questioning. Either way it was a surefire way to spook Chopra into making a hasty move.

"You already know what we talked about," Jack said. "Everyone knows the phones in the visitors room are bugged."

Terry tried on a look of righteous indignation. "The sheriff's department runs the jail, not SFPD. Monitoring is at their discretion. They do it when they think a prisoner could be sending coded messages like ordering a hit against another gang member. The transcripts are handed over to the district attorney long before they're shared with city police. Even then they're subject to redaction to safeguard a prisoner against inadvertent self-incrimination."

"Whoa, Terry. I didn't know you were taking another night school shot at Golden Gate Law." Jack dropped the grin. "That's what the legal code might say but we both know how it really works. If you weren't listening in while Katie and I were talking with Laura then a guard looking to get a parking ticket fixed handed you a podcast before we left the building."

"I should run you in for conspiracy."

"And we both know you'd wind up with another false arrest ding on your sheet." Jack made a show of sniffing the air. "You say you want me to help you out? Okay, here's a tip. This pile of fish stays in the sun any longer the mayor will get wind of it. If you don't want to take the blame when the tourists start complaining on TripAdvisor you better get back to work."

33

The private entrance for ballplayers at AT&T Park was located between the team parking lot and McCovey Cove where kayakers fought over splash hits. Billie Worthington worked the door ever since the stadium was built. She did the same when the Giants played at Candlestick. Legend was she'd dated Willie Mays and "The Count" John Montefusco. Whenever people asked she'd smile and say in a voice that grew more honeyed with age, "I'm not the sort of girl to kiss and tell."

Billie had a soft spot for Jack. He never showed up without bearing a gift. This time it was a crystal owl to add to her collection of glass figurines.

"Ah, it's so cute," she said.

"Reminds me of you. Wise and wonderful."

"You better hope your wife don't hear you sweet-talking like that. She's likely to get the wrong idea."

"It'd be the right one, don't you know?"

"Go on with you. You sound like your father. Irish firemen, don't get me started."

Billie waved him through without asking for a pass or a ticket. Not that Jack didn't buy them from time to time. Even then he rarely sat in a seat. As much action was going on around the concession stands as on the field, and given the Giants had won three rings in five years meant plenty of opportunities for people like Jack.

A glass elevator carried him up to Anchor Plaza behind the center field scoreboard. Food stands ringed rows of picnic tables. It was still an hour before first pitch, but the place was already packed and a party was in full swing. Jack spotted Wonder Boy sitting at a table. The statistician extraordinaire was hunched over a notebook, fastidiously entering numbers with a pencil. His penmanship was so precise, he could've written The Declaration of Independence on a grain of rice.

Jack bought a couple of Steams and ferried them over. "You got a prediction on the outcome?"

Wonder looked up. "One run game. Giants. Biggest threat comes in the eighth. Dodgers load them with nobody out. Lopez gets the first on a two-s-s-seamer. S-s-sergio gets the final two on s-s-sliders, the last hitter takes him full count and fouls off s-s-six."

"Torture. It's why we keep coming back." Jack slid one of the beers in front of him. "Especially when LA's in town. I never miss."

"That's because you like s-s-seeing a big money team lose. You get a kick that they s-s-spent all that money on marquis players and s-s-still can't buy the championship."

"You know me. It's why I only ran grifts on deep pockets. It's not because they're rich. It's because they got where they are by cutting corners and don't think anybody will try cutting theirs."

Wonder bobbed his head. "*You can't cheat an honest man.*"

"It's a fact of life. It's what keeps me in business. Kept." He paused. "Have you found anything on that pair from Arch Ventures I asked you to look into? Specifically, who they're working for."

Wonder started bobbing. It was what he did when he was putting his thoughts together and trying to match them to the right words. "S-s-sorry it's taking s-s-so long. Nobody s-s-seems to know anything. All I got is s-s-some history."

"That's more than me. Spill it."

Wonder licked the tip of his pencil and studied his notebook some more. "Tomasz Radic and Jeremy Werthing. Those are their real names. They arrived at S-S-SFO on a flight from Las Vegas but they're not from there. Tomasz is from the Balkans. He s-s-served in the paramilitary."

"I figured that. He has that genocidal smell about him. *Ethnic cleansing.* Talk about the king of all euphemisms."

"Jeremy is younger by a few years. He's from back East. He s-s-studied engineering at Rensselaer Polytechnic."

"Now that's an odd couple. Smart and Dumber. How did they hook up?"

"Atlantic C-c-city. A New Jersey mob hired them after s-s-someone took a s-s-slot machine for a million dollar jackpot. The mob thought they had it rigged s-s-so it would never pay off, but it did s-s-so they knew s-s-somebody hacked it. Computers run s-s-slots now. The computers drive s-s-step motors to run each reel by s-s-sending digital pulses. Jeremy had a reputation as a whiz kid at his s-s-straight job at Bell Labs. The mob offered him a lot of money to discover how their s-s-slot got ripped off. He not only did that, but he figured out who. Tomasz was brought in to teach the hacker a lesson."

"Ouch." Jack grimaced. "Don't tell me. It was love at first sight. Jerry got a thrill out of associating with bad guys—it was more fun than punching a clock. What he really dug was watching Tom beat the shit out of people. It didn't take long before he was into dishing out punishment himself. Voila. Tom and Jerry. A marriage made in hell."

Wonder nodded. "Their names got around. Other enterprises with s-s-special problems like hacking and patent hijacking needed their s-s-services. You'd be s-s-surprised how many."

"Not really. Tech may sell itself as clean as a whistle, but it still uses all sorts of nasty chemicals and buys off corrupt officials when it comes to getting their merchandise made offshore, not to mention bringing it back for sale. Plus there's the never-ending problem of industrial spying and workers running off with intellectual property and customer lists. After a while the guys in the C-Suite grow impatient with slapping underlings with polite memos drafted by an HR department worried about violating the employee handbook."

"The word on the s-s-street is Tomasz and Jeremy often go a lot further than what their contract calls for."

"That's because they like their job too much. But the people paying them can hardly complain or ask for their money back, can they?"

Wonder stared at his notebook again.

"Any ideas on who they're working for now?"

"Nothing that's c-c-certain. Only s-s-speculation."

"Anybody speculating about Capital Dexterity? How about a VC operator named Arjun Chopra? He's Mumbai mafia by the way." Jack took a gulp of beer.

"S-s-sorry. All I got is what I told you." He looked around. "That and where they're s-s-staying."

Jack nearly choked. "You were saving that one, weren't you? Funny guy. Okay, where?"

Wonder did something few people ever saw him do—he

grinned. "The Mandarin. They're s-s-sharing a s-s-suite on the top floor."

JACK BOUGHT a plate of garlic fries and found an empty spot on the bench among the bleacher creatures. The game started out as Wonder Boy had predicted, a real pitcher's duel with lots of ground balls and no runs. That was fine with Jack. It gave him plenty of opportunity to admire the infield turn double plays and make cross-diamond throws. It was his favorite part of baseball and took him back to when he played shortstop at St. Joseph's with Hark behind the dish and Terry on the mound. The altar boy-turned-cop was the team's star and carried the highest batting average. He was also the school's leading scorer in basketball and the quarterback.

Between innings Jack ran down what he knew and didn't about Dexter's murder and all the rest. Knowing where Tom and Jerry were staying was a help but he had to figure out how to play it. Catching Chopra off base and doubling off that pair of wack jobs was going to be harder than turning a 6-2-3.

The bleachers kept filling and the young woman sitting next to Jack squeezed closer. Her blonde bangs hung beneath a Panda hat that looked all the more ridiculous since the pudgy third baseman had defected to Boston. She elbowed Jack. "Is that a phone vibrating in your pocket or are you happy to see me?" Her breath reeked of peppermint schnapps. She burst into hysterics. So did her companion who was also wearing a Panda hat. This one dyed orange.

Jack checked the text. It was an incoming from Hark. *Guess who showed up at my abuelita's? We're on but you better get over here quick before I stuff his ass in the trunk.*

Posey was at the plate. The crack of the slugger's bat reached

Jack at the same time the faithful jumped to their feet. A hundred bare hands reached up to snag the big fly coming their way. As much as he wanted to watch the Giants beat LA, Jack knew Hark wouldn't remain patient for long. The echo of the stadium's foghorn signaling a home run followed him out of the park.

34

A *Cerrado* sign dangled in the window of Abuelita's Café. Jack tested the front door, but it was locked. He walked around the corner to Hark's garage. A dim light seeped beneath the partially lowered bay door. Jack ducked under and pulled it closed behind him.

Hark was sitting on a stool. The big man clenched a shot glass in his fist.

Jack nodded at the open bottle of Cazadores sitting among the tools and paint cans littering a workbench. "Didn't your grandmother warn you about drinking alone?"

"I'm self-medicating so I don't lose my temper and bust him one. You know I never liked him. There are rules, *ese*, and he breaks each and every one every time. Always has, always will." Hark threw back the tequila, slammed the shot glass down, and wiped his mouth with the back of his fist.

"Where is he?"

Hark hooked a thumb at the spray booth. "I got a Bonneville ragtop in there. Six coats of hand rubbed acrylic. Midnight blue with stardust."

"Are the booth's dryers on?"

"You think I'd bake his stink into a customer's ride?"

"He in the trunk?"

"The back seat. I must be getting soft. I even left the stereo on. His choice. Bruno Mars." Hark made a face. "I duck taped his hands together. Didn't want him to scratch the new upholstery."

Jack opened the booth's double doors. Fluorescent lights bathed the newly painted lowrider. Its luster was as deep as the universe and the Milky Way had nothing on the metallic highlights that sparkled and swirled. Bobby sat upright, his head keeping time to the retro pop pumping through the door speakers and concealed subwoofer. He had a grin on his face that mimicked the grille on the vintage Pontiac.

"I don't know what you're smiling about," Jack said. "Hark's working up to taking a belt sander to your hide. You'll need a dustpan to scrape your tan off the floor."

Bobby beamed. "Why so noir, bro? I got everything worked out."

"Yeah, and how you going to do that wearing gray tape cuffs?"

"Tone down the tunes a touch and I'll tell you. You're going to like what you hear."

Jack slid into the front seat and silenced the car's stereo. "I'm listening."

Bobby held up his hands. "How about a little help here? There's got to be a razor blade around someplace. They use them to scrape off overspray."

Jack studied his old running buddy. No way he could ever trust Bobby again after he threatened to post the photos of Little Buddha. "You tell me what you want to tell me, and then we'll see about cutting you loose."

"Whatever." Bobby placed his hands on his lap. "I talked to Kim right after you hung up on me, which you got to admit was inconsiderate after all I've done for you over the years. He's up for taking my little golden friend back. He already has a buyer lined up."

"And how's that going to happen?"

"He's going to meet me in Tijuana. Kim hands over a brief-case and I hand over the statue. He flies back to Thailand, and I go home to my place on the beach. *Adios* San Francisco Police Department and hello pretty young things wanting to learn how to kiteboard."

"What's in it for me?"

Bobby fashioned a hurt look. "Sorry, bro, but you opted out of the game from the get-go. What were your words again? 'I'm legit now. I got a business and tax returns to worry about.' I offered you twenty percent of the take to sell him for me but you didn't deliver on that. I couldn't wait any longer. I have to take care of number one."

"Except you're forgetting one thing, aren't you?"

"What's that?"

"Little Buddha? I'm holding him and you're not."

"Have you forgotten the pictures up in the cloud?" A stare down ensued but Bobby lost. "Relax, you know I'm not going to stiff my best friend. There's a fee in it for you. Not as much as if you'd sold him for me but I'll give you a taste. Of course I will. For old times. Now all I need is for you to go get him and bring him to me."

"And how do you expect to get to Tijuana? Terry Dolan and the SFPD are looking at you for Cotswold's murder, not to mention the paper you're still riding from that job you pulled in Ross. Don't look so surprised. Terry told me."

"Talking to cops? That hurts, bro. Really hurts. But I'll forgive and forget. Why do you think I came here? I knew you couldn't turn your back on your old partner. Plus Hark's Mexican. He's bound to know a coyote who'll do a backwards run across the border."

Jack didn't need to turn around to know who was standing in the open double doors of the spray booth.

"Forget the trunk," the big man bellowed. "I'm going to stick you in a drum of paint thinner. Melt you down like a dried-up brush."

Bobby slipped down in the Bonneville's backseat. "Whoa, I meant that as compliment. Since when did you get all *la raza*?"

Jack wasn't about to get in the middle. The bad blood boil over was right on cue. Hark was to the car in two strides. He yanked Bobby straight out and held him off the ground.

"I never liked you. I never trusted you. I put up with your shit all these years out of respect for Jack. But that's over. No one's going stop me from doing what needs to be done."

Bobby blanched. "Ten large," he gasped. "That's what I was going to give you as a handling fee for arranging my transportation. Come on, Hark. You know I respect you. I always have. Was I being culturally insensitive? I apologize. Sincerely. How about it? We cool here?"

The metal wall of the spray booth clanged as Hark slammed Bobby against it. "You don't got ten small much less ten large. Once a bullshitter always a bullshitter."

"I do. Well, I will soon once I make the trade with Kim. *Fast pay makes fast friends*, that's always been my motto."

"You're not my friend. That's my motto." Hark cocked his fist.

"Wait," Bobby shouted. "If you knock my teeth out, I won't be able to tell Jack what I know about the murder. What I really saw that night. What I've been holding back for just the right occasion. Well, the right occasion is right now."

"More bullshit," Hark said through clenched teeth.

"I know who killed Cotswold." Bobby's words poured out fast. "I can prove it."

Hark hesitated. Jack jumped out of the front seat and put a hand on his friend's elbow. "I won't stop you and I won't blame you if you rip his head off, but Bobby might know something that could help us take down those fuckers who shot you and tried to flatten Katie and me."

The ticktock from a shop clock hanging among *Lowrider Magazine* centerfold pinups echoed in the metal booth. Seconds passed. A full minute.

Hark let go of Bobby. "You want to listen to him gas you, be my guest. But you know you can't believe a word he says." He stalked off.

Bobby straightened his shirt and ran his fingers through his curly locks. "Dude's always had a temper."

Jack held up a warning finger. He took a deep breath. "I'm not going to ask why you held back on me, all I'm going to do is ask for the truth. You do that and I'll go retrieve Little Buddha and get you a ride to Tijuana. You'll be there in time for *heuevos rancheros*. So what did you see? Who did it?"

Bobby's eyes brightened and his smile returned. "Sure, no problem. I'll tell you as soon as I see Little Buddha." He shrugged. "I want to make sure he's not scratched or anything."

Jack grabbed Bobby by the shirtfront. "You fucking little weasel."

Bobby's smile didn't slide off this time. "Come on, Jack. If it were the other way around, you'd do the same. *Trust but verify.* It's the code we live by."

Jack kept hold of Bobby and counted to sixty in his head. Then he blew out air and let go. "Fine. I'll be right back."

"No way I'm going to stay here while you run home. I'm coming with you."

"No need. Little Buddha's in the car. He goes with me every-where. Hang on. I'm parked right around the corner."

Jack exited the spray booth. Hark was sitting on the stool at the workbench nursing a tequila. Their eyes met but they didn't say a word. Didn't need to. They didn't say anything either when Jack went back into the spray booth with a black backpack slung over his shoulder.

The Bonneville's stereo was blasting again and Bobby mimicked Bruno Mars's dance moves. Step, touch, flick. Step, touch, flick. "All right," he said when Jack came back. He tipped an imaginary porkpie hat and did a scoot. "Let me see him."

Jack cut the tape binding Bobby's wrists and then handed over the backpack. Bobby set it on the ground and made a show of unzipping the top. He stuck both hands in and lifted the statue. He held it up and turned it around and around, examining it closely for the telltale blemish on the bottom. Each rotation caught the spray booth's fluorescent lights and made the gold figure gleam.

"Buddha's fingerprint," he said with a cheer. "You know what this is?"

"The stuff dreams are made of."

"No, bro. Freedom. My freedom." He slid the statue back in the black backpack and executed another step, touch, flick.

"Little Buddha's yours. Now your end. What did you see that night?"

Bobby shook his head. "You said you'd arrange a ride to TJ, too."

Jack pulled out his phone, scrolled through the contacts, and found Jimmie Fang's number. He put the phone on speaker. The Chinatown gangster answered on the third ring.

"Hello, Jack. Long time no talk to."

"It's been awhile. How you doing?"

"Busy. You have no idea what it's like managing a booming business. Since you helped retrieve our smart chips, our gross is up forty-two percent across the board. Legitimate enterprises and not so legitimate. My old man finally retired and turned over the reins." His voice dropped a notch. "You'd think he'd let up on me, but it's like I can't do anything right."

"Fathers. What you going do?"

"Tell me about it. What can I do for you?"

"I got a friend needs a ride south. No questions. No passport."

Jimmie harrumphed. "That all? The Triad still owes you big."

"Any chance you can fly him in under the radar? He's in a bit of a hurry."

"Easy. We'll take him down in the company Lear. Land at the private airport in Otay Mesa on the U.S. side. A car will drive him across. Sound good?"

"Now I owe you one."

"Give me the address where he's at. I'll send a Mercedes to pick him up within the hour."

Jack did and hung up. Bobby was back doing his Bruno Mars moves and singing the lyrics to "It Will Rain."

"You forgetting something?" Jack said.

"What's that?"

"Your end? What you saw that night at Cotswold's mansion."

Bobby stopped dancing. "It's like I said before, bro. That Laura, she's always been one sick chick."

35

The way Bobby told it, on the night of the murder the Cotswold driveway was busier than a takeout window at an In-N-Out. It was around seven thirty that evening when he and Laura rolled in from their "Two for the Road" excursion to Napa. Dexter wasn't home yet so she invited him in. He left the rented convertible parked out front and gave himself a self-guided tour while she went upstairs to change. His first stop was the library.

"You know how it is," Bobby said. "You always pull a couple of slot machine handles when you walk through a casino in case someone left a spin behind. You never know. You might hit it big on somebody else's nickel, but you wouldn't if you didn't believe you might."

"Did the library door come up sevens?" Jack asked.

They had moved from the spray booth to Hark's front office waiting for Bobby's ride. The back seat of a '56 Nomad served as a couch. Bobby took a seat and set the black backpack on the trunk lid of a '77 Eldorado that doubled as a table. Jack sat next to him.

"No, the library was closed up tight. Dexter had the palm

scanner turned on so there was no way to get in. But that was fine by me. I had my go-bag in the trunk of the rental and figured it was better to stick with the original plan."

"Don't can a good plan or you could wind up in the can."

Bobby grinned. "A golden rule to live by. It's why I've never served a day inside. But things started going sideways right from the start, so I had no choice but to deviate."

"What happened?"

"Laura."

Bobby went on to explain that his former girlfriend came back downstairs, wearing a purple negligee. Her hair was done up in pigtails and her cheeks smeared with rouge.

"Her lipstick was all wrong. There was way too much of it. She looked like a little girl who'd gotten into Mommy's makeup. Baby doll stuff."

"What did she say?" Jack asked.

"Now I'm the first to admit, I don't shy away from a ride that's rough and ready but she..." He shook his sun-bleached curls. "Way-off my diet, if you know what I mean. I told her I had to go. I'd been putting her off all day as it was. She got pissed and told me to get the fuck out. Said she got all the sex she wanted anyway because she was three-timing her husband. She told me the way I was acting I was no better than him. You know, short in the testosterone department. Not that I am. There's plenty who'll say otherwise."

"Laura tell you who the other guys were?"

"Not their names or anything. Only that they were rich, smart, powerful, and a lot more fun than I was turning out to be."

"Nothing more than that?"

"I didn't ask. I really didn't want to know. All I wanted was to grab Little Buddha when the time was right and head home to Baja."

"Did you believe there were really two guys or do you think she was inflating the count to make you feel bad?"

"Maybe she was. Who knows? Why do I care? But I'll tell you this, the entire time we were in Kathmandu together, she was always the eager beaver. The high altitude did nothing to slow her down. And you know me, I can go all day, all night as long as I'm properly hydrated."

Jack waved him off. He didn't want to hear Bobby defend his prowess in the prow department. "Did you ask if Dexter knew about her lovers?"

"As a matter of fact, I did. She laughed in my face, but she was really laughing at him. She said Dexter thought he was such a good businessman, but couldn't see what was going on right in front of his nose."

"Meaning one of the lovers or both, if there really were two, were associated with his business."

"Now that you say it, I suppose so." Bobby paused. "Why do you care?"

"I need to nail down all the facts if I'm going to get Terry off my ass. Cut to the chase. You said you knew who killed Dexter. Could prove it. Who was it?"

Bobby hesitated. His chin dipped. "I may have overstated that a bit. I mean, Hark was going to knock my block off after all."

Jack exhaled loudly. "What part's overstated? The what you saw part or the who the killer is?"

"Hold on. I may not know a name, but I can definitely narrow down the field."

"Then walk me through it. Laura comes downstairs and then what happened?"

"I started backpedaling. Like I said, I had a job to do, and the last thing I wanted was to risk it. You know, hubby coming home and getting the wrong idea, which would have been the right idea. So I said my goodbyes and off I went."

"But not too far off."

"No. I had my plan and I was sticking to it. I stashed the rental and made myself comfortable in the woods and waited for the right time. Only it was a lot longer in coming because of the parade."

"What parade?"

"All the cars. First up was a little red number. It roared up the driveway and screeched to a halt. The front door of the house swung open and Laura ran out still in the purple nightie. By the time the driver got out, she'd already jumped on him. Arms and legs wrapped around him like a starfish. He had to carry her inside."

"A red car? I thought you said the Tesla was black."

"I did and it was. But it wasn't first up. This was a red Audi. One of those high end sports coupes built on a Lamborghini frame."

"What did the driver look like?"

"I couldn't see his face because it was buried in Laura's tits but he was definitely a rich techie."

"What makes you say that?"

Bobby grinned. "Who else in California would spend that kind of money for a car that can hit two hundred miles an hour? Hello? Gridlock? Six gears and you never get it out of third. He had a personalized license plate. *IPOBALLR*. Talk about liking to stroke it in public."

Jack's memory bank paid a dividend: Alta Mesa Cemetery. He'd parked behind the car at Dexter's funeral.

"Was the Audi still there when the black Tesla showed up?"

"No. But the Tesla wasn't up next. A Jag was. A sedan. The driver slowed down, checking out the red Audi, and then went straight to the garage. Door opened automatically, Jag drove in, door came down."

"Dexter," Jack said. "Home from the office."

"Exactly my take. If he thought he was going to find Laura greeting him at the door with a martini and dinner in the oven, he was in for a big surprise."

"Did you see Dex go inside?"

Bobby shook his head. "The garage is attached to the main house. But it was him all right."

"How can you be sure?"

"Because I snuck over and looked through the window. This was turning out better than watching TV. No, make that a train wreck. You know how you can't turn away? I could've been the one onboard if I hadn't left." He faked a shudder. "Discretion is the better part of valor."

Jack asked what Dexter did when he caught the pair *en flagrante.*

"That's just it. He didn't. It was like he didn't want to. He went straight to the kitchen and made a lot of racket, putting on a teapot. Remember those monks blowing those big horns and banging cymbals? They were less noisy than he was. He poured himself a cup and toddled off to his library. I figured it was a gift horse of some sort."

"So you went back inside."

"Naturally. You would've, too. The front door was still unlocked. I went in and made for the living room across the hall from the library to keep an eye open for an opportunity."

"Did he leave the door open?"

"Partially. I heard him rummaging around but had to duck because Laura got her pants back on and was coming down the stairs with her boyfriend in tow. They were heading right for the library."

"You get a look at the guy then?"

"No. It wasn't like I could pop up from behind the couch and say, 'Sorry, I dropped my keys.' "

Jack asked if he could hear what Dexter said when Laura and the mystery man joined him.

"Nothing distinct. The walls in that mansion aren't exactly like the ones you and I grew up with in the Mission. But I could tell from the tone, everybody knew everybody. Lots of 'hey, how are you doing, good to see you, can I get you a drink' buzz going on." Bobby reached over and touched the backpack as if to make sure it was still there. "Then everything went silent. Somebody closed the library door. I took that as my cue to go back outside and wait until later to make my drop down the chimney."

"The Audi left before the Tesla showed up?"

"Yes. It was about an hour later. The Audi took off the same way it came. The driver got that big V-10 revving, slammed it into gear, and fishtailed on out."

"Where was Laura?"

"I didn't see her. She didn't send him off with a kiss. I didn't think much about it. But then the Tesla showed. And then everything came down like I told you before. Word for word. The driver got out of the car. Someone let him in the front door. I couldn't see who. He didn't stay very long and off he went. So I went back in again. Library was open. Dexter was dead. I grabbed Little Buddha and had to duck behind the couch again when Laura showed. Then out I went."

"That doesn't move the ball downfield very much. The killer could be any one of them. Even you, for that matter."

"Well, you can eliminate me because it wasn't me. It was one of those three. Had to be. My money's on the guy in the Audi. Or Laura."

"Why don't you think it was Tesla man?"

"He wasn't there very long. I think he took one look and got the hell out of Dodge."

Mobsters and murder went together like fish and chips, but Jack was starting to have second thoughts that Chopra was the killer. Maybe it was Audi man or maybe Terry had locked up the right suspect after all.

A car horn sounded. "That could be your ride," Jack said.

Bobby jumped up and went to the window. "A Mercedes. Sweet."

"It's dark. You'd better make sure before you go outside. Can you see the driver?"

Bobby pressed his nose against the glass. "He looks Asian."

"Sounds like one of Jimmie Fang's crew all right. You're good to go."

Bobby turned around, picked the black backpack off the table, and swung it over his shoulder. He stuck out his hand. "All right, bro. I'm out of here. I'll send your cut after Kim makes good. Wire it to the Caymans through Anders, right?"

Jack got off the couch. "That'll work." He ignored Bobby's hand.

Bobby tried a fist bump this time. "We all right?"

"Keep your head down," is all Jack said.

Bobby shrugged and left.

Jack moved to the window and watched as Bobby got into the backseat. The Mercedes eased away and slipped into the night.

Hark entered carrying two full shot glasses and handed one to Jack. "That was fun. Everything go slick?"

"So far so good. Jimmie will let me know when they drop Bobby off in Tijuana."

"Good riddance," the big man said.

He knocked back the tequila. Jack did the same.

Hark said, "Were you counting on getting the 411 on what he saw the night of the murder or was that a bonus?"

"It's like you said, Bobby's incapable of telling the full story until his back's against the wall."

"Good call on your part. What's your next move?"

"Chase down the driver of a red Audi sports coupe."

"That shouldn't be too hard. Not that many of them."

"Especially with a personalized plate."

"Need my help?"

"Always."

Jack set the empty shot glass on the Eldorado trunk lid. He reached under the Nomad couch where he'd been sitting and dragged out a backpack identical to the one Bobby left with.

Hark watched, bemusement growing in his eyes. "You sure you want to stick to the straight and narrow? Looks like you still got the touch when it comes to making a switch."

"You still play a mean role, too." Jack started for the door, carrying the backpack.

"You think Bobby will look in the bag he took?"

"All the way down to TJ, but he'll only see what he wants to see."

"Like all the pigeons do." Hark toyed with his shot glass. "Hey, *ese*. Tell Henri hi for me next time you see him. He hasn't lost his touch either. I'm honored to have sprayed and baked his piece."

"I'll let him know. You got the Buddha fingerprint down pat."

Hark grinned. "I'd sure like to see Bobby's face when Kim tells him he's holding a gold brick. Maybe the statue's curse is real. First Dexter gets killed and now Bobby gets burned for all the shit he pulled."

"Karma," Jack said. "Sometimes it's a bitch."

36

The next morning Jack raced up the stairs to his fourth floor office. He hurtled the trash can propping open the emergency exit door and sprinted down the hall. Moana stood with her prized tin watering can clasped to her breast.

"You were already too late before I called. Look what those *fai hoosi* did to my baby." The overgrown philodendron was hacked off at the stalk. Tendrils drooped from the water pipe and once bright green leaves had lost their luster. "I catch who did this, I'll cut their *lalo* off with a cane knife."

The office was a wreck. Desk drawers were yanked out and dumped on the floor. File cabinets lay on their sides. A hole the size of a fist marred Moana's computer screen.

Jack sucked his teeth. "Where's Do Pray?"

Moana frowned from beneath her straw fedora. "He wasn't in when I got here. I saw we'd been ripped off and called you. I tried his cell but no answer. He didn't do this if that's what you're thinking."

"I'm not."

Do Pray's cubicle looked as if Hurricane Katrina had rolled

through. A rack that once held stackable storage drives containing all the coding files was empty. The thieves wouldn't need to hack them if they had grabbed Do Pray, too. He wouldn't hold out for long if grilled for the password. Jack pictured Tomasz Radic wielding a blowtorch while Jeremy Werthing watched through the smoky lenses of a new pair of sunglasses.

"*Que paso?*"

Jack turned around. Hark had gotten his 911. He stood in the doorway holding the Beretta at his side.

"Our friends from the other night paid me an office visit."

"You sure it's not some junkies? No matter how hard the city tries dressing up Mid-Market, it's still Mid-Market."

"It was them all right. Tom is about as subtle as a litter box on a dining room table."

Hark tucked the gun beneath the tails of his flannel shirt. "They take anything or was it only a trash job to send a message?"

"The drives holding the blueprints to my app are gone along with the programmer who drew them."

"And don't forget what they did to my baby," Moana said.

Hark gave her the once over. "Nice hat."

Moana did the same. "What's your name, big boy?"

"Uh, it's Hark."

"You sure about that?"

"Pretty sure."

"You look like you can handle yourself."

"I do all right."

"You help me find the *lemus* who cut down my jungle plant, I'll do a fire dance for you so hot flames will shoot out your ears."

She chucked him under the chin with the tip of the watering can. The move showed off the bands of tattoos circling her upper arms.

A big dopey smile spread across Hark's face.

"We got bigger problems here than a dead philodendron," Jack said.

Moana whipped out her phone. She tapped the screen and held it out for Jack to see. "You think I fell off the pineapple truck? The racks are all backed up on the cloud. I already changed the password and sent a *delete all* command to the network drives they stole. They got nothing."

"Except Do Pray."

Her face sunk. "Who are they?"

Jack gave her the highlights, but left out the parts about the Mumbai mafia and Tingly Meyers swimming with the fishes.

"You mean Arch Ventures isn't going to give us any money? I was counting on that to pay for the Heilala Festival."

"They're not VC. Not even close."

She crossed her arms. "Then I say we call the cops."

"All in good time. Whoever's behind this is rich, powerful, and connected. I don't know how far his influence goes. Best bet is to trip him up so he gets locked up and stays locked up." Jack took a breath. "First off we find Do Pray."

"Maybe they took him down to the building in Oyster Point," Hark said.

"I doubt it. The guard would've told them about our visit. They know it's burned."

"How about tracking the kid through his phone?"

"Tom is rock stupid but not Jerry. He would've thought of it and crushed it." Jack looked around the room. "But you might have something there. Maybe we can track them through theirs."

"You got their number?"

"I don't but Moana does."

Moana's fedora tilted. "I do?"

"Remember, they called to set up the lunch meet down on the Embarcadero. It's probably still on your phone's Recents."

She scrolled. "Here it is."

"Call it," Hark said. "They put a cap in me. The sooner I find them the sooner I can return the favor. It's about respect."

"You got shot?"

Hark gave an aw-shucks. "You wanna see it? It's got a little bandage that might need changing."

Jack exhaled loudly again. "A little help here. I'm going to have to triangulate the call if they answer. And that's a big *if*."

"Not necessarily," Moana said. "The boys in the next office have an app that can track a cell that's been turned off or flushed down the toilet. It works pretty good, too."

"And you know this, how?"

"I had an ex I needed to track." She shot a glance at Hark. "Not in a stalkerish sort of way, mind you."

Jack threw up his hands. "Is there anybody not building a killer app?"

"Us if we don't find Do Pray."

"We?"

She crossed her arms. "You better believe *we*. They killed my plant. They snatched my one and only direct report. I got skin in the game."

Hark gave her the once over again. "True that."

THE OFFICE next door was even more disheveled and it hadn't been ransacked. Skateboard posters covered the walls. The Offspring howled from a pair of lopsided speaker towers. The place reeked of pot and dirty socks. A yellow dog on a dingy brown sofa performed autofellatio.

Moana introduced two twentysomethings whose beards had

more vacation spots than Maui. "This is Timmy and he's called One Shot."

"What's the dog's name?" Jack asked.

"Doesn't have one," Timmy said. "We found him in the alley. Cool, huh?"

Jack rolled his eyes. "Moana tells me you're working on an app that can pinpoint phones without going through the carriers' protocols."

"Maybe," One Shot said. "What's it worth to you?"

He was taller than Timmy and wore a Camp Kill Yourself T-shirt. His left wrist was wrapped in a blue cast and fresh scabs decorated his elbows.

"Two hundred bucks," Jack said.

The young men laughed. One Shot dug into the front pocket of his baggy jeans and fished out a roll of bills as thick as a skateboard wheel. "Two hundy? I spent more than that for this T-shirt. An angel investor laid one milla skrilla on us." The pair bumped knuckles.

Hark stepped between Jack and One Shot. "That's a lot of money for a T."

One Shot sneered through his peach fuzz. "It's a collector's item. I got it on eBay."

"Is it bulletproof?"

"What are you talking about?"

Hark drew the Beretta and leveled it between Camp and Kill.

One Shot shrieked and stumbled backwards. "Dude, mellow out!"

Moana touched Hark's gun hand. "Easy big boy." She turned to Timmy. "Some lowlifes snatched Do Pray. The only way to find him is by tracking their phone. Help a fellow coder out, would you?"

One Shot's eyes were blinking faster than a strobe as he fixated on Hark's gun. "Is that thing real?"

"One way to find out," Hark said.

The punk glanced at his partner. "Dude's, like, authentic. Cool, huh?"

Moana said, "Are you going to help or not?" When Timmy nodded she gave him the number.

He keyed the digits into a laptop. Jack looked over the skater's shoulder. The screen filled with the image of a satellite map. It quickly zoomed in on a crosshatch of streets. A red dot flashed.

"Figuring out the different carrier codes was easy," Timmy said as he fingered a mouse. "It's like they didn't even try to make it complicated. All the different brands of handsets basically use the same manufacturer in China. We wrote a pattern analyzer code to group the ESNs, turned it loose on a Friday night, drove down to Santa Cruz for some serious partying, and when we came back on Monday, a thousand terabytes locked and loaded. Assigning the satellite search and find function and matching the last known grid and probability of location based on the user's usage profile was a walk in the freaking park. Cool, huh?"

One Shot edged closer to Hark. "Sick neck tat, brah. What inkster do you use?"

Hark growled.

Timmy clapped his hands. "Here you go, neighbors. The phone's not even turned off. It's in a, here, let me zoom in." He drove the mouse and clicked a key and the grid turned into a street view of the front of a three-story stucco residence.

"Russian Hill." Jack said it before Timmy could. "That's Filbert Street." He shoved the coder aside, logged into the city's property tax website, and typed in the address. The record showed the building belonged to a limited liability company based in Hong Kong. "That's the same name as one of the shells I traced the Oyster Point warehouse to. Bet if we dig deeper, we'll find the ownership is stacked like Russian dolls."

"So that's why they call that neighborhood Russian Hill." One Shot grinned. "Awesome."

Moana stopped Hark from slapping the punk upside the head. "He can't help it. He fell off his skateboard one too many times."

37

Moana led the way on her red Vespa. Hark and Jack followed close behind. They drove up Larkin, past the Asian Art Museum, through the Tenderloin, and over Nob Hill.

"Katie was right," Hark said as he steered the Impala around cars and gunned it through yellow lights to keep up with the scooter. "My kind of woman. The *chica* can drive."

"You might want to let her know that's a compliment. If she thought you meant chick, she's likely to bust you one."

"Like I said, my kind of woman. Opinionated." Hark hit the gas as another green turned yellow, and the lowrider's twin pipes yowled.

They turned onto Filbert. Moana pulled over a couple of blocks from the address Timmy had pinpointed. Hark brought the Impala right alongside.

Jack leaned out the open window. "Most of these blocks have little half streets and alleys running through them so people can access garages. Hark and I'll take the front. You go up and wait on Union. If they try to run out the back, call me. We'll come running."

Moana eyed Hark. "Don't let my boss get shot. He owes me a lot of back pay." She twisted the scooter's accelerator handle and turned the corner.

Hark parked. He reached over and popped open the glove box. "I know you don't like to carry, but I wouldn't want to piss her off before we get a chance to go out. There's another nine behind those cassettes."

"This is a terrible place to stash a gun," Jack said.

"How's that?"

"A cop stops you and looks in there he'll wonder what these are." Jack held up one of the cassettes. "No way he'll believe it when you tell him something this size only holds one album worth of music."

"Take the gun, *ese*. How you want to do this thing?"

"It'd be nice if they opened the front door all friendly, but they know what I look like. Chances are they won't recognize you from the night you were trading shots with them. How about you go ahead and play deliveryman at the wrong address?"

"You mean if they do recognize me, I'll be the first one to take a cap."

"You're the one who said it was about respect."

The building was a yellow stucco three-story. Hark raised his hand as if to give the front door a rap and then grinned at Jack. "How we did it in the 'Stan." He proceeded to kick in the door.

Jack scrambled fast to keep up. They entered with their guns out. The door opened to an empty foyer with a staircase leading up. Hark pointed his gun at it and mimed covering the stairwell and Jack to start climbing. When they were both on the first landing, they started clearing. No one was in the living and dining rooms. The kitchen was empty, too. It didn't smell like anybody had been cooking. A hallway led to a TV room and a half bath. Another stairway rose at the end of the hall.

"Probably leads to the bedrooms upstairs," Jack said.

"If anybody's here they got to be somewhere. Let's do it."

This time Hark led the way up. They checked every room. No one was hiding under a bed. No one jumped out of a closet.

"Maybe we got the wrong address," Hark said. "Maybe those skater punks' app isn't so good. I sure hope Moana didn't invest in it."

Jack pulled his phone and called her. "Dial Arch's number again."

Two seconds later they heard ringing. Jack pointed with his gun. "Downstairs."

A cell was lying beside a remote control next to the television set. Jack answered it. "It's me, Moana. There's no one here. You might as well head back to the office. We'll catch up with you later."

"How do you read this?" Hark asked.

"Like someone wanted us to track them. Someone wanted us here so they could deliver a message."

Hark looked around. "How?"

Jack picked up the TV clicker and hit power. Do Pray's face filled the screen. One of his eyes was swollen shut. Dried blood tracked from his nose. His lip was as fat as a ballpark hotlink.

The camera pulled back to show the programmer was tied to a chair with rope. Not much of the room showed but Jack spotted a shadow moving. There was at least one other person besides whoever was holding the camera. He didn't have to wait long to know who was who.

A voice-over began. It was Jeremy Werthing.

"Ah, Mr. McCoul. Not as technologically illiterate as one might have assumed. As you can see, your young employee is proving to be rather uncooperative. We hope you won't prove likewise."

The shadow moved behind Do Pray. A hand appeared in the screen and slapped him hard against the side of his head.

"You ordered a vicious attack on our client's network. That was a poor decision. Now you can see the consequence. If you hope to see your employee again, you need to provide an antidote. We also need you to restore all the data on the network drives we acquired. Consider the forfeiture of your application's design as the penalty for the damage you have incurred."

The voice-over stopped. The camera drew back to reveal a man standing behind Do Pray. His face was purposely kept out of the frame but Jack knew it was Tomasz. This time both hands came into the picture. One cupped Do Pray's chin and yanked his head back. The other held a knife.

"No doubt you're thinking heroic thoughts," Jeremy started again. "Or maybe you're thinking your employee is expendable and you can hire another. But the one thing you should not be thinking is that we won't exact penalties should you ignore to do what we ask."

The knife drew quickly. Do Pray screamed as a thin red line appeared on his neck. The cut wasn't fatal nor was it as viscous as the slash in Tingly Meyers' throat but it had the same effect on Jack as when he and Katie were nearly run over. A cold fury sharper than the knife's blade rose in his gorge.

"You have work to do," Jeremy said. "You had better get to it. We'll be in touch."

The screen went dark.

"It's a recording," Hark said. "The kid is probably already dead."

"Maybe but I got to act like he isn't." Jack felt around the TV set's frame and found a thumb drive stuck in the USB. He pulled it out and slipped in in his pocket. "That's how they played the tape."

"So where do we start looking for him?"

"Wonder Boy got a bead on them. He says they're booked into a suite at the Mandarin."

"Punks are accessing a lot of high price real estate for a couple of out-of-towners. Oyster Point. Russian Hill. Now a luxury hotel in the FiDi." He pointed his gun at the TV. "I've never been to the Mandarin."

"Now's your chance."

"Don't tell me you want me to play deliveryman again. What, rolling a room service cart this time?"

"We may have to come up with something a little more subtle. Let's head back to my office and check out what else might be on this drive. It could give us an edge."

"Moana going be there?"

Jack nodded. "But don't say I didn't warn you."

38

They badged him as soon as he entered the lobby. Both were in plainclothes. One wore a windbreaker over a black T-shirt, the other a sport coat. They had on jeans. They could've been Twitterites.

"Keep your hands where we can see them," the cop in the sport coat said.

"Okay if I leave them attached to my wrists?" Jack said.

"Funny guy. They told us you have a mouth," sport coat said.

"A big mouth," windbreaker said.

"Helps with eating and drinking," Jack said.

"Check his ID," sport coat said.

Windbreaker snapped his fingers and stuck out his palm. Jack fished out his wallet and handed over his driver's license. The cop gave it the once-over. "It's him all right."

Jack was glad he'd put the nine back in the Impala's glove compartment. He was also glad Hark had dropped him off out front and went to find parking, never an easy search in any neighborhood, especially Mid-Market. Hark always packed and that would've made the lobby feel even smaller than it did now.

"You want to tell me what this is about?" Jack asked.

"You'll find out when we get where we're going," sport coat said.

Windbreaker provided a theatrical "*Dun du dun dun.*"

"Are you boys moonlighting for Uber? Sorry to disappoint but I didn't ping for a ride."

"Funny," windbreaker said. "Not."

"If you're arresting me aren't you supposed to read me something?"

"Nobody's arresting nobody," sport coat said. "Give him back his ID."

Windbreaker held out the driver's license. When Jack reached for it the cop let it go. "Oops."

Jack knew what was coming if he bent down to pick it up. He let it stay where it lay. "If I reach for my phone to call my lawyer, are you going to shoot me?"

Windbreaker started breathing heavy. Sport coat's eyes never left Jack's. "Save your minutes. It's why we're here. We're taking you to Broadass compliments of Inspector Dolan. He thought you might get lost along the way."

"Terry's at Broadshank's office?"

"That's for you to find out."

Windbreaker went with the "*dun du dun dun*" again.

They hustled him out to the street and toward a baby-shit-brown sedan parked a couple of doors down. Hark was walking their way. Jack waved him off with a glance. They passed without a word. Jack knew Hark made the pair as cops. He also knew the big man wouldn't wait around. He'd dive right into planning Do Pray's rescue.

~

WINDBREAKER DROVE. He used the bike-only lane to pass streetcars as they sped down Market. The cops talked football the whole way.

"You do know it's baseball season," Jack said.

"So what?" sport coat said. "Game's too slow ever since they stopped runners from being able to knock the catcher on his ass."

"For pussies," windbreaker said. "Like watching ice skating."

"Remind me how many world championships have the 49ers won recently? Any in the last, say, twenty years?"

"Shut up," both cops said in unison.

They double-parked in front of a sand-colored office building on Sutter a block past Montgomery. It was one of the Financial District's oldest high-rises. Its age and Late Gothic Revival style put it on the Register of Historic Places. That kept it from being demolished to make way for another one of the soulless test-tube towers sprouting up all over downtown. Windbreaker stayed behind the wheel as sport coat escorted Jack inside.

"I can take it from here," Jack said as he punched the elevator button. "I promise I won't get lost."

"As if I got a choice," sport coat said. The elevator door opened. "Get in."

Jack pushed 20. The elevator began to rise. "You know I went to school with Terry," he said.

"So what?"

"So I know what it's like with Terry giving orders. He was a hardass back at Saint Joe's. Always has been. Always will be."

"FYI, douche-bag, I don't take orders from Dolan. We're equal rank."

That told Jack what he wanted to know. Whoever was waiting upstairs with CB had a lot of clout, enough to get the police commissioner or chief of police barking down the chain of command.

"Must be an important meeting," he said.

"Dolan told me you'd try to bleed me. Yeah, I know who you are. And, yeah, I know he used to date your wife. Everybody in Robbery Homicide does." He chuckled. "We got a pool. Everybody picked a month and year when we'd finally put you away. Guess what? I got this month."

The cop was still grinning as the doors opened. Broadshank, Hicklin, and Wong, LLP shared the floor with a nonprofit environmental activist group. Katie was one of its most ardent supporters. She was always making online donations to help them save wolves and whales and sue greedy polluters.

Broadshank's receptionist wore eyeliner and a pantsuit to match. He ushered Jack and sport coat into the main conference room. Whatever Jack was expecting it wasn't this. Terry Dolan sat on one side of the table. Cicero Broadshank sat at the head, and sitting across from Terry was Arjun Chopra.

"Jack, my boy, glad you could find time to join us," Broadshank bellowed. "You know everyone here? Of course you do. Take a seat. Refreshments?"

A platter of chocolate chip cookies was within arm's reach of the lawyer. Each was as thick as a hockey puck. Jack ignored the fresh-baked smell and sat down. It was like they were getting ready to play poker. In a way they were.

Broadshank picked up a cookie. From the look of his shirtfront, it wasn't his first. He waved it at sport coat. "Thank you, detective. Martin will show you out."

Sport coat didn't budge. Terry said, "Thanks, Chip. I'll see you back at the station."

Jack winked at sport coat and mouthed, "orders."

The detective scowled and stalked out.

"Okay," Jack said. "You got my curiosity. What gives?"

The lawyer took a deep breath. "First, I must remind everybody that this meeting has no agenda nor is it a formal proceeding. It is the result of a suggestion made by a member of the mayor's staff. Its very existence should not be construed as an endorsement of a position or a legal opinion of either the mayor or the mayor's staff. I have been asked to serve as mediator for this meeting at the suggestion of the mayor's office. My presence does not preclude Mr. Chopra from representation by an attorney of his own choosing should he so desire. Mr. Chopra's presence is strictly voluntary, and whatever he may or may not say does not constitute a formal statement. Inspector Dolan is here as lead investigator of the homicide of Mr. Dexter Cotswold, late of Woodside, California. Mr. McCoul is here because, well, because Jack appears to have prompted a chain of events that led to this meeting. To wit, a conversation held with Mrs. Cotswold that was recorded. While that recording was legal, Mr. McCoul must consent to its use and be present for it to be shared with a third party who is not a sworn officer of the law, namely Mr. Chopra. In sum, this conversation, for all intents and purposes, is intended to serve as a means for correcting misperceptions and clarifying actual events that may or may not benefit the San Francisco Police Department's investigation, as well as may or may not benefit Mr. Chopra, whose personal reputation may or may not be impinged by said investigation and said misperceptions."

Broadshank took out a yellow silk handkerchief and dabbed the sweat beading on his brow. Next he took a bite of cookie, chewed noisily, and then wiped a gooey chocolate chip that had collected at the corner of his mouth.

Jack raised an eyebrow. "You're like a freelance writer who gets paid by the word, CB. We get it. Terry listened to the tape of my visit with Laura and called Chopra for a friendly chat. Chopra reached out to the mayor to remind him of his last campaign contribution. So here we are. What you didn't say was how all of this may or may not benefit Laura. She's the one stacking time at the Hall."

"I'll do the talking here," Terry said curtly. He shifted in his chair so his shoulders were aligned directly with Chopra's. "You understand that anything you say today despite this being *informal* will need to be corroborated. It doesn't mean no one believes you, it's simply a matter of investigative protocol."

"Of course," Chopra said. "It is only logical. Mr. Broadshank gave me an overview of the process before you arrived, so please ask any questions you may have. As you will find, I have nothing to hide and everything to gain as my objective is the equivalent of yours, and that is to bring swift justice to whoever is responsible for my late business partner's death."

Jack was glad he wasn't eating a cookie or he would've choked. "Does this mean the cops haven't talked to you until now?"

Chopra turned his hawklike gaze on him. His eyes did not blink.

"Don't answer that," Terry said.

Broadshank nodded. "Jack, please. Let the inspector do his job."

Jack couldn't resist. "Proceed."

That earned him another warning look from Terry.

"Mr. Chopra, one of my team already interviewed you, correct?"

"Yes, a female officer. I do not recall her name. She asked about my history with the company. When I joined, what I did, how well I knew Dexter, that sort of thing."

Terry glanced at a manila folder open in front of him. The murder book. "Officer Liu. That's who questioned you. She also asked you if the victim had any enemies and your opinion on who might have been the perp." He caught himself. "Perpetrator."

"Yes, I imagine it is in your notes. I told her that in our business it is not unusual to have disappointed some people, be they investors, a start-up seeking funding, individuals wishing to become partners. Ours is a fast-paced business reflecting the nature of the industry we fund. While we always strive to conduct activities in a respectful manner, we do not always have the luxury of time to go back and assess how our decisions may be perceived by others."

"So who do you think killed Dex?" Jack said.

Chopra swiveled his head toward Jack then returned to look at Terry. "I did not offer an opinion. I had none. I still do not."

Terry shuffled his notes loudly to draw attention back to him. "Officer Liu doesn't appear to have asked for an accounting of your whereabouts the night of the murder."

Chopra was expressionless. "Should she have? Perhaps she assumed as I did that I was not a suspect."

"Do you mind answering the question now?"

Broadshank put his cookie down. "Mr. Chopra, I must strongly advise you to consider conferring with legal representation before answering. You do have rights."

"I do not need counsel to advise me on this. The answer is simple. The truth always is. I was attending a biotech conference in San Diego. The firm has been looking to expand our investment portfolio beyond software and hardware for some time." Chopra reached into the inside pocket of his dark gray suit jacket that offset a cream turtleneck. He pulled out a phone and scrolled. "Yes, here is my schedule for that day. I flew down at two pm, attended a reception at the Grand Del Mar that evening, and had dinner with a group of CEOs. I spent the night at the hotel as I was to be the keynote speaker at the breakfast plenary."

"And did you?" Terry asked.

"Did I what?"

"Give a speech."

"Unfortunately, no. Early that morning I received a call informing me my partner was dead. I went straight to the airport and flew home."

"Who called you?"

"Mr. Cotswold's executive assistant, Miss Nash. She was quite distraught. Understandably so."

"No doubt," Jack said, earning himself stern looks from both Broadshank and Terry. Chopra didn't acknowledge him.

"And all that can be corroborated. Airline tickets, hotel bills, witnesses, that sort of thing," Terry said.

"Everything except for an airline ticket. I flew private. Of course a flight plan would have been filed. I'll have the office send a copy." Chopra keyed his phone and the whoosh of a sent text sounded. He slipped the phone back.

"What kind of car do you drive?" Jack asked.

Chopra answered before Terry could issue another warning. "My principal automobile is a Tesla. Our firm was an early investor. We like to show loyalty to our partners."

"Black?"

The slightest of frowns turned Chopra's lips. "Yes."

"Did you leave it at the airport overnight?"

Chopra turned to Terry. "Should I be answering Mr. McCoul or you?"

"Me." Terry paused. "So did you park it at the airport?"

"No, I did not. I flew out of San Carlos. Despite being in the heart of Silicon Valley, the airfield has a minimum number of parking stalls equipped with recharging stations for electric vehicles. They are usually occupied, especially by the afternoon. I was dropped off and picked up."

"We'll need to corroborate that. For the record," Terry said.

"You will need to speak to Miss Nash. She drove me."

"In your car, the Tesla?" Jack said.

Chopra nodded. "Yes. We left from the office. My overnight bag was already in the trunk. I was running late and it was quicker to take my car rather than transfer my bag. My parking space is right in front."

"Executive privilege," Jack muttered.

Broadshank waved a cookie at him. "Jack, my boy, please."

Terry studied his notes some more before looking up. "I want to thank you, Mr. Chopra. That's all the questions I have."

"You got to be shitting me," Jack said. "That's all you're going to ask him? What about the black Tesla seen coming and going from Dexter's driveway that night? How about that he and Laura have been doing the twerk? Come on, Terry. Private jet? He could've flown back and forth to San Diego three times that night."

"Shut it," Terry said. "We're done here."

"Seriously? How hard is the mayor coming down on your boss?"

Terry stood up so quickly, he knocked his chair over. "And I'm warning you not to say another word. Period."

"Gentlemen, please," Broadshank said. "I must insist on propriety. This interchange goes way beyond the intended informality of this meeting."

"And who are you representing, CB? Laura or this guy? She's the one in jail. She's the one who's going to have to take a mouthful of gas if you don't do your job."

Broadshank turned crimson. Cookie crumbs blew off his lips as he sputtered. Jack stole a glance at Chopra to see if his outburst was going to pay off.

The venture capitalist remained perfectly calm. "You say a Tesla was seen at the Cotswold home that evening? I can see why you might jump to conclusions. But obviously my presence in San Diego in the company of others precludes me from having driven it myself. That does leave the possibility of another driver. But how can anyone be positive the vehicle was mine? Did anyone note the license plate number?" Chopra waited. When no one responded he said, "I am not the only Tesla owner in the region. True, my automobile is black but it is also the model's most popular color. I can tell you from experience that the other Tesla colors are often confused with black at night—not only the midnight blue but also the brown, the dark gray, and the green. There are many stories about valets bringing the wrong car to the wrong owner at the end of a Silicon Valley party. You can read them on the Tesla forum. Most amusing."

"Nice explanation," Jack said. "Almost believable. But it still doesn't cover the fact that you and Laura were having an affair. What happened, Dexter finally got wise?"

"Don't answer that." Broadshank's voice started to rise to its well-known courtroom crescendo. "I must insist. Jack, your allegations and speculations are appalling. They have no standing in a court of law. Mr. Chopra is entitled to his privacy, the same as everyone else. His personal life is no one's business but his own. That is the law and I will defend it with every core of my being no matter who my client may be or whatever the charge."

Terry got in Jack's face. "Get out of here. Now."

Jack threw up his hands and stormed out. "Am I the only here who hasn't been bought off?"

39

Jack gave himself a standing ovation for his performance. Not only did he need to exit stage left before Terry could ask him about Bobby Ballena's whereabouts, but he wanted a head start on Chopra. The elevator passed the lobby and stopped at the underground garage. Jack got out and went straight to the parking attendant booth.

"Black Tesla? Came in within the hour? I'm meeting a friend. He's right behind me."

"You got the ticket?" the attendant asked.

"No, he does." He put on a grin. "Don't worry. He's a big tipper."

"You want me to bring it around?"

Jack smiled to himself. Chopra's car was there. "No need. I'll walk up the ramp and meet him on the street. Gives me time to have a smoke."

He didn't have to wait long. The Tesla purred up the ramp. As Chopra stopped to wait for the automatic gate to rise, Jack stepped from behind a pillar and hopped in. "You mind giving me a lift?"

Chopra stayed cool. "You certainly are most unconventional. I assume you have more questions."

"Plenty. I don't know what you got over Terry and CB but I'm not buying what you're selling."

"Be that as it may, everything I said was true. I am not responsible for Dexter Cotswold's death."

"It's the stuff you left out that interests me."

There was an opening in the traffic and Chopra pulled onto Sutter. The car showed tremendous acceleration as they made the light at Kearny and beat out a UPS truck trying to double-park.

"I have never been hijacked before, so you will have to tell me where it is I am taking you," Chopra said. "Or are we to keep driving until you are satisfied with my answers?"

Jack had to give it to him—he was unflappable. "It's *carjacked,* but that's not what I'm doing. This is called me doing someone a favor."

"A favor for Laura, I assume."

"Her, too. But right now it's mostly for my employee Do Pray Davis. Your soldiers took him and now they're holding him. But here we are. I see a prisoner exchange. How about you?"

For the first time Chopra's calmness cracked. "Soldiers? Oh my, are you unwell?"

Jack twisted in his seat so he could grab the wheel if Chopra tried anything. "You think I'm crazy? You're damn right. I get good and crazy when someone orders a hit on my patent lawyer, shoots my friend, trashes my office, and kidnaps my programmer. For what? An app. You call yourself a successful businessman? All you and Dexter had to do was invest some seed capital in my start-up. If you wanted it so much you could've bought it outright. It would've saved you the expense of having to hire psychos like Tom and Jerry."

Chopra took his eyes off the road. The pupils were dilated

either with fear or surprise. "I have absolutely no idea what or who you are talking about." He turned his attention back to the car in front and braked as they approached a flashing yellow at Powell Street. A cable car clanged by. "I concede I do know about your mobile application." Chopra's voice turned calm again. "Dexter showed me the business plan you provided him but it was incomplete. I am the one who rejected it."

"You?"

"It was my job. Your business model is problematic. To begin with, you must successfully leverage information about the illicit activities marketplace for your application to succeed. Gambling, sex, and alcohol consumption in countries where it is restricted or prohibited by law?" He made a face as he listed them. "The legal fees required to defend your product will far outstrip any hoped for profit margin. And then there is preexisting competition. Your app will have to supplant long-established mechanisms that are already in place for customers to access these markets. Be that as simple as the taxi driver from the airport or the bellman at the hotel. Furthermore, the information is already widely available for free on the internet, promoted by the very establishments and purveyors themselves as part of their self-marketing. All one needs to do is to know of the areas of the cyber world in which to find such information."

"It's all disorganized and hardly as quick as one-stop shopping," Jack said. He could hear how defensive the words sounded.

The light changed. Chopra accelerated. "I had a difficult time convincing Dexter we should not consider it. I told him we had our reputation to think about and the risk of a sound return was much too high. I suppose Dexter's tenacity was out of loyalty to his wife and yours."

"Dexter liked it?"

"He allowed friendship to blind him."

Jack started to feel the earth shift beneath him. It was time to throw the changeup. "So when did he find out about you and Laura?"

"I am sorry but what exactly was he supposed to find out?"

"What I said earlier. That you are lovers."

Chopra sighed. "I do not talk about my private life. I lack the courage of a Tim Cook. But if it helps Laura with her case and ends this malicious speculation on your part, I suppose I have no choice. You see, I am gay. Mr. Broadshank and Inspector Dolan already know that."

A car pulled out in front of them. Chopra neatly swerved to avoid being sideswiped.

"Did Dexter know?"

"I suppose so, but you must realize we were business partners. It is not the same as being friends. We did not share personal histories or anything personal for that matter. My ethnicity proved a barrier to that."

"You being Indian and Dexter being cut from the same cloth as Prince Philip. You're saying that didn't exactly make for besties."

"Dexter is not the only person with racist or sexist tendencies in Silicon Valley. The tech industry is hardly a level playing field. In many respects it does resemble a boys club."

Jack hoped another changeup would nail him. "I know about the Mumbai mafia."

Chopra frowned. "Apparently Dexter is not the only one prone to stereotyping."

Jack batted it away. "I found out about Whydah. It links to you and it links to organized crime in Mumbai. Tell me how I'm wrong thinking you're connected?"

Chopra's sigh was loud and painful. He pulled the Tesla into an empty bus stop and stared at the dashboard. The lights were blue and soothing. The speedometer went up to 160 miles per hour.

"Actually, you are not wrong, but I am only connected by birth," he said quietly. "My grandfather and his brothers started in that... that line of work. It was how our family was able to survive in the ghetto. An American such as you has no idea what life there is like. My father had no choice but to join the family *business*. I on the other hand was given a choice. My mother insisted that I escape the bondage of our family's heritage. My father reluctantly acquiesced. I was sent to boarding school and then to the Indian Institute of Technology. You surmised it earlier. From there to the London School of Economics and then MIT and postgrad at Stanford."

"You've never been back to Mumbai? Never were forced to join the mob?"

Chopra's laugh was soft but had pain in it. "I am hardly a Michael Corleone. My home is here. My work. And then there is what some people would call my *lifestyle*. It is easier for everyone for me to live here."

Jack understood. "Fathers," he said. "What you going do?" They sat in silence for a while. "So what is Whydah?"

"A mother's love," Chopra replied. You see my mother was a very strong woman. When I was a young boy, she used to read to me all the time. My favorite books were pirate stories. She created a trust fund for me and called it Whydah after the pirate ship. It was our little secret. No matter where I went or lived, she could sleep at night, knowing I would have sufficient financial resources, especially after my father cut me off. My mother died several years ago. I continue to use the name as an LLC in her memory."

"Do the holdings include any real estate? Say a warehouse in Oyster Point, a house on Russian Hill?"

"Perhaps. I do not know the full extent of the portfolio

anymore. I am at the point financially where I must rely on professional money managers. My lawyer would know more than I."

"Let me guess. Winston Cheatham."

Chopra nodded. "Indeed. Why do you ask?"

"Just filling in some blanks."

A bus pulled in behind them. The driver honked. Chopra gave a wave in acknowledgement and hit the turn signal.

"Are we finished? I have a business meeting and a dinner engagement later."

"Sure, I'll get out at the next light. But before I go tell me this, if my app is as worthless as you say it is, then why is someone going through all this trouble to try to steal it from me?"

Chopra thought for a minute. "The key to success in venture capital is to study an investment from every possible angle. Perhaps you are looking at yours the wrong way."

"How so?"

"What if it is not acquiring your application somebody wants to do but to protect the information it could expose?"

40

T he cable car picked up speed after it crested Nob Hill and started its descent down California Street. Jack looked like the gaggle of tourists standing on the running boards and hanging on to the handrails. It was night but everything was crystal clear now. The lights in the buildings downtown shined as bright as the cosmos. He kept his eyes fixed on the twin spires of a skyscraper at the bottom of the hill. The top eleven floors were luxury hotel rooms.

"You believe him?" Hark asked again, bringing Jack back to the moment.

He had the volume turned up high on his phone so he could hear over the whir of the cable running beneath the tracks and the screech of the grip as the gripman threw the big lever to tighten and then loosen it to control their speed. The clattering metal wheels and ringing bell added to the only-in-San-Francisco symphony.

"I do," he said. "Chopra holds the key to the Silicon Valley magic kingdom. He doesn't need my app. Still, I feel sorry for him. All that money and he can't buy his father's love because of who he is."

"Do you mean who his old man is or who he is?"

"Both."

"He needs to get over it. I didn't even know my old man, but I don't lay awake at night, worrying about it. You got to lead your own life, right *'mano*?"

Jack's father was a son of a bitch through and through who did most of his parenting with his fists, especially when he came home after fighting a fire and drank to douse the flame that was always burning in his soul. Jack knew Gavin had shaped who he was. There was no escaping it, no denying it, but he also knew if he ever had kids himself, he'd learn from it.

"Are you sure Tom and Jerry are at the Mandarin right now?" he said.

"Yeah," Hark said. "I got the word from a cousin who works as an assistant manager there. Get this, they're staying in the Taipan Suite. Place's bigger than my crib. You know what it goes for a night?"

"More than Katie and I pay a month for our loft."

"These guys got a serious bankroll behind them. My cousin Manny talked to housekeeping. They're living on room service and drinking the minibar dry. They keep one of the closets locked and tell the maids not to try and open it."

"I'm almost there. Where should I meet you?"

"There's a bar on the ground floor. We're already there."

"We?"

"Yeah. Moana and me."

"That a good idea?"

"Hey, she's the one who came up with the plan. It's pretty good, too. You'll see."

~

IT WAS A GOOD PLAN. Hark's cousin announced he was feeling ill mid-shift and had to go home, conveniently providing himself with an alibi and leaving the front desk shorthanded. But before he left, he gave Hark and Moana hotel uniforms and Jack a key to the general manager's private office.

Moana commandeered a housekeeping cart that was left in a hallway and knocked on the door of the Taipan Suite. Tomasz answered.

"You want turn down service, mint on pillow?" she said in her best pidgin.

"Yeah, clean this shit up. And leave a whole box of candy this time. The least we should get the money we're paying for this dump."

Jeremy was sitting on the couch in the suite's living room and playing video games on the TV. Moana went about straightening the rooms and then went into the master bathroom, shoved a roll of toilet paper in the john, and kept flushing until water flowed over the top of the bowl.

"So sorry," she cried. "The toilet overflowed. I call maintenance. They fix it, *wikiwiki*."

"Stupid bitch," Tomasz said.

"You're probably to blame," Jeremy said to him. "Every time you use the bathroom it needs to be fumigated."

Moana used one of the suite's phones to call Hark.

He knocked on the door two minutes later. The uniform was too small and the tool belt barely buckled around his waist but Tomasz and Jeremy didn't seem to notice. He went into the bathroom and started banging on the pipes.

He came back out. "Whoa, we got a big mess in there. It's going require snaking and a whole lot more. Hotel policy says you need to leave while we're fixing it. Health code stuff."

"No fuckin' way," Tomasz said. "Fix the damn crapper or else."

"I can't start if you're still here," Hark said. "It's my job if I let you stay. You want to talk to the manager? Maybe he'll make a special exception."

"And they call this a five-star?" Tomasz said. "We're not leaving."

Moana stepped in. "You ever been in swimming pool and little kid poops? Lifeguard makes everybody get out, scoops it up with net, then pours in chemicals. You can't go back in water for half hour. This same thing. We don't know what floor poop come from. Call manager."

Jeremy put down the video controller and picked up the phone. He punched zero. The switchboard routed the call automatically to the GM's office.

Jack answered using a German accent. "Good evening, Hans Klinkenberg speaking. How may I be of assistance?" He listened to Jeremy. "That is correct. Your health and comfort is our utmost concern. We humbly apologize for the inconvenience, but not only does the hotel policy require guests to temporarily vacate during such an unfortunate but rare incident, San Francisco Health Code mandates it."

He listened some more. "I am looking at the computer right now and I am terribly sorry, Mr. Werthing, but all our suites are booked or else I would move you immediately. However, I am also corresponding with the head of engineering as we speak and am assured the repairs can be made in less than one hour. Would you please be my personal guest at dinner at the Brasserie downstairs? Everything is complimentary, of course. I recommend the duck breast and comfit. By the time you finish dining, the repairs will be completed and the suite completely sanitized. The night's stay is gratis, of course." Jack listened again. "*Ich danke Ihnen.*"

Two minutes later his cell buzzed with an incoming text from Hark. *They're in the elevator.*

Jack slipped out of the manager's office, quickly walked to

the connecting tower, and rode the elevator up. Glass enclosed catwalks connected the top eleven floors of the twin towers; they were the hotel's architectural signature. He crossed back over to Tower One and knocked on the door.

Moana opened it. "We found him. He's pretty beat up."

Hark had carried Do Pray to the bed. Jack gently pulled the gag out of the young man's mouth.

"You're going be okay. I'm sorry this happened."

Do Pray looked groggy. His face was bruised, his lips swollen. "They wanted the password to the NAS. Then they saw it got wiped clean by remote. That's when they really started in on me."

"We can talk about it later," Jack said. "First we need to do is get you out of here."

"*Wikiwiki*," Moana said. "Before they get back."

"You and Hark take him," Jack told her. "Remember, don't go back to the office. Stash him at your relative's house in South City like we talked about."

"You'll be safe there," she told Do Pray. "Mostly Pacific Islanders living on that street. If these *lemus* come around, they'll stick out like conch shells on wet sand."

"What are you going do?" Hark said.

Jack pulled out the thumb drive he took from the house on Russian Hill. "It's about time somebody snapped a trap on Tom and Jerry."

"If you're staying, I'm staying. I'll take Do Pray down the other elevator and be back before those *gueros* finish their main course." The big man turned to Moana and handed her his car keys. "Meet us on the Battery Street side of the building and whatever you do don't flip the red toggle switch on the dash. It fires the hydraulics. You'd be hopping all the way down the road."

She grinned. "Now that sounds fun. Tell you what, I'll let you ride my scooter sometime."

HARK WAS CARRYING MORE than a pipe wrench in the tool belt. He'd packed his Beretta and the glove box nine. Both were trained on Tomasz and Jeremy as they walked into the suite. Jack was hiding beside the door. He closed it behind them.

"And how was your dinner?" he said in the German accent.

"You're fuckin' dead," Tomasz growled. "You have no idea who you're fuckin' with."

"Sure we do," Jack said in his normal voice. "Now if you would be so kind, we have a couple of seats waiting for you. The movie's about to begin."

Hark waved the guns and ushered them into the living room. Two straight-backed chairs were positioned in the middle, back-to-back. "Sit down or you'll fall down."

"Fuck you," Tomasz said.

Hark didn't shoot him. He didn't need to. His kick to Tomasz's knee was a blur. It dropped the genocidal germ into the chair. Jeremy squealed and sat down behind him.

"There is no need for violence," he said. "We can work this out."

"It's already worked out," Jack said.

Jack took a roll of duct tape from the plumber's tool belt and strapped the pair to their chairs while Hark covered him. He fashioned a double-ended noose from the tie of a hotel bathrobe and slid it over their heads. He pulled the knots close to their throats.

"If you start rocking in your chairs, you're likely to hang each other before the cops get here," he said.

"What cops? Why would you do that?" Jeremy said. "Come on. We can work something out. How much do you want?"

"Too late. If killing Tingly Meyers wasn't reason enough, you tried running me over. Shot the big man here. Kidnapped my employee and beat the shit out of him. *Let's Make a Deal* time is long gone. You're going down."

"This is California. Everything is always on the table. Name your price."

"There's nothing you can tell me. You don't even know the name of the person who hired you. You've never even met him. Everything's been done remotely. Even this room here. It's being paid by a numbered account. I checked when I was in the GM's office. Tell me I'm wrong."

Jeremy bit his upper lip. "You're right but we can turn this around. We'll help you find out who he is."

"Too late. I already know."

Hark looked at Jack. "You do?"

"Yeah. I got it."

"Right, the license plate. Good one."

Tomasz hissed at Jeremy. "Don't listen to him. You know he's a grifter. He's bluffing."

"You killed Tingly and you're going to suck gas for it," Jack said. He lifted a pillow off the couch and carried it over so the pair could see it. A knife lay on it.

"You ever heard of Richard the Third? English king back in the Middle Ages. A twisted sort, physically and mentally. He met his match at Bosworth Field and was buried on the spot where he fell. Five hundred years later, it's a parking lot. Workers are digging a hole and discover some bones. DNA confirms it's old Sick Dick, the last English monarch to die in battle." Jack paused. "Think what the lab rats at SFPD will be able to find on this blade. Tingly Meyers's DNA. Tom's here. My programmer's when you nicked his neck."

"You planted that knife. No way to prove it's mine," Tomasz shouted.

"Funny, I found it in your kit. But the cops don't need to take my word for it. They can see for themselves."

Jack put the pillow down, picked up the TV clicker, and hit power. Do Pray's face filled the screen as the knife was drawn across his neck.

"Now I know what you're thinking. So what. Tom's face is always conveniently cropped out of the frame in the video. Who's to say that Jerry here is the narrator?" Jack adopted a late night TV product announcer's voice. "But wait, wait, there's more. A lot more. In your rush to copy the video over to the thumb drive, you also copied the outtakes. Sure, you realized your mistake and deleted them. But guess what? Nothing's ever really deleted. It can always be rescued if you know how. And guess what? There's an app for that."

He clicked fast forward. The recovered outtake recorded the camera being set on a table and Jeremy joining Tomasz to untie Do Pray from the chair and yank him upright.

"Right out of *Bloopers*, eh boys? And Tom, that sure looks like the same knife you're cutting the ropes with as the one right here."

"So what," Tomasz said. "Most they got is false imprisonment. They can't link us to whoever paid us, so there's no way to prove we're hired cleaners."

Hark kicked him in the knee. "That's for shooting at me." He kicked him again, this time harder. "And that's for being stupid. No one's going skate on this. You're going down for murder one. And the dude who paid you? He's going down even harder."

Jack picked up the hotel phone and dialed. "*Inspektor* Dolan? Hans Klinkenberg here, General Manager of the Mandarin Hotel. Housekeeping found something most unusual in one of our suites. Could you please come over right away? It appears to have to do with a murder. *Auf wiedersehen*."

Jack hung up and set the TV playback on continuous loop. "Some entertainment while you're waiting for the cops to get here."

Hark slapped gray tape across their mouths and tested the double noose to make sure it was good and tight. "You better hope we don't get an earthquake. This building will shake harder than a maraca."

Jeremy's eyes widened. Tomasz tried to swear but the tape kept the words stuck in his craw.

Jack uncapped a marker and printed *Tom* and *Jerry* on the pair's respective gags. "That's all, folks," he said with a wave and sidestepped out the door.

41

A pair of heavy black frame reading glasses perched on the tip of Katie's nose. Books covered the dining table. A spreadsheet filled the display of her laptop. She didn't hear Jack open the front door.

"Such a pretty nose to be buried in a book," he said.

She pushed up the bridge of the glasses with her fingertip. "Did you know if I open another yoga and workout gym, I could increase my net by twenty-five percent by applying economies of scale to inventory, marketing, and labor? Think of it, not only could I help more women achieve health and happiness but also add to my bottom line."

"I'm all for more bottom." He looked over her shoulder at the laptop. "And where are you thinking of expanding your empire?"

"All that redevelopment in Mission Bay? Besides the UCSF Hospital campus, most of what's being built are apartments and condos. And then there's the old shipyard in Hunter's Point. Thousands of new residences are going up and a good portion of it will be affordable housing. People need to exercise and eat healthy. I can help."

"Good for you, my entrepreneurial do-gooder. You'll need some working capital for rent, building out the gyms, and hiring instructors."

"I thought of all that. It's on the spreadsheet here." She tapped the screen. "I have an appointment with a bank tomorrow morning to discuss a business loan. Part of my plan is only to hire people who live in those communities. There's been a huge lack of jobs ever since the shipyard closed."

Katie stood. "I think it will work. I like what I do and I'm good at it."

"The key ingredients to any business," Jack said.

"And while your start-up is sure to do great, we can't put all our financial eggs in one basket, can we?" She smiled shyly. "We need to think about the future."

"Funny you should mention my start-up."

"Why, what happened?"

Jack told her about his conversation with Arjun Chopra.

"I can't believe we were so wrong," Katie said.

"About the app?"

"About Arjun. I was sure he was Laura's lover and the murderer." She put a hand on her throat. "I feel terrible we jumped to conclusions. That's awful. The poor man."

"We didn't jump. We were pushed by what we knew at the time."

"Now what are we going to do? Laura's never going to get out of jail."

"I still have a card or two up my sleeve. All I need is some time before I can play them."

"How much time?"

Jack looked at his watch and calculated flight times. "Enough for me to double-check your bottom line if you want."

Katie laughed and took off her glasses.

IT WAS THE FOLLOWING NIGHT, and Jack hadn't been back to
Woodside since he'd dropped down Cotswold's ventilator shaft
and looked for Little Buddha. He followed Woodside Road
through town and up the east side of the Santa Cruz Mountains.
Skyline Boulevard followed the ridgeline all the way to San
Francisco but Jack turned onto a private road before he reached
it. The road ran parallel and the houses built along it were
spread far apart. All had 180-degree views of the valley below
and the bay beyond. The enclaves were built for privacy. Most
housed technology titans. Ironically, high technology mapping
and satellite imagery rendered their privacy moot.

Jack pinpointed Winston Cheatham's house. The structure
was all glass and steel beams. It perched on the hillside like the
crow's nest of a ship. Jack didn't bother ringing the doorbell. He
crept quietly along the wraparound deck until he found an
unlocked sliding glass door. He slipped in and turned on the
lights.

"It's Jack McCoul," he called loudly. "Wake up, Winston. It's
time we talked."

It took a few minutes for the lawyer to appear. Sleep hadn't
mussed his blow-dried hair any. He wore a black tracksuit and
Italian leather slippers. He brandished a phone as if it were
a gun.

"The house has a silent alarm," he said. "They're going to
call here right away. If I don't say the correct password, this place
will be swarming with police. Don't say I didn't warn you. You'd
better leave."

"You'll be lucky if it's the cops who show up first."

"What's that supposed to mean?"

"It's over. I talked to Arjun Chopra. Tom and Jerry are under arrest. They might not be able to ID you as their *client,* but it doesn't matter."

"I don't know what you're talking about."

"Really? If you squeeze that phone any harder, you're likely to pop a vein. Sit down and let's talk. We still have a few minutes before they get here."

"Who?"

"Who do you think? The organization you've been skimming."

"I told you I don't know what you're talking about."

"So sit down and I'll explain it to you. It'll give you time to think up something to say to them to try and save your sorry ass even though I don't think they're going to be in a listening mood."

Winston's lower lip trembled. He sat on a couch. Jack sat in an Eames chair across from him. A glass coffee table separated them.

"You know, Silicon Valley is a lot like Hollywood," Jack said. "Everybody wants to be a director, even the actors. IP lawyers are no different. A thousand dollars an hour billing rate still makes you nothing more than a wage earner. The real money is building and selling start-ups. It must eat at your soul to see kids half your age making billions, designing and selling a game. Am I right?"

Winston offered a glare and silence.

"I've got to admit, I couldn't resist the siren call myself. So I came up with an idea for an app that played upon some things I had more than a passing familiarity with in my previous career. Kind of like that advice you always hear writers give: write what you know. So I cook up an idea for an app and go looking for venture capital. I try my wife's best friend's hubby. But old Dexter didn't get where he got on his gut instincts alone. He relied on advice. He showed my business plan to his managing partner who nixed the idea because of all sorts of reasons. Chopra wasn't the only one he talked to. He gave the plan to you, too, because of the legal complications it might bring."

Jack took a breath. He looked around the room. The furniture was chrome, glass, and black leather. A Warhol litho of dollar signs decorated the one wall that wasn't a floor-to-ceiling window. If it was a knock-off, then someone nearly as good as Henri LeConte had forged it.

"You took one look at my plans for an app and realized it had more than potential, it had real possibility. So you hired a couple of programmers in Bangalore or someplace to code it."

Winston's phone rang.

"Go ahead and answer it," Jack said. "It doesn't matter what password you give. They're still coming."

Winston pushed talk. His voice quavered. "Yes, I'm Winston Cheatham. It was a false alarm. An open window. The code is IPOBALLR. Right. Thanks."

"Like your license plate. Now that's easy to remember."

The lawyer scowled. "And your story is only a story. Are you finished?"

"Almost. Before you stole my idea for an app, you'd already discovered who Arjun Chopra was. More to the point, who is family was. It wasn't that hard. Research is part of what lawyers do. Plus it's easier than ever. The internet has made secrets an endangered species."

Winston put the phone on the glass coffee table and leaned back in a casual, if not bored, manner.

"So you reached out to Arjun's dad and told him about your app, that you could optimize it so it would drive traffic to any establishment of his choosing like a regular search engine does for paying customers. You told him you could bench test it in India to prove it would work. But what you didn't tell him was you added a hidden feature to it, a backdoor tracker that allowed you to ID customers so you could skim off their credit cards and wire transfers."

Jack shook his finger at him. "What were you thinking? You were dealing with the Mumbai mob. Don't you know criminals are hardwired to think about how to commit crimes? It was only a matter of time until Chopra's dad got wise. Everything was going along fine until I came back into the picture. Your first attempt to back me off by siccing the patent trolls on me wasn't working, so you fortified your defenses and hired Tom and Jerry."

"You seem to think you know it all." Winston faked a yawn. "Are you finished yet?"

"You know what finally gave you away? A kid from Louisiana. You tried hacking my system and he hacked you right back. Allowed me to ID your server. Come on, you know better than to try to out hack some kid. They're the ones who keep coming up with the next big thing."

Winston glared.

Jack didn't give him time to talk. "Did Laura know what you were doing or were you screwing her as cover for pillow talk intel on Dexter? The app business wasn't your first stroll down Crooked Lane. You'd already been manipulating Arjun Chopra's personal portfolio, Whydah. What were you nibbling from Dex? Was it insider trading information or straight up embezzlement?"

"Your imagination is running away with you," Winston said. "I admit Laura and I were lovers. If she hasn't told that to the police already, I'm sure she will. But an affair is no crime. And in no way did I have anything to do with Dexter's murder, if that's what you're insinuating."

"I'm not because I know you didn't do it. You never kill a golden goose. But you did order Tingly Meyers killed when he found out you were behind the patent trolls and threatened to expose that you were ripping off users. And you did have Tom and Jerry try to kill Katie and me." Jack felt the cold fury rise. "For that you're definitely going to pay."

Winston jabbed his hand behind a couch pillow and came up with a silver Smith & Wesson. "I'm already on record with the alarm company tonight," he said with a sneer. "When I shoot you, it will set it off again. I'll say there was an intruder hiding in the house the whole time, and I had no choice but to defend myself. Everything else you say I did? There's nothing that connects me. I made sure of it."

"It's really too bad you didn't, because that would've given me the choice of calling the cops instead."

Winston pulled the trigger.

It clicked. It continued to click as he pulled again and again.

Jack held out the gun's clip. "Guess what? I'm hardwired that way, too."

He stood and started for the door. It was already opening when he reached it. Two men dressed in black suits entered. One carried a Glock, the other a machine pistol. They acknowledged him with the barest of nods as they passed by.

In the driveway, a pair of black Range Rovers was parked next to Jack's Prius. Another man in a dark suit sat behind the wheel of the closest one. He eyed Jack carefully. The rear window rolled down. A man with a silver brush cut and wearing a turtleneck beneath a suit jacket leaned forward from the back seat.

"Did you learn what you needed, Mr. McCoul?" His eyes were piercing, his voice matter-of-fact.

"Enough. You know, Mr. Chopra, your son's a good man. You should be proud of him, what he's accomplished with his life and career here in the Valley."

"Who is to say that I am not?" He dipped his head. "Sadly, in my world there are always those who would seek to exploit vulnerability, thus I must show none to remove all possibility of repercussion."

"That's a steep price to pay," Jack said.

"I take it you are not a father or you would know that one must always make sacrifices."

Jack hooked a thumb at the house. "What's going to happen to Cheatham?"

His eyes did not blink. His smile was enigmatic. "Is it any of your concern now?"

"Not any longer."

"I thought not."

Jack opened his car door and started to get in.

"One other thing," Chopra Senior said, making a steeple with his hands beneath his chin. "The acquisition of your mobile application and associated patents is now complete. The proceeds have been deposited in your Caymans account." He paused. "You will destroy all the coding as agreed, yes?"

He did not wait for an answer. The window rolled up.

Jack drove away and never looked back.

42

The dawn was turning golden and more steam was rising from the to-go cup than there was mist in the sky. Jack sipped coffee while parked on a quiet street in Palo Alto. A beat-up Nissan with a loud muffler was making its way toward him. The driver was tossing newspapers onto driveways. He bypassed more houses than he threw to, and Jack knew he was witnessing a custom's waning days, a reminder that he, too, kept one foot in the past and one in the future. He read the daily paper online except on Sundays. That one he would keep having delivered as long as they printed them. Few things were sweeter than a lazy morning, lounging in bed with Katie and swapping sections while the rain beat against the window or the fog rolled by or the sun streamed in.

Marriage had taught him about the power of passion and that the heart could make people do things that neither doctors nor scientists could explain. He wouldn't lose a moment's sleep for handing Winston Cheatham over to the Mumbai mob. Arjun Chopra's father was wrong; Jack did know what it took to protect those he loved, and he would do it again in a heartbeat.

Tingly's murder and the attempts on his and Katie's lives had been about money but that, in and of itself, was unusual. Homicide was mainly a crime of passion, a one-sided relationship where love had given over to pain and anger. The odds of being killed by a stranger were less than drowning in a bathtub as a family member or acquaintance committed most murders. Jack reasoned Dexter's death was no different. It had all the markings of the flip side of love. He had turned his back on his killer either out of scorn or out of indifference. The force of the blow to his skull was fueled by a red-hot emotion only the heart could produce. It was rage not robbery. The murderer had taken only one thing, the weapon. And that was either to hide the evidence or reclaim a treasured keepsake. Jack was betting on the latter.

The car radio was dialed to NPR and the volume was soft but the news harsh. More madness in the Mideast, more evidence of climate chaos, more stalemates in Washington. Jack turned it off and looked at his watch. It was time to go. He waited for a woman walking her Labrador retriever to pass before opening the door and crossing the street.

The house was a brown shingle bordered by a low wooden fence abloom with star jasmine. Mixed among the pavers leading to the front porch were stepping-stones engraved with Chinese figures and their English translations: love, destiny, water, home, peace. A statue of a Korean lion dog stood watch in the garden. A miniature orange Shinto shrine gate hung over the front door. The doorbell sounded like Tibetan chimes.

Miss Nash answered.

"Mind if I come in?" Jack said.

The executive assistant backed up wordlessly. She was wearing a kimono and straw sandals. The house smelled like sandalwood incense. Scroll paintings hung on the walls. A row of jade animal figurines marched silently across the mantle.

"What... what do you want?"

"Tea would be nice," Jack said. "Along with the truth."

Miss Nash kept backing up and he kept following. They entered the kitchen. It was neat and orderly. A Siamese cat looked up from its perch on a covered window seat.

"I'm getting ready for work," she said. "I'm late."

"Let's have that tea first. The office can wait."

"No it can't." Her voice became shrill. "Nothing gets done there without me."

"You've worked at Capital Dexterity a long time, haven't you?" Jack spoke in a low, soothing voice.

"Since the beginning. I worked for Mr. Cotswold before he started the firm." She grasped the cowl of her kimono and pulled it tight. "He was... he was a genius at business and antiques."

"But not so smart about personal stuff." When she didn't bite he said, "I see you share his appreciation of Asian art."

"Of course. I had to study it thoroughly. I assisted Mr. Cotswold in the acquisition of his collection."

"Did you travel with him on buying trips?"

She nodded. "He relied on me for everything. Travel arrangements, meeting coordination, making sure the works of art were properly insured and documented for shipment."

"Even after he got married?"

Her frown formed a slash. "I already told you I have to go to work."

"You love your job."

"Yes, it's very fulfilling. I'm sorry but I can't be late."

Jack sat down at the kitchen table. "What about now? You're Arjun Chopra's executive assistant. How's he as a boss?"

"It's not the same." She said it quickly. "He's... I suppose it will take some getting used to. For me and for him as well."

"Can I ask you a question?"

"What?" It sparked with exasperation.

"What's your first name?"

She tugged on the kimono again. "That's none of your business."

"The first initial is *E*. Should I guess what it stands for?"

"How do you know that?"

Jack eyed the table. "You have a lot of unopened mail piled here."

"I've been busy ever since…"

"Since Dexter died. Is it Elizabeth?"

"What?"

"Your first name. *E* for Elizabeth. Or how about Evangeline?"

"Don't be absurd." She huffed. "It's Edwina if you must know. There? Are you satisfied? Now please, I really must be going."

"My mother had a traditional first name, too. It was Aideen and people always mistook it for Aileen. Listening to my old man, you wouldn't have known what her name was. It was either *Hey* or *Shut up* or *Fetch me another* or *I'm warning you*." Jack shook his head. "He treated her like shit. Ran around, came home drunk whenever he did bother to show up, whupped on her and us kids. Still, she loved him til the day she died. Cancer. It was heartbreaking. Wasted away in front of my eyes. She died in her own bed. The whole time she was sick she wouldn't let go of two things, her bible and this tiny model of the Eiffel Tower. Da gave it to her as a wedding present. Told her it was an IOU for the honeymoon they were going to take someday. Of course, they never did. We buried her with that toy tower clutched in her hand. I guess she wanted to hold onto something forever that reminded her he'd loved her once upon a time."

Miss Nash backed up against the refrigerator. Her eyes darted like fish.

"You gave Dexter a bronze statue of Benzai-ten, the Japanese goddess of love, language, wisdom, and the arts. Well, the goddess of everything. Kind of like an executive assistant. I saw it on his desk the first time he invited me in. I could tell that it wasn't an antique like his other artifacts but it was priceless to you, wasn't it?"

"You have no business prying," she said. The words came in short breaths.

"I bet if I looked around I'd find it here, but it doesn't matter. I don't believe you meant to kill him. I think you went there to do what you've always done, to support him, be there to dot the i's and cross the t's, pick up after him. After you dropped Arjun off at the San Carlos airport, you kept his car. Later that night you got a call from Dexter to come to the house. He let you in. Laura had already gone to bed. You and Dexter went to his library. Maybe he asked you to bring him some papers to sign or pick up. One thing led to another and you told him about Laura and Winston. You'd known awhile. It wasn't like they were trying to hide it. Everything you'd bottled up came pouring out. *Why did he put up with her? Why couldn't he see it was you who really loved him?* His response wasn't what you hoped. Maybe he even laughed. He turned his back on you. It was the final straw. You took back the Benzai-ten statue you'd given him. He didn't deserve it. But then holding it you could feel every sleight, every time he took you for granted, forgotten your birthday, all the hurt and loneliness. The statue burned in your hand and when it was over, it was all you had left to remember him by."

Miss Nash rocked back and forth in her straw sandals, clutching her kimono to her throat. A low moan came from somewhere deep inside her.

"I guess it's true what the torch singers say when they sing about love," Jack said. "Sometimes it lasts and sometimes it hurts."

"What are you going to do now?" Her voice was small and distant.

"You've already put yourself in a hell worse than any prison but there could be a way out for you."

"What, commit *jigaki*?"

"No, that's the easy way." He placed Terry's card on the kitchen table. "Tell him what happened. They'll go easier on you if you turn yourself in. A murder committed in the heat of passion is always ruled second degree. You'll probably get ten years, be out in seven."

She choked and started to sob.

"And while you're deciding what to do, don't forget about Laura. Sure, she cheated on Dexter and that was lousy of her, but that's all she was guilty of. He did love her and she loved him as much as she's capable of loving any man, considering what her father did to her."

43

Sunday was living up to its name. There wasn't a cloud in the sky and San Francisco was buzzing with human electricity. It was as if every neighborhood was holding a street fair—a leather event on Folsom Street, Italian opera in one meadow of Golden Gate Park, bluegrass in another, outdoor hip-hop concerts in Visitacion Valley, a Chinese wedding parade in the Inner Richmond, and food booths and cook-offs in Japantown. Everywhere people were mixing and celebrating, creating a huge mulligatawny of art, music, and lifestyle that reflected the city's heart and soul.

The Mission District was hopping, too. Dolores Park was filled with picnickers. Church bells rang from the tower at St. Joseph's. The restaurants on Valencia were packed. Mission Street was crowded with hipsters and Latinos. *Mariachi* music poured from open windows.

Jack and Katie strolled among the crowd. She was sucking a fresh fruit ice pop she'd bought from a sidewalk vendor.

"I can't believe you're still hungry after that huge lunch," Jack said.

"I couldn't resist when I saw he was selling mango *paletas*. I'm craving sweets lately. Want a taste?"

Jack gave her a look as she held out the frozen treat. Earlier he noticed she'd passed on a margarita at lunch.

"Hear from Laura?" he asked as he wiped the sticky tropical fruit from his lips.

"She texted me. She's down in Malibu. Something about a beach party."

"Maybe she'll marry a movie star."

"Be nice," she said. "Laura's still healing."

"So is everyone else down there. She'll feel right at home."

A horn honked. It belonged to a '64 Impala pulling to the curb. Hark was behind the chrome chain steering wheel. Moana was riding shotgun.

"I love the flower behind your ear," Katie said. "What kind is it?"

Moana's lips were as red as the blossom. "A heilala. It's the Tongan national flower."

"I'm surprised you can find fresh ones."

"They're grown in greenhouses, especially this time of year because of the festival today and so many people from the Islands living here." She turned to Jack. "You sure you don't want to come with us? They'll treat you like you were King Tupou himself since you made Do Pray and me rich. I paid for all the roast pigs."

"Next year," Jack said. "We got something else we got to do."

"What could be more important?" Moana asked.

"Even I don't know," Katie said. "Jack's acting very mysterious. At first I thought he was taking me on a picnic because he's wearing that silly backpack, but then we went out to lunch."

Hark and Jack exchanged glances. The big man gave a knowing nod. "We better get going ourselves. We don't want to miss the tattoo booth. I'm thinking of getting a pair of volcanoes inked on my chest. See you round, 'mano. Later Katie."

Jack looped his arm through Katie's and steered her onto Twenty-Second Street. Halfway down the block they stopped in front of a red and gray three-story building topped with Gothic spires. It stood between two Victorians. Eight stairs led to bright red double doors adorned with lion-head knockers. Gold Chinese symbols were painted on either side of the entrance.

"What is this place?" Katie asked.

"A Buddhist temple," Jack said. "Want to go inside and take a look around?"

"So this is your surprise. You're so sweet. It takes me right back to Nepal."

The lights were low and the air thick with smoke from incense. Ember-tipped sandalwood sticks as plentiful as quills on a porcupine stuck out of trays filled with sand. The sound of chanting rolled from the shadows and in the distance came the thonking echo of a wooden drum.

"It's so beautiful," Katie whispered. "I never knew it was here."

"It used to be a German Lutheran church when I was a kid growing up around the corner," Jack said. "It became Buddhist about ten years or so ago."

"I thought all the temples were in Chinatown."

"Started that way during the gold rush when the Chinese came to work in the mining camps and build the railroad, but they're scattered throughout the city now. Japanese immigrants built their own temple downtown but it burned to the ground after the great quake. They rebuilt it on Pine Street. It's enormous."

"You sound like a tour guide." She tightened her arm around his.

"Been doing my research," he said.

"How come?"

He hesitated. "The main hall is up on the second floor. Let's check it out."

They entered a large room lit by candles. A dozen nuns with shaved heads and dressed in yellow and gray robes sat cross-legged on the floor. Some chanted. Others wore earbuds. Jack figured someone had come up with an app for playing Buddhist mantras. A twenty-one-foot-high Buddha sat at the far end of the room. Offerings of flowers, oranges, grapefruit, boxes of raisins, and candles were stacked in front.

"Look at all those glasses of water," Katie said. "There must be a thousand."

"They refill them every day."

"Do the nuns live here?"

"There's a parish house next door."

"Would they mind if I lit some incense?"

"They'd love you to. See that incense stand over there next to the monk pounding the fish drum? It's for worshippers and visitors alike. Help yourself."

Jack watched her go. When her back was turned, he went up to the main altar and slipped off the backpack. He unzipped the top, reached in, and pulled out Little Buddha.

"Sorry for the roundabout journey," he said. "They'll take good care of you here. Welcome home."

He set Little Buddha at the foot of the big Buddha and moved a few oranges around on the altar so it looked like the 400-year-old, foot-high gold statue had always been there. Katie came up behind him. She had a handful of unlit incense sticks.

"What are you doing?" she asked.

"Just making things right," he said.

"What sort of things?"

"Something from before."

She eyed him carefully. "Well, in that case I'm happy. There are leaflets by the incense stand. They're written in different languages. Did you know Buddhism shares a belief in karma with Hinduism, Taoism, and other religions?"

Jack did but didn't say so.

"Good deeds and good intent can insure good karma and future happiness," she quoted. "Do you want to burn some incense, too? It's supposed to clear away evil spirits."

"Sure, hand me a stick."

So they lit them. Katie closed her eyes and meditated. He watched the smoke curl upward and thought about the future. Whether or not Little Buddha would smile on his actions was anybody's guess. But one thing was for certain. Whatever came next, Jack wouldn't leave it to chance.

A NOTE FROM THE AUTHOR

Thank you so much for reading *BAD KARMA*. I'd truly appreciate it if you would please leave a review on Amazon and Goodreads. Your feedback not only helps me become a better storyteller, but you help other readers by blazing a trail and leaving markers for them to follow as they search for new stories.

To leave a review, go to the *BAD KARMA* product page on Amazon, click "customer reviews" next to the stars below the title, click the "Write a customer review" button, and share your thoughts with other readers.

To quote John Cheever, "I can't write without a reader. It's precisely like a kiss—you can't do it alone."

GET A FREE BOOK

Dwight Holing's genre-spanning work includes novels, short fiction, and nonfiction. His mystery and suspense thriller series include The Nick Drake Novels and The Jack McCoul Capers. The stories in his collections of literary short fiction have won awards, including the Arts & Letters Prize for Fiction. He has written and edited numerous nonfiction books on nature travel and conservation. He is married to a kick-ass environmental advocate; they have a daughter and son, and two dogs who'd rather swim than walk.

Sign up for his newsletter to get a free book and be the first to learn about his next novel as well as receive news about crime fiction and special deals.

Visit dwightholing.com/free-book. You can unsubscribe at any time.

ALSO BY DWIGHT HOLING

The Nick Drake Novels

The Sorrow Hand (Book 1)

The Pity Heart (Book 2)

The Shaming Eyes (Book 3)

The Whisper Soul (Book 4)

The Jack McCoul Capers

A Boatload (Book 1)

Bad Karma (Book 2)

Baby Blue (Book 3)

Shake City (Book 4)

Short Story Collections

California Works

Over Our Heads Under Our Feet

Made in the USA
Columbia, SC
05 August 2024

39990230R00186